A Woman's Life

("Une Vie")

A WOMAN'S LIFE
by Guy de Maupassant

Translated from the French by
Marjorie Laurie; with an introduction by
Edmond Jaloux, and illustrations
by Edy Legrand

London,

The Nonesuch Press

& The Heritage Press, New York

The introduction by
EDMOND JALOUX

WHY SHOULD the choice of the committee called on to select the ten best French novels have fallen on Guy de Maupassant's *Une Vie* (A Woman's Life) rather than on any other of his works? I should like to begin by answering this question, giving some of the reasons for our selection of *Une Vie* rather than *Bel-Ami, Mont-Oriol, Fort comme la Mort, Pierre et Jean,* or *Notre Coeur.*

Bel-Ami which, along with his story *Boule-de-suif* published in *Les Soirées de Médan,* and *La Maison Tellier,* brought Guy de Maupassant to the literary forefront, is a study of "manners" which hardly goes beyond an anecdotal picture of everyday life, and of all Maupassant's novels is the only one which strikes us now as "dating." And it "dates" precisely for this reason: that in it the author had not yet risen to the height of taking a bird's-eye view of things and people; that, for all his experience of life, Maupassant still betrayed in it a certain ingenuousness and, under a veneer of cynicism, positive naïveté. The contrast between the moral laxity of the characters, the superficial boldness of dialogue and incidents, and the author's state of relative innocence as regards Parisian *mores*—Maupassant's knowledge of which at this period was still very far from adequate—makes the work seem out of plumb, and tells against its permanence.

There is a lack of balance of another order in *Mont-Oriol,* in which a double plot pursues its course on parallel lines; on the one hand we have a very tender and touching love-story, on the other a quite arbitrary picture of the creation of an hydropathic spa. Had Maupassant been an adept of the light, fantastic touch, we should have had no reason to reproach him for having made a thorough-going comedy, almost a farce, of his description of a wa-

ix

tering-place and the doctors attached to it. But Maupassant set
out to be, and indeed was, a realist and, this being so, we cannot
accept from him a narrative conditioned by mere imagination and
little short of a caricature.

Passing to *Fort comme la Mort* and *Notre Coeur*, we are confronted with a new Maupassant, a man who is already somewhat
unbalanced by the onset of the malady that was to carry him off.
(He was barely thirty-nine when he had to give up writing, and
died at the age of forty-one.) The Maupassant of that period had
become a man of the world, somewhat under the influence of his
friend Paul Bourget—but a worldling always ill at ease. He could
never feel quite at home in the society in which his lot had fallen;
its sophistications and feminine coquetries went against the grain of
a temperament that had still its moments of puerility and a certain
natural uncouthness. For this reason *Fort comme la Mort* and *Notre
Coeur* lack that tranquil forcefulness and perfect adaptation of
form to subject, that feeling for life seen steadily and whole, and
for the tragedy of the everyday, which we find in those two mas-
terpieces *Une Vie* and *Pierre et Jean*. The latter falls into line with
the most classical traditions of the French novel, those aspects
which reveal it as a derivative of Tragedy. By this I mean that,
unlike those in Anglo-Saxon fiction, the situations in the French
novel are created by the characters and not by that all-embracing,
flooding tide of life which makes characters, situations and all the
myriad incidents of every day seem less the consequence of any individual effort than of the resistless march of Time. In a typical
French novel such as *Pierre et Jean* the clash of personalities is such
as to lead to dramatic situations, whose violence inevitably pro-
vokes catastrophe.

Une Vie, however, is built to the measure of those long, leisurely
narratives in which we see a human life shaping its slow course over
a long span of years, with its promise and performance, its vital
trends and sorrows, its faltering plans, its failures. It is a book on
the scale of *Wilhelm Meister's Apprenticeship*, of *The Mill on the
Floss*, or *l'Education Sentimentale*. Guy de Maupassant was not a
particularly cultured man and I do not suppose he ever made the
acquaintance of *Wilhelm Meister* or *The Mill on the Floss*. But he
was Flaubert's pupil and it is obvious that the *Education Sentimentale* impressed him no less deeply than did his teacher's theories.

Introduction

As readers will see, *Une Vie* is a model of equipoise, proportion and observation. In this novel, aptness of "tone," veracity in the description of the relations between the various characters, the art that "holds a mirror up to life"—all are brought to a pitch of perfection that, we make bold to say, can never be excelled. The more novels one reads, the more apparent it becomes that *Pierre et Jean* and *Une Vie* are supreme examples of nice adjustment and finished craftsmanship. Terms that are apposite to handicraft, and I have chosen them deliberately; for in Maupassant the art of composition—of "fitting things together"—which plays so large a part in the novelist's art, is not only plain to see but makes us realise its indispensability.

If one asks oneself what is the real theme of *Une Vie*, the answer can but be that this great book has none other than the constant ebb and flow of life: its tragic wear-and-tear and its eternal power of self-renewal, rejuvenation. The book opens on a marvellous glimpse of a woman in the springtime of life, of all the unsuspected treasures of emotion that a young, ardent creature, vibrant with longings, haunted by her dreams and aspirations, can cherish in her heart. The closing years of adolescence have perhaps been treated by romantic writers with still greater tenderness and rapture, but no realistic writer has conveyed their gentle glamour with such warmth and reverence. As the tale proceeds, we see what life, ruthless in its task of slow erosion day by day, makes of this woman whose whole being yearned for beauty, love, devotion. It is very evident that the man Jeanne de Lamare married was a "second-rater," of almost aggressive mediocrity; but there was nothing really exceptional about him. And when the young wife learns that her husband has played false to her in the most revolting manner and her father, Baron Le Perthuis des Vauds, infuriated by such baseness, wishes to thrash his son-in-law, the local curé quietly remarks:

"Come, come, Baron; between ourselves, he has been no worse than anyone else. Do you know many husbands who are faithful to their wives? Why, I bet that even you have played your little games." And adds in a tone of good-humoured banter: "Come, your hand upon your heart, isn't that true?"

The Baron stares, flabbergasted, at the priest, who continues:

"Yes, yes, you have done like the rest. Who knows even whether you have never amused yourself with a little baggage like that? I tell you all the world does as much. And your wife has been none the less happy, none the less loved for all that, has she?"

But then, as we continue reading, we come on the following passage:

"The Baron was so overcome that he did not stir. It was true that he had done as much, often enough; in fact, as often as he could; he, too, had not respected the conjugal roof; and, when they were pretty, he had had no scruples in regard to his wife's servants. Was he, therefore, a scoundrel? Why, then, should he condemn so severely the conduct of Julian, when he had never dreamed that his own conduct was blamable?

"On the lips of the Baroness, still out of breath with sobbing, hovered the shadow of a smile at the memory of her husband's frolics; for she was of that class, sentimental, readily moved, kind-hearted, for whom love affairs are an essential element of life."

There speaks the voice of mature age, and thus experience gives its "dusty answer" to the dreams of youth, hot for the certainties of ideal love. In this passage each sentiment is voiced by a different character and implies a different knowledge of life. The first derives from observation and the habit of the confessional; the second from memory of the speaker's personal lapses; the third from suffering and resignation. To reach this stage of disillusioned acquiescence Jeanne in her turn has to undergo a long-protracted martyrdom. Her husband is unfaithful, and she becomes shamefully inured to his infidelities; she loses her father and mother; one day her husband is murdered by a man with whose wife he is having an intrigue, and she mourns his loss; then the son, too, on whom she dotes, forsakes her. She loses her money and the one friend now left to her is the companion of her childhood, the maid who was Julian de Lamare's first mistress. Her only son marries unwisely, yet when the wretched creature he has married dies, Jeanne, old and hopeless now, takes rapturously to her bosom the child this woman has brought into the world.

Then, Maupassant writes: "She was overwhelmed by a boundless emotion. Swiftly she drew away the covering, and looked for the first time on the face of this child, her son's daughter. And when the frail little atom, roused by the bright light, opened her eyes and moved her lips, Jeanne embraced her passionately, clasping her to her bosom and showering kisses upon her."

And so at last all the misfortunes, disappointments and frustrations of the past are blotted out. Life begins anew for Jeanne, and, with life, love returns and the glad promise of a better day. This sombre, disillusioned novel ends on a glow of dawn.

Guy de Maupassant, like the men whose lead he followed, the *naturalistes*, set out with the intention of depicting characters he had actually observed, unexceptional people only, neither good nor bad, such as one meets with in the ordinary course of life. Still he did not wholly succeed in preventing a romantic element from creeping in. Thus Count and Countess de Fourville, and above all the vengeance of the country squire with whose wife Julian de Lamare has an intrigue, remind us more of the stock characters and situations in the works of Octave Feuillet, author of *M. de Camors* and *Julie de Trécour*, than of those of a friend of Flaubert and Octave Mirbeau. Not that the characters are wholly "fictional"; but they add a touch of somewhat romantic colour that seems out of keeping with the deliberate greyness of this novel, dedicated to "the humble truth." True, such great novelists as Balzac, Stendhal and Barbey d'Aurevilly, who combined realism with romance, were still not far removed in time. And Flaubert himself, the better to eliminate from his work any and every element that did not derive from the most scientifically accurate observation of real life, allowed his imagination, by way of counterpoise, to play truant on the grand scale and run riot in his *Tentation de St. Antoine, Salammbô*, and *La Légende de St. Julien-l'Hospitalier*.

There is no figure in *Une Vie* that is not fashioned in the round, with a well-marked personality. If Jeanne strikes us as a somewhat colourless character this is precisely because she is the most universal of them all, a woman like so many of her sisters, not so much virtuous or faithful as incapable of loving any other man than her first love.

It would be a mistake to think that this type of woman has altered during the fifty-five years that have elapsed since *Une Vie* was written. We need only visit the French provinces to find another sensitive, austere Jeanne de Lamare, the Le Perthuis des Vauds family, the Abbé Picot. Abbé Tolbiac, however, represents a type of country *curé* very different from the country *curé* of today. And we are inclined to think that Rosalie, though still to be found, is a less common type. The Fourvilles nowadays would have modernized their outlook; a crime of passion such as Count de Fourville's would strike us to-day as being something quite exceptional in that particular social *milieu*. Needless to say, we do not claim that such happenings are wholly inconceivable; but the fact that nowadays they are improbable prevents them from appearing so fundamentally true to life as they still did when Maupassant wrote *Une Vie*. As for Julian de Lamare, with his egoism, his gross sensuality and meanness, there is no reason to regard this sort of man as less prevalent in modern times than half a century ago.

If this brief estimate of the extent to which the pattern of man's life has changed, during a period that has seen so many changes, be correct, we have yet another reason for admiring *Une Vie;* for the picture it displays of life is so vigorously drawn and apposite that it is no more "out of date" in its handling of that human element than in its superb craftsmanship.

A Woman's Life

("Une Vie")

A Woman's
L I F E

1

JEANNE, having finished her packing, went to the window to look
out. But there was no abatement in the downpour. All night long
the rain had rattled on roof and window-pane. It was as if the lowering, rain-laden sky had burst and was emptying itself upon the
earth, churning it into pulp, melting it like sugar. Squalls, violent
yet warm and oppressive, succeeded one another. In the deserted
streets the water roared down the over-flowing gutters, and the
houses absorbed like sponges the penetrating moisture, which
exuded later on all the walls, from cellar to attic.

On the previous day Jeanne had bidden farewell to her convent.
She was free at last, free for ever, ready to embrace all the joys of
life, of which she had so long been dreaming. But now she feared
that, unless the weather improved, her father would be reluctant to
set forth homeward, and for the hundredth time that morning she
scanned the horizon.

She noticed that she had forgotten to pack her calendar in her
travelling-bag. She took down from the wall the little square of
cardboard, with its divisions for the months. It bore the date of the
current year, 1819, in gold letters in the middle of an ornamental
design. With her pencil she struck out the first four columns, scor-
ing out separately the Saints' names, until she came to the second
of May, the day on which she had left the convent.

"Jeannette," called a voice at the door.

"Come in, Papa," replied Jeanne, and her father entered the
room.

Baron Simon Jacques le Perthuis des Vauds was an aristocrat of

3

the old school, worthy, but eccentric. An enthusiastic disciple of Jean-Jacques Rousseau, he had a lover's passion for nature, for fields and woods and animals. Of noble birth, he held in instinctive abhorrence the events of the year 1793. None the less, being a philosopher by temperament and a liberal by education, he would express his detestation of tyranny with declamatory but harmless violence.

His great strength, and at the same time his great weakness, lay in his kindness of heart—a kindness that had not arms enough for all the caresses and gifts and embraces it longed to bestow; a kindness that was creative, yet diffused and yielding; an atrophy of the will, as it were, a defect of power, almost amounting to a vice.

A slave to his theories, he had thought out for his daughter a complete scheme of education, which should render her happy, virtuous, upright and affectionate. Until her twelfth year she was brought up at home. At that age, despite her mother's tears, she was sent to the Convent of the Sacred Heart. Her father had kept her there, rigorously cloistered and secluded, aloof from and ignorant of all the facts of life.

It was his wish that she should be restored to him at seventeen in perfect innocence, so that he himself might administer to her a baptism of poetic common sense. In a rural atmosphere, with the fertile fields around them, he hoped to see the flowering of her soul, and to enlighten her, through the contemplation of the ingenuous affections and unconstrained love-making of animals, on the placid ordinances of life.

And now she had left the convent, radiant, full of vitality, eager for the happiness, the joys, the enchanting possibilities which she had pictured to herself during idle days and long, long nights, in a solitude of dreams.

In appearance she recalled a portrait by Veronese. Her skin, an aristocratic skin, delicately tinged with pink, seemed to have caught from her fair hair a glistening lustre; it was shaded with a light down, peach-like, which was faintly noticeable when the sunshine glanced on it. Her eyes were of china blue, like those of the quaint little men in Dutch faïence.

On her left nostril she had a small mole, and on the right side of her chin another, with some hairs on it, of a pale colour like her skin, and almost imperceptible. She was tall, her bust well-devel-

4

oped, and her figure supple. At times her clear voice sounded somewhat shrill, but her unrestrained laughter rang out with infectious gaiety. She had a little trick of raising her hands to her temples, as if to smooth her hair.

She ran to her father, threw her arms round him, and kissed him. "Well, are we going?" she asked.

He smiled, and shook his somewhat long and already whitened locks. Pointing towards the window, he exclaimed, "How can you expect to travel in weather like that?"

But she coaxed and entreated. "O Papa, do let us go, I implore you. It is sure to be fine in the afternoon."

"Your mother will never agree."

"Yes, I'm sure she will; I'll answer for her."

"If you can persuade your mother, I am quite willing to go."

She darted into her mother's room. Jeanne had been looking forward with ever-increasing impatience to this day of their departure. Since her admission to the convent, she had never been out of Rouen, for her father had refused to allow her any distractions until she reached the age he had named. Twice she had been taken to Paris for a fortnight; but Paris, too, was a town, and all her dreams were of the country.

Now she was going to spend the summer on their property, *Les Peuples*, an old family seat, situated on the cliffs near Yport. She had promised herself an infinity of delight in the free life by the seashore. It had, moreover, been agreed that the estate was to be hers, and that when she was married she would always live there. The rain, which had never ceased since the previous evening, was the first serious annoyance in her life.

In three minutes' time, however, she ran out of her mother's room, calling through the house, "Papa! Papa! Mamma consents. Order the carriage."

The downpour showed no sign of abating. On the contrary, when the carriage came round to the door, it seemed to increase in severity. Just as Jeanne was ready to enter the carriage, her mother descended the steps. The Baroness was supported on one side by her husband, and on the other by a tall, strapping maid, as limber as a boy. The maid, who was from the Caux region in Normandy, looked at least twenty, although she could not have been more than eighteen. She had been Jeanne's foster-sister, and was treated in

5

the family almost like another daughter. Her name was Rosalie.

Her principal duty was to attend her mistress whenever she moved about. Of late years the Baroness had grown enormously stout, in consequence of a hypertrophy of the heart, of which she never ceased complaining.

Panting, the Baroness reached the perron of the old mansion, and looked down into the courtyard, which was running with water.

"Really, it is absurd," she protested.

Her husband replied with a smile, "Why, it was you who insisted, Madame Adelaide." To the imposing name Adelaide he always put the prefix "Madame," with an air of respect in which there was a touch of mockery.

At that she moved on, and climbed laboriously into the carriage, whose springs yielded beneath her weight. The Baron took his place beside her, while Jeanne and Rosalie seated themselves with their backs to the horses.

Ludivine, the cook, brought an armful of coats, and arranged them over the travellers' knees, while two large baskets were stowed away under their feet. Then she clambered up on to the box beside old Simon, and rolled herself up from head to foot in a large rug. The porter and his wife took leave of the family, and received parting instructions about the luggage, which was to follow by cart. Then the door was closed, and the carriage drove away.

Old Simon, the coachman, with head bowed, sat hunched up in the rain, almost lost to sight in his driving-coat with its triple cape. The storm howled and beat against the windows, and the highroad was like a running stream.

Drawn by its pair of horses at a fast trot, the carriage bowled briskly along the quay, where great ships forlornly reared into the dripping sky their masts, yards and rigging, like leafless trees. Then it proceeded down the long Boulevard of Mont Riboudet. Presently the way lay through open country, and here and there a half-drowned willow, with a corpse-like inertness in its drooping branches, stood out in funereal relief against the watery mist. The horses' hoofs clattered, and the wheels splashed through the mud.

There was no conversation. The travellers' spirits seemed affected by the universal dampness. The Baroness was leaning back with closed eyelids, while the Baron contemplated with melancholy gaze the dreary and sodden landscape. Rosalie, who held a parcel on her lap, had sunk into a condition of animal reverie, common in her class. But Jeanne felt revived by the warm rain, like an indoor plant which has been brought out into the fresh air.

The intensity of her joy was as a leafy screen, which protected her heart from sorrow. Although she was silent, she longed to sing, to put her hand outside in order to collect the rain-water and drink it. She enjoyed the rapid pace at which they were driving, the dreary aspect of the countryside, and the sense of being sheltered in the midst of a deluge. The horses' shining cruppers were steaming in the pitiless rain.

Gradually the Baroness fell asleep. Her face, in its frame of six carefully arranged curls, slowly subsided upon the soft support of her three immense double chins, whose lowest folds were lost in the vast expanse of her bosom. At each breath, her head was jerked upwards and then dropped down again. Her cheeks were puffed out and from her half-open lips issued a resonant snore. Her husband leaned towards her and gently placed a little leather hand-bag in her hands, which were crossed over her ample waist.

His touch awoke her. She looked at the bag with dazed eyes, in the bewilderment of a person suddenly startled out of sleep. She dropped the bag, and it burst open. Gold and notes were scattered over the floor of the carriage. This roused her completely, and her daughter broke out into mirthful peals of laughter.

The Baron picked up the money, and laid it in his wife's lap.

"Look, my dear," he said, "this is all I have left out of the sale of my farm at Eletot. I sold it for the repairs to *Les Peuples*. We shall be there a good deal now."

She counted the money, six thousand four hundred francs, and quietly put it away in her pocket.

This was the ninth farm they had sold out of thirty-one bequeathed to them by their parents. But they still derived an income of twenty thousand francs from property which, in capable hands, could easily have yielded thirty thousand. Their income would have been sufficient for their simple mode of life had it not been for the existence of the bottomless and ever-yawning pit of benevolence. It was this that drained away their ready money, as the sun drains a marsh. The money slipped through their fingers,

7

melted away and vanished, no one knew how. One or the other was continually exclaiming, "Somehow I spent a hundred francs to-day, without buying anything of any consequence."

This passion of generosity was, however, one of their chief joys in life, and their unanimity on this subject was exquisite and touching.

"Does my house look nice now?" asked Jeanne.

"You will soon see, little girl," replied her father gaily.

Gradually the violence of the rain abated, until it was hardly more than a mist, a drifting drizzle of rain. The vault of clouds was rising and growing less dense, and suddenly through an invisible rift a long slanting ray of sunshine shot down upon the fields. Patches of blue showed through the rift, which widened like a torn veil, and a sky of deep clear azure was gradually disclosed.

A fresh, gentle breeze, like a sigh of content, was wafted over the earth; and from garden and copse came the blithe song of a bird, drying its feathers.

Evening descended. Except Jeanne, everyone in the carriage was asleep. Twice a halt was made at an inn to rest and water the horses, and give them a feed of oats.

The sun had set. In the distance the church bells were ringing. At a little village they drew up to light the carriage lamps, and from the sky came the answering twinkle of a myriad stars. Here and there the lights of a house flashed forth, piercing the darkness like fiery shafts. Suddenly, above a hill-slope, rose a great red drowsy moon, shining through pine branches.

The air was so mild that the carriage windows were left open. Jeanne had had her fill of happy dreams and fancies, and was now resting. But sometimes she awoke from a cramped position, and opened her eyes. Then she would look out into the starry night, and see the trees of a farm glide past, or cows lying here and there in a field, and raising their heads. Then she would move into a new posture, and try to recapture some fleeting dream. But the persistent rumbling of the carriage sounded in her ears and wearied her brain, and she closed her eyes again, with a sensation of mental and physical stiffness.

At last the carriage drew up, and men and women came to the doors with lanterns in their hands. The travellers had reached their destination. Wide awake in an instant, Jeanne jumped out quickly.

One of the farmers held a light for the Baron and Rosalie, who had almost to carry the Baroness between them. She was completely exhausted. She uttered groans of distress, and repeated again and again in a faint, expiring voice:

"O Heavens, my poor children!"

She refused to eat or drink; went straight to bed, and fell asleep immediately.

Jeanne and her father had supper together. They smiled at each other, and clasped hands across the table. Full of childlike joy, they then explored the house.

Les Peuples had been recently restored. It was one of those lofty and spacious Norman structures, half farm, half mansion, built of white stone which had turned grey with age, and roomy enough to house a whole tribe. The immense central hall, which was of the full depth of the house and divided it into two sections, had two great doors, opening front and back. There was a staircase on each side of the vestibule; these left a clear space in the centre of the entrance hall, and united on the first floor like a bridge. On the ground floor, to the right, was a spacious drawing-room, hung with tapestry, bearing a design of birds flitting among foliage. Every article of furniture was decorated with tapestry in fine needlework, illustrating La Fontaine's fables. Jeanne gave a jump of joy when she recognised a favourite chair of her nursery days, which represented the fable of the Fox and the Stork.

Next to the drawing-room came a library full of old books, and then two unused rooms. On the left lay the dining-room, newly wainscotted, the linen-room, the servants' hall, the kitchen, and a small bathroom.

A corridor ran the whole length of the first story, with the doors of ten rooms opening on to it. At the far end, on the right, was Jeanne's bedroom, which Jeanne and her father entered. The Baron had had it redecorated, using for this purpose some hangings and furniture that had lain neglected in the attics. The bizarre figures in the ancient Flemish tapestry had the effect of making the room seem full of people.

When Jeanne caught sight of the bed, she uttered cries of rapture. Four great birds in black polished oak supported the corners of the bed as if guarding it. The sides of the bedstead were carved to represent broad festoons of flowers and fruit. Four delicately fluted columns, surmounted by Corinthian capitals, bore a cornice of roses and Cupids interlaced. Its aspect was monumental, and yet elegant, despite the austerity of the woodwork darkened with age.

Counterpane and canopy glittered like starry skies. They were made of antique silk of a dark blue colour, spangled with *fleur-de-lis* embroidered in gold.

When she had duly admired the bed, Jeanne raised her candle in order to examine the tapestry and discover its subject. A young lord and lady in grotesque dresses of green, red and yellow, were conversing in the shade of a blue tree with white fruit on its boughs. A fat rabbit of the same colour was nibbling the grey grass. Immediately above the figures, in a conventional perspective, were five small round houses with pointed roofs; and still higher, almost up in the sky, a windmill in red. Between and around all these details wound a great floral pattern. Two other panels bore a close resemblance to the first, except that four little men, dressed in Flemish fashion, emerged from the houses, raising their hands to heaven in a gesture of extreme astonishment and wrath. The last picture, however, represented a tragedy. Near the rabbit, which was still nibbling the grass, lay the young man, apparently dead. The damsel, her gaze fixed on him, was piercing her bosom with a sword, and the fruit on the tree had turned black.

Jeanne despaired of unravelling the story, when she perceived in a corner a microscopical beast, which the rabbit could have devoured like a blade of grass, but which, for all that, turned out to be a lion. She realised then that it was the tale of Pyramus and Thisbe, and although she smiled at the artlessness of the designs, she rejoiced in this story of passion, which would ever speak to her of cherished hopes, and would bring the atmosphere of bygone love to brood over her nightly slumbers.

The rest of the furniture was a medley of totally different styles. Each generation in a family contributes its quota of furniture, until an ancient house comes to resemble a museum with a little of everything in it. A magnificent Louis XIV chest of drawers, with shining copper fittings, was flanked by two Louis XV armchairs, still with their original covers of flowered silk. A rosewood writing table stood opposite the mantelpiece, which was adorned by a pendulum clock of the Empire, under a glass globe. The clock represented a beehive in bronze, and was supported on four marble columns above a parterre of gilded flowers. At the tip of a slender pendulum, which hung down from the beehive through a narrow slit, a small bee with enamelled wings swung backwards and forwards unceasingly above the parterre. The dial was of coloured faïence and was set in the side of the beehive. This clock struck eleven, and the Baron kissed his daughter and retired to his own room.

Reluctantly, Jeanne went to bed. She cast one last glance round the room, and then blew out her candle. The head of the bed rested against the wall. Through a window on the left a flood of moonlight streamed into the room and formed upon the floor a pool of radiance. It cast reflections on the walls, pale reflections that played faintly upon Pyramus and Thisbe spellbound in their love-making. Through a window in the wall beyond the foot of the bed, Jeanne saw a great tree, all bathed in the soft light. She turned on her side, closed her eyes; but presently opened them again. She still felt the sensation produced by the jolting of the carriage, and the rumbling of the wheels echoed in her ears. For a while she lay motionless, courting sleep by this semblance of repose, but soon the agitation

11

of her mind communicated itself to her whole frame. Her limbs were seized by a feverish and ever-increasing restlessness. Presently she rose, with bare arms and feet, and, looking like a phantom in her long nightgown, she crossed the pool of light which lay upon the floor. She opened the window and looked out. The night was so radiant that everything was as plainly visible as in broad daylight. Jeanne recognised all the features of the countryside which she had loved in childhood. In the immediate foreground lay a wide lawn, creamy yellow in the moonlight. In front of the mansion stood two huge trees, a plane tree to the north and a lime to the south. The great lawn extended as far as a little thicket, forming one of the boundaries of the estate, which was protected from ocean storms by five rows of ancient elms, twisted, battered, worn, bent over like a roof by the force of the ever-raging sea wind.

The park was bounded on the right and left by two long avenues of tall poplars, called *peuples* in Normandy. They separated the grounds of the mansion from the two adjacent farms, one of which was occupied by a family of the name of Couillard, the other by a family called Martin. It was from these poplars that the property derived its name. Beyond the enclosed grounds extended a great barren, wind-swept moor overgrown with gorse, where the sea-breezes whistled and howled day and night. The coast fell away abruptly in a sheer white cliff three hundred feet high, with its base in the sea.

Jeanne gazed at the distant expanse of rippling water, which slumbered in the starlight. In the soothing absence of the sun, all the scents of the earth were wafted abroad. The climbing jasmine that twined around the windows mingled its penetrating fragrance with the subtler perfume of young leaves. Little puffs of wind blew past, charged with the strong tang of the sea, and the exhalations of viscid seaweed.

Jeanne gave herself up to the mere joy of breathing; the peacefulness of the country calmed her like a bath of cool water. Nocturnal animals, whose mysterious existence is cloaked by the tranquillity of night, filled the twilight with a noiseless agitation. Great birds, like blots or shadows, winged their way silently through the air. The murmur of invisible insects fell upon the ear; soft feet stole over the dewy grass and the gravel of the deserted paths.

Only some melancholy toads addressed to the moon their brief, monotonous croak.

Jeanne's heart expanded; it seemed, like the moonlight night, full of murmurous sound; teeming with a thousand vagrant thoughts like those creatures of night that troubled the air around her. She felt an affinity with all this living poetry, and in the soft radiance of the night, she was conscious of supernatural shudders, intangible hopes, something that resembled a breath of happiness.

She fell into a dream of love. Love! For two years she had felt the increasing agitation of its approach. At last she was free to love. She had only to meet the hero of her dreams.

What would he be like? She had no clear idea of him and did not even try to form one. He would simply be himself. All that she knew was that she would worship him with her whole soul, and that he would love her with all his heart. On such evenings as this they would wander together, with the shining star dust showering down upon them. They would go hand in hand close to each other, listening to the beating of their hearts, conscious of the warmth of each other's shoulders, their love mingling with the soft radiance of summer night, and in such unity that by the mere force of love each would penetrate to the other's most sacred thoughts.

And this state of bliss would last indefinitely, in the serenity of a love inexpressible.

Suddenly it seemed to her that she felt him there beside her, and she was thrilled by a vague and sensuous tremor. Unconsciously she pressed her arms to her bosom as if to embrace her dream, and she felt a sensation which nearly made her faint. It was as if the spring air had pressed a kiss of love upon the lips that she offered to the unknown.

Suddenly in the distance, on the road behind the house, she heard footsteps. With an impulse of her overwrought mind, in an ecstasy of faith in the impossible, in providential coincidences, divine presentiments, romantic contrivances of destiny, she wondered if this could be he. She listened eagerly to the rhythmic tread, convinced that the wayfarer would pause at the gate and ask for hospitality. When the steps passed on she had a sense of disappointment. But she smiled as she realised the fantastic nature of her hopes. She subsided into a calmer mood, and her musings turned

13

in a more practical direction; she endeavoured to probe the future and to map out her life. She would live here with him, in this quiet mansion by the sea; and she would have two children, a son for him, a daughter for herself. She imagined them running about on the grass between the plane tree and the lime, while their father and mother watched them rapturously, and over their heads exchanged passionate glances.

She remained at the window a long, long time, lost in her dreams, until the moon had traversed the sky and was sinking in the sea. The air was cooler, and a faint light suffused the eastern sky. In the farm to the right a cock crowed, and was answered by others in the farm to the left. Their raucous voices rising from the poultry yard seemed to come from very far away. The great vault of the sky was gradually lightening, and the stars were fading.

A bird's tiny chirrup was heard. From the leaves came timid twitterings, which soon grew bolder, and spread, vibrant and joyous, from branch to branch and tree to tree.

Suddenly Jeanne was conscious of a bright light all round her, and raising her head from her hands, she closed her eyes, dazzled by the splendour of the dawn. From a bank of purple clouds, half hidden behind the wide avenue of poplars, blood-red light poured down upon the awakening earth. And gradually, rending the luminous mists, deluging with fire the trees, the moor, the ocean and the whole wide landscape, the flaming orb of day rose into view. Jeanne felt wild with delight. Her heart was overwhelmed by a delirious joy, an infinite emotion, at the glory of the universe. This sun was hers; this dawn was hers; they were the beginning of her life, the morning of her hopes. She stretched out her arms towards the radiance as though to embrace the sun. She longed to speak, to utter words worthy of the divine dawn; but she remained dumb in an exaltation that she could not express. She bowed her face on her hands; her eyes filled, and she wept delicious tears.

When she raised her head the glory of dawn had already faded. Her enthusiasm had subsided; she felt chill and a little weary. Without closing the window, she lay down on her bed, nursed her dreams for a few more minutes, until she fell into so deep a sleep that she did not hear her father calling her at eight o'clock, and only woke up when he entered the room.

He wanted to show her the improvements in the house, this house which was her own. The mansion faced the grounds, and an enclosure planted with apple trees lay between it and a branch road, which ran on between the peasants' apple orchards and met, a mile away, the highroad between Havre and Fécamp. A straight path led from the wooden fence to the perron of the mansion. Along the two sides of the enclosure, for the whole length of the farm dykes, stood a row of roughcast out-buildings with thatched roofs.

Fresh blinds had been put up, the wood-work entirely restored, the walls repaired, the rooms repapered and the whole interior repainted. New silvery-white shutters and patches of recently applied plaster chequered the great grey façade of the weather-stained old mansion. One of Jeanne's windows opened on to the back of the house, which commanded a distant view of the sea across the copse and the ranks of wind-beaten elms.

Arm in arm, Jeanne and the Baron inspected everything, without missing a single corner. Then they took a leisurely stroll down the long avenues of poplars, which enclosed what was known as the park. A green carpet of grass had grown up beneath the trees. The copse at the end of the avenues was charming, with its maze of little paths which wound their way between leafy barriers. A hare sprang up suddenly, startling Jeanne; it jumped the bank and scampered away into the rushes towards the cliff.

After luncheon Madame Adelaide, who was still exhausted, announced her intention of resting. The Baron suggested walking to Yport, and he and Jeanne set out. Their way led through Etouvent, the hamlet in which *Les Peuples* was situated. Three peasants wished them good-day as if they had known them all their lives. They entered the woods that slope down towards the sea, following the line of a winding valley. Soon they reached the village of Yport. Women sat mending clothes on their doorsteps, and watched them as they went past. The street, which was built on a declivity with a stream running down the middle and rubbish heaps at every door, had a strong salty odour. Brown fishing-nets, with shining scales clinging like small silver coins to the meshes, were drying on the doors of hovels, whence issued the reek of large families herded together in a single room. A few pigeons were strutting about the banks of the stream, picking up their sustenance.

To Jeanne's gaze, all this had the interest and novelty of a scene at the theatre.

Suddenly as they turned a corner, she beheld the solid and glassy blue of the ocean stretching away beyond the range of sight. They stood on the beach and looked at the view. Sails, like white wings, were moving across the open sea. On either hand rose tall cliffs. On one side the prospect was cut short by a high promontory; on the other the coast line ran on and on until it faded into a distant blur.

In one of the nearer gullies houses and a quay were visible, and tiny waves, fringing the sea with foam, broke on the shingle with a low murmur.

Boats of the country were hauled up on the sloping shingle and lay sunning their shiny, tarry hulls, while fishermen were making them ready for the evening tide.

A sailor brought some fish for sale, and Jeanne purchased a brill, which she proposed to carry home herself. The man then offered to take them out in his boat, and repeated his name several times to impress it on their memories.

"Lastique, Joseph Lastique."

The Baron promised to make a note of it. They turned towards home. The fish was too heavy for Jeanne, so she passed her father's walking-stick through its gills, and each held one end of it. They climbed the hill gaily, their faces to the wind, bright-eyed and chattering like a couple of children, with the brill, which gradually tired their arms, trailing its thick tail through the grass.

2

JEANNE now led a life of enchanting liberty. All by herself she roamed, reading or dreaming, about the countryside. Lost in a reverie, she wandered slowly along the roads, or skipped down the little winding valleys, whose sides were cloaked in a golden fleece of flowering gorse. The strong sweet scent, drawn out by the heat, intoxicated her like fragrant wine, and her soul was lulled by the distant murmur of waves breaking on a beach.

At times, in a languorous mood, she would lie at full length on a turfy slope. Now and then, when a vista at a bend in the valley afforded her a sudden glimpse of a triangle of sea, sparkling in the sun, with a sail crossing the horizon, an extravagant sensation of joy would steal over her, as if some mysterious happiness were hovering above her. A love of solitude possessed her amid the delights of this unspoiled tract of country, and soothed by the calm of those far distant prospects, she would sit so long on a hilltop that the little wild rabbits would scamper past her feet. Often she would run along the cliff, stimulated by the exhilarating breezes of the uplands, and thrilling with exquisite joy in movements that tired her no more than a fish in the sea or a swallow in the air.

In every spot she scattered memories, as one scatters seed upon the ground, memories that take root and endure till death. It seemed to her that in every fold of these valleys she left behind her something of her heart. She bathed enthusiastically. A strong, bold swimmer, without thought of danger, she swam out of sight of shore. She felt at home in the cradle of the cold, clear, blue water. When she was far out from shore, she would lie on her back, cross her arms on her breast, and plunge her gaze into the deep azure of the sky, crossed now and then by a swift flight of swallows or the white silhouette of a sea bird. She could hear nothing but the distant murmur of the waves breaking on the beach, and the muffled, confused, and almost inaudible landward sounds that reached her across the water. Then she would change her position, and in an ecstasy of joy, utter shrill cries of glee, and beat the water with her hands. Sometimes, when she had ventured too far, a boat would come after her.

17

She would return home, pale with hunger, but buoyant and alert, with a smile on her lips and happiness in her eyes.

The Baron, for his part, was nursing great agricultural schemes; he wished to make experiments; to initiate progressive methods, test new implements and acclimatise foreign breeds. He spent part of the day in discussion with the peasants, who shook their heads and regarded his efforts with scepticism.

Often too he went out with the Yport fishermen. When he had explored the grottos, springs and pinnacles in the neighbourhood, he wanted to go fishing like an ordinary seaman. On breezy days, the swelling sail bore the broad-beamed boat swiftly over the crest of the waves, with the long, running line sinking at each tack to the bed of the sea, and pursued by shoals of mackerel. His hands quivering with excitement, the Baron would hold the line, which thrilled to the resistance of a fish on the hook. On moonlight nights he went out to pull up the nets that had been set the previous evening. He loved to hear the creaking of the mast, to breathe in the fresh night breezes which whistled through the rigging. After tacking about for a time in an attempt to find the buoys, taking his bearings from a ridge of rocks, a church-tower and the Fécamp lighthouse, he delighted to remain motionless, watching the first rays of the rising sun as they glanced on the slimy backs of diamond-shaped skate and the plump bellies of turbot.

At each meal he discoursed enthusiastically about his expeditions, and the Baroness rejoined by telling him how many times she had walked up and down the whole length of the avenue of poplars. She favoured the right hand one, by the Couillards' farm, the other not having sufficient sun.

As the Baroness had been advised to take exercise, she became passionately devoted to walking. As soon as the day had warmed up, she came downstairs, leaning on Rosalie's arm, with a cloak and two shawls round her, her head smothered in a black hood, and over that a red knitted scarf.

By dragging her left foot, which was a little heavier than the other, she had already worn in either direction, the whole length of the avenue, two dusty tracks where the grass had been trampled down. She would set out on her interminable journey, in a straight line from the corner of the house as far as the first bushes of the coppice. She had had a bench placed at each end of the path, and every five

minutes she stopped and said to the poor maid, who was patiently giving her her arm:

"Let us sit down, child. I am rather tired."

Each time she rested, she deposited on one bench or the other first her scarf, then one shawl, then the other, then her hood, then her cloak, and these garments formed at each end of the avenue a great pile of clothing, which Rosalie carried home on her spare arm at luncheon time. The Baroness spent her afternoons in a more leisurely fashion. Her rests became longer, and she even dozed for an hour at a time on a couch which was wheeled out of doors for her. She referred to "her exercise," just as she alluded to her disease as "her hypertrophy."

A doctor, whom she had consulted ten years before about certain attacks of breathlessness from which she was suffering, had mentioned the word hypertrophy. Ever since then this term, the significance of which she did not understand, had fixed itself firmly in her head. She insisted on the Baron and Jeanne and Rosalie feeling her heart, of which the pulsations could not be discerned, buried as it was in the redundance of her bosom. She positively refused to allow

19

herself to be examined by another doctor, for fear he should discover other ailments. She spoke of her hypertrophy at every opportunity and with such frequency, that it seemed as though the affliction were peculiar to herself, something unique to which no one else could lay claim.

The Baron alluded to "my wife's hypertrophy," and Jeanne to "Mama's hypertrophy," as though they were saying "her gown, her hat, her umbrella."

In her youth she had been extremely pretty, and as slender as a reed. She had waltzed with all the officers of the Empire; she had wept over *Corinne*, and her mind was still noticeably affected by that romance.

In proportion as her body increased in girth, her soul indulged more and more in poetic transports, and when she was confined to an armchair by her obesity, her vagrant thoughts revelled in romantic incidents, of which she imagined herself the heroine. There were certain favourite interludes on which she dwelt continually in her reveries, like a musical box which has been set so that it repeats the same tune over and over again. Those languorous romances, in which figure captives and swallows, never failed to bring tears to her eyes, and she had a fondness even for certain ribald songs of Béranger's, because even they are the vehicle of regret.

Often she remained motionless for hours, lost in dreams. *Les Peuples* had a great charm for her, because it afforded a setting for the romances that thrilled her soul. Its surroundings of woods and barren moor and its proximity to the sea, were coupled in her mind with the works of Walter Scott, which she had for some months been reading.

On rainy days she shut herself up in her room and looked through what she called her treasures. These were all her old letters, her father's and mother's, those that the Baron had written to her during their engagement, and other letters besides. She kept them in a mahogany writing table ornamented at the corners with copper sphinxes. She would say, in a tone reserved for this occasion:

"Rosalie, my child, bring me the drawer with my souvenirs."

The little maid would open the desk, take out the drawer, and place it on a chair beside her mistress, who would slowly read the letters, one by one, occasionally dropping a tear upon them. Sometimes Jeanne took Rosalie's place and accompanied her mother on her walks, and the Baroness would relate memories of her childhood. The girl recognised herself in these tales of other days. She was struck by the similarity of their ideas, the common origin of their desires. For each human heart imagines itself to be the first to quiver with that host of emotions which thrilled the breasts of the first created beings, and will be still distracting the bosoms of the last surviving man and woman. Their slow steps kept pace with the slow course of the narrative, which was often interrupted by a passing physical oppression. Jeanne's thoughts would, in these intervals, leap away from these interrupted tales, and would fling themselves headlong into the joys and hopes of the future.

One afternoon when they were resting on the further bench, they saw a stout priest coming towards them along the avenue. From a distance he raised his hat, and smiled, and when he was a few steps away he bowed again and called out:

"Well, Baroness, and how are we?" It was the parish priest.

The Baroness, born in a philosophical age, and brought up in the days of the Revolution by a somewhat sceptical father, never went to church, although she had a liking for priests, due to a religious instinct common in women. She had quite forgotten Abbé Picot, her parish priest, and reddened when she saw him. She apologised for not having forestalled his visit. But the good man did not seem to have taken offence. He looked at Jeanne, congratulated her on her appearance, sat down with his three-cornered hat on his knees and mopped his brow. He was very fat, very red in the face, and he perspired profusely. From his pocket he continually drew a huge check handkerchief, soaked with perspiration, and passed it over his face and neck. But he had hardly restored the square of damp linen to the recesses of his gown, when new drops formed on his skin and rolled down, and mingling with the fine dust off the roads, formed little round spots on his cassock.

He was a genuine country clergyman, merry, tolerant, talkative and kindly. He told stories and discussed the neighbours, and seemed unaware that his two parishioners had not yet appeared at church. The Baroness's indolence accorded well with her unsettled beliefs, and Jeanne was only too delighted at her release from the convent, where she had had her fill of pious ceremonies.

The Baron joined them. His pantheism rendered him indifferent to dogma. But he was kind to the Abbé, who was an old friend, and made him stay to dinner. Men of the most mediocre ability, who are summoned by the hazard of circumstances to exercise authority over their fellows, acquire unconsciously a certain astuteness. By dint of his life-long manipulation of souls the priest had learnt the art of pleasing. The Baroness made much of him, drawn to him, perhaps, by one of those affinities that unite kindred natures. His red face, shortness of breath and stoutness appealed to her, panting under the burden of her own obesity.

Towards the end of dinner, he attained a mood of priestly joviality, and the easy familiarity which is induced by a merry meal.

Suddenly, as if struck by a happy thought, he exclaimed:

"I have a new parishioner, Viscount de Lamare, whom I must present to you."

The Baroness, who had all the heraldry of the province at her fingers' ends, asked:

"Does he belong to the Lamares of Eure?"

The priest assented. "Yes, he is the son of Viscount Jean de Lamare, who died last year."

Madame Adelaide, who had a passion for aristocracy, asked a great many questions, and learned that after paying his father's debts and selling his ancestral estate, the young man had made a temporary home for himself in one of three farms he owned in the township of Etouvent. The income derived from this property amounted in all to five or six thousand francs. But the Viscount was of a prudent and economical turn of mind, and intended to live quietly for two or three years in his little cottage, until he had saved enough to make a suitable appearance in society and to marry advantageously, without running into debt or mortgaging his farms.

"He is a very charming fellow," added the Abbé, "so steady and quiet. But he finds it dull here."

"Bring him to see us, Abbé," said the Baron, "it might amuse him now and then."

The conversation passed on to another subject.

When they had had coffee and entered the drawing-room, the priest asked if he might go for a stroll in the garden, as he had the habit of taking a little exercise after his meals. The Baron accompanied him. They paced slowly up and down, from end to end of the white façade of the mansion. Their shadows, one lean, the other round and surmounted with a hat like a mushroom, moved with them, now behind, now in front, according as they faced or turned their backs on the moon. The priest chewed a cigarette which he extracted from his pocket. He explained its purpose with the frankness of a countryman.

"It assists my digestion, which is somewhat slow."

Suddenly he looked up at the bright moon sailing across the sky.

"That's a sight of which one never tires," he exclaimed. Then he returned to the house to take leave of the ladies.

3

ON the following Sunday the Baroness and Jeanne, prompted by a delicate feeling of deference for the priest, went to church.

After service they waited to invite him to luncheon on Thursday. He emerged from the sacristy with a tall, well-dressed young man, who linked arms with him with an air of familiarity. As soon as the priest saw the two ladies, he made a gesture of surprise and delight.

"What luck!" he exc.aimed. "Baroness, Mademoiselle Jeanne, allow me to introduce your neighbour, Viscount de Lamare."

The Viscount bowed, said that he had been looking forward to meeting them, and entered into conversation with the ease of a man of the world. He had one of those handsome faces of which women dream, but for which men have an instinctive aversion. His curly black hair shaded a smooth sun-burned forehead; his eyebrows were as symmetrical as if they were artificial, and gave a deep and tender expression to his dark eyes, of which the whites had a bluish tinge. His long, thick lashes lent to his gaze the passionate eloquence which disturbs the peace of mind of the fair and haughty lady in her drawing-room, and makes a girl, tripping along the street with cap and basket, turn her head to look. The languorous charm of his eyes gave an impression of profound thought, and invested his slightest utterances with meaning. His thick, glossy, silky beard concealed a somewhat pronounced jaw.

They parted on friendly terms. Two days later Monsieur de Lamare paid his first visit. He arrived just as his hosts were trying the effect of a rustic seat which had been placed that morning under the great plane tree outside the drawing-room windows. The Baron wanted to balance it with another seat under the lime. But his wife, who disliked symmetry, would not hear of it. The Viscount was asked his opinion, and agreed with the Baroness. Then he talked about the surrounding country, which he pronounced very picturesque. On his solitary walks he had discovered many enchanting spots. From time to time, as if by chance, his eyes met Jeanne's. This sudden, fleeting glance, which revealed a tender admiration and a dawning sympathy, made a curious impression upon her.

The Viscount's father, Monsieur de Lamare, who had died the previous year, had chanced to know an intimate friend of the Baroness's father, Monsieur des Cultaux. The discovery of this common acquaintance resulted in an endless conversation full of details of marriages, dates, and relationships. The Baroness performed wonderful feats of memory, settling points relating to the ancestry and the posterity of different families, and never losing her way in the complicated labyrinth of genealogies.

"Tell me, Viscount, have you heard of the Saunoys de Varfleur? Gontran, the eldest son, married a Mademoiselle de Coursil, a Coursil-Courville; the younger son married one of my cousins, Mademoiselle de la Roche-Aubert, who was related to the Crisanges. Monsieur de Crisange was an intimate friend of my father's and must have known yours, too."

"No doubt, Baroness. Was it not this Monsieur de Crisange who emigrated, and whose son came to grief?"

"The very same. He proposed to my aunt after the death of her husband, Count d'Eretry, but she refused him because he took snuff. By the way, do you know what has become of the Viloises? They left Touraine about 1813, after some misfortunes, with the intention of settling in Auvergne, and I have never heard anything more of them."

"I think the old Marquis was killed by a fall from his horse. One of his daughters married an Englishman, and the other some man in business called Bassole, said to be rich. He had seduced her."

Names they had heard mentioned in their infancy by old relations came back to them. And the marriages of these persons who were of their own class had for them the importance of events of great public interest. They spoke of people whom they had never seen as if they knew them well; precisely as those people in other parts of the country would speak of them. Even at a distance there was a certain bond between them, almost as if they were friends and connections, due solely to the fact that they belonged to the same class and caste, and were of the same quality of blood.

The Baron, who was somewhat shy by nature, and unfitted by his education for the tenets and prejudices of his class, hardly knew even the families in the neighbourhood. He questioned the Viscount about them.

"Oh, there are not many of the aristocracy in this district," replied Monsieur de Lamare, just as he might have said, "There are not many rabbits about here." He went into details. There were only three families within a convenient radius, the Marquis de Coutelier, the nominal head of the Norman aristocracy, Viscount and Viscountess de Briseville, people of very good family but keeping very much to themselves, and finally Count de Fourville, a boorish fellow who was supposed to plague his wife to death, and who lived for nothing but hunting. His country-house, *La Vrillette*, was built beside a lake. Some upstarts who were always quarrelling among themselves had bought places here and there. But the Viscount did not know them.

When he took leave, he directed a parting glance at Jeanne, as if he were bidding her an especially tender and cordial farewell. The Baroness thought him charming and praised his manners. The Baron replied:

"Yes, he's certainly a well-bred young fellow."

He was invited to dinner the following week, and after that he came regularly. As a rule he arrived about four in the afternoon, joined the Baroness in her avenue, and offered her his arm. When Jeanne was at home she supported the Baroness on the other side, and all three walked slowly backwards and forwards from end to end of the long, straight path. He did not talk at all to Jeanne, but his velvety black eyes would often meet Jeanne's eyes of agate blue.

Sometimes both of them went to Yport with the Baron. One evening when they were on the beach, old Lastique came up to them. Without removing his pipe, the absence of which would have been almost more noticeable than the disappearance of his nose, he said:

"If this wind holds, sir, you could sail to-morrow to Etretat and back without any trouble."

Jeanne clasped her hands. "Oh, Papa, do let us go."

The Baron turned to Monsieur de Lamare. "Will you come, Viscount? We could have luncheon over there."

The expedition was at once arranged.

Jeanne was up by dawn. She waited for her father, who took his time over his dressing, and then they went together, first over the dewy grass, and then through woods vibrant with the singing of birds. The Viscount and old Lastique were seated on a capstan. Two other sailors helped in the launching. Putting their shoulders to the bulwarks, the men heaved with all their might, but the boat hardly moved over the level beach. Lastique slipped rollers of greased wood under the keel, and then, returning to his post, he chanted his long-drawn "Heave ho!" to which the others timed their efforts. But when the slope was reached, the boat suddenly leapt forward and slid down over the shingle with a loud noise like the tearing of cloth. She stopped short where the little waves were breaking. The party took their seats, and the two sailors stayed behind and pushed her off.

A light, steady breeze, blowing from the sea, caressed and ruffled the surface of the water. The sail was set, and bellied slightly, and the boat sailed quietly along, rising and falling gently on the waves.

At first they sailed straight out to sea. On the horizon, sea and sky melted into one. On the right the tall cliff, indented here and there with sunny slopes of turf, cast a deep shadow upon the water at its base. In the distance, behind them, brown sails were leaving the white quay of Fécamp, while before them lay a curiously shaped rock, rounded and perforated, and resembling the head of a huge elephant plunging its trunk in the waves. This marked the entrance to Etretat.

Jeanne, gripping the gunwale with one hand, and somewhat dizzy with the rocking of the waves, gazed into the distance. It seemed to her that there were only three wholly beautiful things in creation — light, and space, and water.

No one spoke. Lastique, who was holding tiller and sheet, took an occasional pull at a bottle which he kept hidden under the seat, and he continued to smoke, without a pause, his apparently inextinguishable stump of a pipe. A thin cloud of blue smoke rose from the bowl, while another emerged from the corners of his mouth. Yet he was never seen to relight or refill the ebony black clay. Sometimes he grasped it with one hand and removed it from his lips, and spat into the sea. The Baron was in the bows attending to the sail, taking the place of a boat hand. Jeanne and the Viscount, neither of them quite at ease, sat side by side. They kept raising their eyes at the same moment, as if prompted by some unknown force, some affinity. Already between them flowed the current of that vague and subtle sentiment which is so quick to establish itself between two young people, when the man is not unprepossessing and the girl is attractive. Each felt happy in the other's proximity, perhaps because the thoughts of each were on the other.

The sun mounted in the sky as if to contemplate from a greater altitude the vast stretch of sea beneath. Then, as if in coquetry, the sea veiled itself in a thin transparent golden mist, which hung low but concealed nothing, merely shrouding the distance in a soft haze. Presently the sun's rays attained their full strength and dissolved this luminous vapour. Smooth as a mirror, the sea lay flashing in the sun. Deeply moved, Jeanne exclaimed: "How beautiful it is!"

"It is indeed," replied the Viscount.

The serene brightness of the morning seemed to evoke a response from both their hearts.

Suddenly the great arches of Etretat were opened out to their view, seeming as if the cliffs had two legs and were striding into the sea, and they were high enough for ships to pass under them. In front of the foremost one a pointed pinnacle of white rock reared itself.

The boat touched the shore. The Baron was the first to disembark, and he moored the boat to the shore. The Viscount carried Jeanne to land so that she should not wet her feet. Then they walked up the rough shingly beach, side by side, still stirred by the brief moment during which she had rested in his arms. Suddenly they overheard old Lastique saying to the Baron:

"It seems to me that they would make a fine couple."

They had a delightful luncheon in a little inn near the shore. The sea, drowsily subduing their voices and their thoughts, had reduced them to silence, but the meal loosened their tongues till they chattered like school-children on a holiday. The merest trifles became incredibly amusing. When old Lastique sat down to the table, carefully stowing away in his cap his still smoking pipe, the others laughed. A fly, doubtless attracted by his red nose, kept settling on it. He was not quick enough to catch it, and whenever he brushed it away with his hand it settled on a fly-blown muslin curtain, eagerly watching his flaming proboscis, and immediately returning to it.

Each time it settled, Jeanne and the Viscount giggled, and at last the old fellow's irritation became irrepressible and he growled: "The beast's devilish obstinate."

They laughed till they cried, doubling up, and stifling their shouts of laughter with their table napkins.

After coffee Jeanne proposed a stroll. The Viscount rose, but the Baron preferred to bask on the beach in the sun.

"Go along, children. You will find me here in an hour's time."

They took a straight line between some cottages, passed a small country house, resembling a large farm, and found themselves in an open valley, which stretched out before them.

The motion of the sea had made them languid and had disturbed their usual poise. The strong salt air had given them a keen appetite, and their merry luncheon had made them lose their heads a little. They felt an absurd impulse to race wildly over the fields. Jeanne had a buzzing in her ears, and was perturbed by sudden and strange emotion. A fierce sun beat down upon them. On either side of the road, the ripening corn was drooping in the heat. Grasshoppers, like blades of grass in number, were chirruping themselves hoarse, uttering their shrill penetrating note on all sides, among the wheat and the rye and the bents on the shore. No other sound rose under the torrid sky, whose shimmering blue had a yellow tinge, as if it were about to turn red, like metal placed too near a brasier. In front of them on their right they saw a little wood and made their way thither. Between two banks lay a narrow path shaded by tall trees that shut out the sun completely. As soon as they set foot there they felt a sensation of damp, musty chilliness which provoked a shudder and penetrated to the lungs. The grass had disappeared for want of light and fresh air, but the ground was carpeted with moss. They walked on.

"We might sit down for a little, over there," she said.

Two old trees had died, and through this gap in the verdure the light poured in, warming the soil, germinating the seeds of grass, dandelions and bindweed, encouraging the growth of spindling fox-gloves and a delicate mist of small white flowers. Butterflies, bees, clumsy drones, enormous gnats like skeleton flies, a thousand winged creatures, red ladybirds with black spots, beetles, some greenish and others black and horned, haunted this warm pool of light, which was like a well let down into the chill shade of the dense foliage.

They sat down with their heads in the shade and their feet in the

sun. As she contemplated all this teeming infinitesimal life, called into existence by a ray of light, Jeanne, with a gush of sentiment, exclaimed:

"How happy life is! How lovely it is in the country! There are moments when I long to be a fly or a butterfly and to hide myself among the flowers."

They talked about themselves, their habits, their tastes, conversing in those subdued and intimate tones in which confidences are made. He confessed himself already weary of society and his own futile existence. It was always the same; one never encountered truth or sincerity. Society! She would have been glad to have had some experience of it, but was convinced beforehand that it was inferior to the country. The more closely their hearts drew together, the more ceremoniously did they address each other. At the same time, they exchanged smiles and their eyes met. They felt themselves possessed by a new instinct of benevolence, a wider affection and an interest in a thousand things for which they had not hitherto cared. They returned to Etretat. The Baron, however, had walked to the Chambre-aux-Demoiselles, a grotto situated high

up on a ridge of the cliff. They waited for him at the inn. He did not
return till five o'clock, after a long walk on the slopes.

They re-embarked. The boat drifted gently, almost imperceptibly, before the wind. The breeze came in soft slow puffs, and the
sail swelled for a moment, then flapped limply against the mast.
The dark water lay lifeless, and the sun, exhausted by its own
ardour, had completed its orbed course, and was now gently sinking towards the sea.

Once more the sea laid its spell upon them and held them silent.
At last Jeanne said: "I should love to travel."

"Yes," replied the Viscount, "but it is dull travelling alone. One
needs at least one companion with whom one can discuss one's
impressions."

She thought for a moment.

"True. All the same, I love going for walks by myself. It is so
sweet to dream when one is all alone."

He gazed at her lingeringly. "You can dream, too, when there
are two of you."

Her eyes fell. Was there intention in his remark? Perhaps. She
scanned the horizon, as if to penetrate beyond. Then in a deliberate
voice:

"I should like to go to Italy. . . . To Greece. . . . Ah yes, Greece!
. . . And Corsica! Corsica must be so wild and beautiful."

He preferred Switzerland because of its chalets and lakes.

"No," she said, "I prefer either new countries like Corsica, or
else very old countries, full of associations, like Greece. It must be
delightful to come upon the vestiges of races with whose history we
have been familiar since childhood, and to see places which have
been the scenes of great events."

The Viscount was in a less exalted frame of mind. "England," he
announced, "has a great attraction for me. It is a country where
there is much to be learnt."

Then they surveyed the attractions of the whole earth, one country after another, from pole to pole, rhapsodising about imaginary
landscapes and the fantastic manners and customs of races like the
Chinese or Laplanders. But finally they agreed that the most beautiful land of all was France, with its temperate climate, its cool
summers and its mild winters, its fertile plains, its green forests,

31

its great, calm rivers, and its cult of the fine arts, a cult which had existed in no other country since the great days of Athens. Then a silence fell upon them.

The sun reddened as it sank. A broad shining track, a dazzling path of light, stretched across the water from the horizon to the wake of the boat. The last puffs of wind died away, every ripple subsided. The sail hung motionless in the sunset light. All space seemed spellbound in an infinite calm, in anticipation of the mating of the two elements. The ocean, its watery bosom heaving beneath the sky, was like a bride awaiting the descent of her fiery lover. Flushed with amorous desire, the sun was sinking more quickly: at last it touched the sea, and was slowly devoured. A shudder passed over the moving surface of the water, as if the sun, engulfed in the ocean, were breathing upon the world a sigh of content.

There was a brief twilight. Then night came down, spangled with stars. Lastique took to the oars, and they saw that the sea was phosphorescent. Jeanne and the Viscount, side by side, watched the trail of light in the wake of the boat. Scarcely a thought crossed their minds; they sat dreamily contemplative, enjoying the evening in a mood of exquisite content. Jeanne's hand was resting on the seat, and the Viscount, as if accidentally, laid a finger on it. Jeanne did not move; she was startled but happy, confused by the light touch of his hand.

Alone in her room that evening, she felt strangely perturbed, under the spell of an emotion which brought tears to her eyes, whatever she looked at. She glanced at her clock, and it seemed to her that the little bee was like a friendly heart beating, that it would be her companion all her life, accompanying her joys and sorrows with its brisk, regular ticking. She stopped it to print a kiss on its gilded wings. She was ready to lavish her caresses on any object. She remembered an old doll of hers hidden away at the back of a drawer. She took it out and welcomed it with the rapture one has on meeting again a beloved friend. Clasping it to her bosom, she showered kisses upon its painted cheeks and towy mop. With the doll still in her arms she fell into a reverie. Could this man be the husband promised to her by a thousand mysterious voices, the husband whom Providence, in its supreme benevolence, had placed in her path? Could this be the mate created for her and to whom she would devote her life? Were they predestined, he and she, to unite, to mingle indissolubly, and blend their affections, so that love might be born? She had not yet experienced those tumultuous impulses of her whole being, the delicious rapture, the profound upheaval, which constituted her idea of passion. None the less she believed that she was beginning to fall in love. For sometimes when she thought of him, and he was continually in her thoughts, she had a feeling of faintness. When he was present, her heart beat. When her eyes met his, her colour came and went, and she trembled at the sound of his voice.

That night she had very little sleep. Day by day she became more completely obsessed by her yearning for love. She was always questioning herself, consulting marguerites and clouds, and tossing up coins.

One evening her father said:

"I want you to look your best to-morrow morning."

"Why, Papa?"

"That's a secret."

The next morning she came down looking young and fresh in a light-coloured frock. The table in the drawing-room was covered with boxes of sweets, and an enormous bouquet lay on a chair. A cart drove into the yard; it bore the inscription, "Lerat, Fécamp. Pastry-cook. Wedding Breakfasts." Ludivine and a kitchen-maid opened a door at the back of the cart, and took out a number of flat baskets, which emitted a pleasant fragrance.

Viscount de Lamare arrived. The ends of his unwrinkled trousers were strapped under dainty patent leather boots, which set off the smallness of his feet. His long coat fitted closely at the waist, and displayed a lace *jabot* at the breast. A fine cravat, wound several times round his neck, made him hold up his well-shaped dark head, with its air of grave distinction. He looked different from usual. He had that unmistakable air with which even the most familiar faces are endowed by the consciousness of being well-dressed. Jeanne gazed at him in astonishment as if she had never seen him before. She thought he looked a perfect aristocrat, a great nobleman from head to foot.

He bowed and said, smiling:

"Well, are you ready, my fellow-sponsor?"

"Why?" she stammered. "What are we going to do?"

"You will soon know," replied the Baron.

The carriage drew up at the door. Madame Adelaide, in festive attire, came out of her room, leaning on the arm of Rosalie, who seemed so deeply impressed by Monsieur de Lamare's elegance that the Baron murmured:

"Why, Viscount, I think you've found favour in the eyes of our maid."

The Viscount blushed up to the ears and pretended not to hear. He picked up the enormous bouquet and offered it to Jeanne. With deepening astonishment, she accepted it. All four entered the carriage. Ludivine, the cook, who was handing the Baroness a cup of cold broth to sustain her, exclaimed:

"Really, Madame, anyone would think it was a wedding party."

When they reached the outskirts of Yport they all alighted from the carriage. As they went through the village, the sailors, all in new clothes which still bore marks of folding, came out of their houses, shook hands with the Baron and fell in behind him as if following in procession. The Viscount had offered Jeanne his arm and was walking with her at the head. A halt was made in front of the church, from whose doors issued the great silver cross held aloft by a choir boy. He was followed by another urchin in red and white who carried a vessel of holy water with the aspergill. Behind them came three old choristers, one of them lame, then a man who played the serpent, and after him the priest, his paunch giving prominence to the golden stole which was crossed over it. He greeted the Baron's party with a smile and a nod. Then, with half-closed eyes, his lips moving in prayer, and his biretta pushed well down over his face, he followed his surpliced acolytes in the direction of the sea.

On the beach a crowd was assembled round a new ship bedecked and garlanded. Its masts, sails, and rigging were adorned with long ribbons which fluttered in the breeze, and the name, *Jeanne*, was visible on the stern in gold letters. Lastique, master of this craft, which had been built with the Baron's money, came forward to the front of the procession. With one accord all the men took their hats off, while a group of pious women, in great black cloaks that fell in heavy folds from the shoulders, dropped on their knees in a circle at the sight of the cross. The priest, with a choir boy on either side, stationed himself at one end of the ship, while at the other, the old choristers, looking all the dirtier for their white robes, with their

34

bristling chins and solemn aspect, kept their eyes fixed on their books of plain-song, and bawled lustily into the clear morning air. When they paused for breath, the serpent player bellowed on by himself, with his small grey eyes almost disappearing in his inflated cheeks. The skin on his forehead and neck was so puffed out with the violence of his exertions as to seem detached from the underlying flesh.

The calm translucent sea appeared to be contemplating composedly the baptism of its ship. Its little waves, no higher than a finger, broke with a soft sound like that of a rake scraping the shingle. Great white sea gulls, with wings outspread against the blue sky, circled with sweeping curves above the kneeling throng, as though they also wished to see what was going on. After an *Amen* of five minutes' duration had been shouted, the singing ceased. The priest, in an unctuous voice, gurgled some Latin words, of which only the sonorous terminations were distinguishable. Then he went all over the vessel, sprinkling it with holy water. After this came prayers, which he murmured standing by the gunwale and facing the Viscount and Jeanne, the ship's sponsors, who remained motionless, hand in hand.

The Viscount's handsome face maintained its gravity, but Jeanne, half fainting in the grip of some sudden emotion, trembled so violently that her teeth chattered. All at once the dream which had haunted her of late assumed, in a kind of hallucination, a semblance of reality. There had been some talk of a wedding, and here was the priest, uttering a benediction. Here were men in surplices, chanting prayers. Was she herself the bride?

Was it merely a nervous tremor in her fingers? Had the obsession in her heart coursed through her veins and communicated itself to the heart of the man at her side? Or, rather, did he understand, did he guess?—was he, like her, carried away by an intoxication of love? Or could it be that he was merely moved by a consciousness, begotten of experience, that no woman could resist him? At that she grew aware that he was pressing her hand, gently at first, then more violently, almost crushing it. Without change of countenance, and without attracting any attention, he said—there was no doubt of it—he said quite clearly, "Oh Jeanne, if you only would, this should be our betrothal."

Very slowly she bowed her head, a gesture signifying, perchance, her acquiescence. The priest, who was still sprinkling holy water, scattered a few drops on their fingers.

The ceremony was over. The women rose from their knees. The return to the village resembled a stampede. The Cross, borne by the choir boy, had lost its dignity. It was hurried along, now swinging from right to left, now toppling forwards. The priest, no longer at his prayers, trotted behind. The choristers and the serpent player had disappeared down a lane, in a hurry to discard their surplices. The sailors hastened along in groups. All were actuated by the same idea, which affected them like a smell of cooking, lengthening their strides, making their mouths water, and rejoicing the inner man. An excellent luncheon was awaiting them at *Les Peuples*.

A long table had been placed in the courtyard, under the apple trees, and sixty people — sailors and peasants — sat down. The Baroness, who was in the centre, had a priest on either side, him of Yport and him of Les Peuples. Opposite sat the Baron, between the mayor and his wife. The latter — a gaunt country woman, no longer young — kept sending little nods in all directions. Her narrow face peeped out from her big Norman bonnet; she had a head like a white-crested hen, and round, startled eyes. She ate with little quick movements, as if she were pecking at the plate with her nose. Jeanne, seated beside the Viscount, was floating in a dream of bliss. She neither saw nor heard, but was silent in rapturous bewilderment.

"What is your Christian name?" she asked.

"Julian. Didn't you know?"

She did not reply, but reflected, "How often I shall say that name to myself!"

After the meal, the courtyard was left to the guests, and the house party crossed over to the other side of the mansion. The Baroness, on her husband's arm, went for her constitutional, with the two priests in attendance. Jeanne and Julian strolled down to the copse and wandered along the little leafy paths. Suddenly he seized her hands.

"Tell me, will you be my wife?"

Her head drooped.

"I implore you to answer me," he entreated.

At that she gently raised her eyes to his, and he read there his answer.

4

ONE morning, before Jeanne was up, the Baron entered her room and seated himself at the foot of her bed.

"Viscount de Lamare has asked us for your hand."

She wanted to hide her face in the bedclothes.

"We have deferred our answer," the Baron continued.

She panted, half suffocated with emotion.

Presently the Baron added, with a smile, "We would not take any steps without consulting you. Your mother and I have no objection to the marriage. At the same time, we have not committed you to anything. You are much better off than he is. But when it is a question of the happiness of a lifetime, one should not take money into consideration. He has no parents. If you married him, we should gain a son. With another man, it would be you, our daughter, who would have to go among strangers. We like the young fellow. Do you?"

She blushed to the roots of her hair, and faltered, "Yes, Papa, I do."

Looking her in the eyes, her father said, with another smile, "I suspected it, young woman."

She spent the day in a trance, unconscious of what she was doing, mistaking one thing for another. Although she had not been walking, her limbs felt quite weak with fatigue. About six o'clock, while she was seated with her mother under the plane tree, the Viscount appeared.

Jeanne's heart beat wildly. The Viscount approached them, showing no sign of emotion. He kissed the Baroness's fingers, then raised the girl's trembling hand and pressed upon it a lingering kiss of gratitude.

Then began the blissful period of their betrothal. They chatted by themselves in a corner of the drawing-room, or on a bank at the end of the copse overlooking the moor. Sometimes they strolled along the Baroness's avenue, he talking of the future, she gazing with downcast eyes at the dusty track worn by her mother's foot.

Once the marriage had been arranged, it was decided to waste no

39

time. The ceremony was fixed for the fifteenth of August, in six weeks' time, and the young couple were to set out at once on their honeymoon. Jeanne was consulted, and decided on Corsica, where they were more likely to find privacy than in the towns of Italy.

They looked forward to the day of their union without undue impatience. None the less, they were enveloped and steeped in an atmosphere of exquisite tenderness; they savoured the delicate charm of light caresses, pressure of hands, passionate glances prolonged till their souls seemed to mingle; and yet they were vaguely troubled by an undefined yearning for a closer embrace.

It was decided to invite no one to the wedding except Aunt Lison, the Baroness's sister, who lived as a boarder in a convent at Versailles. After her father's death, the Baroness had pressed her sister to live with her; but the old maid was haunted by the idea that no one wanted her, that she was a useless encumbrance, and she retired to one of the religious houses which let apartments to the sad and forsaken. From time to time she spent a month or two with her family. She was a small, retiring woman, and seldom spoke. She appeared only at meal-times, and afterwards withdrew to her own room, where she shut herself in. She had a kindly expression, and mild, sad eyes, and looked older than her forty-two years. She had never been of any importance in the family. As a child, she had been neither pretty nor lively, and no one had ever petted her. She had always sat, unobtrusive and gentle, in a corner. Later on her interests had invariably been sacrificed. As a girl, no one had ever taken any notice of her. She was like a shadow or some familiar object, a piece of furniture endowed with life, seen daily, but of concern to no one.

Her sister, who had acquired the family habit, looked upon her as a failure, a person of no account whatever. She was treated with a careless familiarity, which concealed a kindly contempt. She was called Lise, but she seemed ashamed of this sprightly and juvenile name. When it was obvious that she would never marry, Lise was changed into Lison. After Jeanne's birth, she came to be called "Aunt Lison." She was a humble relation, neat in her person, painfully timid even with her sister and brother-in-law, who were fond of her, none the less. Their vague sentiment was compounded of careless affection, unconscious pity, and natural benevolence.

Sometimes the Baroness would fix the date of distant events in her youth by saying, "It was about the time of Lison's escapade."

Nothing more was ever said about it, and a mist seemed to hang over the "escapade."

One night, when Lise was twenty, she had thrown herself into the water, no one knew why. Nothing in her life or her demeanour had prepared her family for this act of madness. She had been rescued half-drowned. Her scandalised parents held up their hands, but, instead of trying to discover her secret motive, they contented themselves with discussing her "escapade" in the same way as they spoke of the accident to their horse, Coco, who had broken his leg in a rut a little while before and had had to be destroyed.

From that time onwards, Lise, soon Lison, was regarded as a person of feeble intellect. The mild contempt with which she had inspired her nearest relations gradually communicated itself to those around her. Even little Jeanne, with the natural instinct of a child, took no notice of her, never went up to kiss her in bed, or even entered her room. Rosalie, the maid, who kept her room tidy, was the only person who seemed to know where it was. When Aunt Lison entered the dining-room for luncheon, the child, from force of habit, presented her forehead to her, but that was all. If she was wanted, a servant was sent to find her. When she was absent, no one wondered about her, or thought of her, or even dreamed of saying uneasily, "Dear me, I haven't seen Lison this morning."

She had no niche in the world. She was one of those beings who remain sealed books even to their nearest, and whose death leaves no gap or blank in a home; one of those beings who have not the gift of entering into the existence and habits and affections of those around them. The words "Aunt Lison" evoked no more sign of affectionate response than if one had said the coffee-pot or the sugar-basin. She walked with short, quick, inaudible steps. She made no sound, but glided past everything without touching it, and she seemed to endue surrounding objects with her own quality of noiselessness. The touch of her hands was as light and soft as if they were made of cotton-wool.

She arrived towards the middle of July, quite overwhelmed by the idea of the wedding. She brought a quantity of presents, which, as they came from her, were hardly noticed. The day after her arrival, no one seemed aware that she was in the house.

She was seething, nevertheless, with extraordinary emotion, and her eyes never left the lovers. She worked at the trousseau with singular and feverish activity, stitching away like a paid seamstress, in her room, where no one ever came to see her.

She was always showing the Baroness handkerchiefs she had hemstitched herself, or towels on which she had embroidered monograms, and she would say, "Will these do, Adelaide?"

And the Baroness, after a careless glance, would say, "My poor Lison, don't give yourself so much trouble."

A sultry day at the end of July was followed by one of those warm, moonlight nights which exalt the soul, fill it with disturbing emotion, and awake all its hidden poetry. Mild breezes from the fields stole into the quiet drawing-room. The Baroness was placidly playing cards with her husband at the table in the circle of light projected by the shaded lamp. Aunt Lison was seated beside them, knitting, and the young people were leaning against the open window, gazing into the moonlit garden.

The lime tree and the plane cast their shadows upon the broad, palely gleaming lawn, which stretched down to the dark copse.

Irresistibly attracted by the exquisite charm of the night and the misty radiance of trees and groves, Jeanne turned to her parents.

"Papa, we are going for a stroll on the lawn."

"Go along, children," said the Baron, continuing his game.

They went out and wandered over the broad expanse of lawn, white in the moonlight, till they reached the little thicket. It grew late, but they did not think of returning to the house. The Baroness was tired, and wanted to retire to her room.

"We had better call the lovers in," she said.

The Baron cast a glance at the spacious, moonlit garden, where the two shadows were quietly wandering.

"Let them alone," he said; "it is lovely out of doors. Lison will wait up for them. Won't you, Lison?"

The old maid raised her restless eyes, and answered in her timid voice, "Yes, certainly."

The Baron helped his wife out of her chair, and, himself wearied after the heat of the day, remarked, "I shall go to bed too."

Together they left the room.

Aunt Lison too rose, leaving on the arm of her easy-chair her unfinished work, her wool and her needles. She leaned against the window and gazed out into the exquisite night.

The lovers continued to stroll up and down the lawn, from the copse to the front steps and back again. Silently they pressed each others' hands. They seemed exalted above themselves, one with the breathing and visible poetry of the earth. Suddenly Jeanne caught sight of the old maid framed in the window, her silhouette thrown into relief by the lamplight.

"Look," she said, "there is Aunt Lison watching us."

The Viscount raised his head, and echoed unthinkingly, "Yes, there's Aunt Lison watching us."

They continued to wander, lost in a dream of love. But the grass was wet with dew, and presently they felt a chilliness.

"We had better go in now," said Jeanne.

They returned to the house.

When they entered the drawing-room, Aunt Lison had resumed her knitting; her head was bent over her work, and her thin fingers trembled a little, as if they were very tired. Jeanne went up to her.

"It's time to go to bed, Aunt."

The old maid raised her eyes. They were red, as if she had been weeping, but the lovers paid no heed. Suddenly, however, the Viscount noticed that Jeanne's thin slippers were wet. He was seized with anxiety, and asked tenderly, "Aren't your dear little feet cold?"

At that, Aunt Lison's fingers trembled so violently that her work slipped from her grasp, and the ball of wool rolled away over the floor. Abruptly hiding her face in her hands, she burst into convulsive sobs.

Dumfounded, the lovers looked at her. Then Jeanne threw herself on her knees, stretched out her arms, and exclaimed in deep concern, "What is the matter, Aunt Lison? What is the matter?"

In a tearful voice, her body rigid with grief, the poor woman faltered, "It was when he asked you, 'Aren't your dear little feet cold?' No one has ever said things like that to me, never, never."

Surprised and compassionate, Jeanne could nevertheless hardly refrain from laughing at the idea of a lover murmuring soft words to Lison. And the Viscount turned away to conceal his amusement. Suddenly Aunt Lison rose, and, leaving her ball of wool on the floor and her knitting on the chair, she fled up the dark stairs, feeling her way to her room.

When they were alone, the young people looked at each other, in mirth mingled with pity.

43

"Poor Aunt Lison," murmured Jeanne.

"She is not quite herself to-night," replied Julian.

They held each other's hands, reluctant to part, and as they stood in front of Aunt Lison's empty chair, softly, very softly, their lips met in their first kiss. But on the morrow they did not give another thought to the old maid's tears.

In the fortnight preceding the marriage, Jeanne was as quiet and calm as if she were exhausted with tender emotions. And on the morning of the auspicious day she had no time to think. She had a curious sensation of emptiness all over her body, as if flesh and blood and bones had dissolved under her skin. When she touched anything, she noticed that her hands were trembling violently. She did not regain her self-possession until she found herself in the choir of the church, with the ceremony proceeding.

Married! She was actually married! All the actions and events that had followed one upon the other since dawn seemed to her as unreal as a dream. It is in such moments that all around us seems changed. The merest gesture takes on a new significance. Even the procession of the hours appears to be disarranged. She felt even more surprised than bewildered. The previous evening nothing in her life was changed. Only that cherished hope of hers had drawn nearer, until it seemed almost tangible. She had fallen asleep still a girl, and now she was a woman. She had crossed the barrier beyond which lay the future, with all its joys and its promise of bliss. She felt that a door was opened to her, and that she was about to enter the region of her dreams. The ceremony was over. The bride and bridegroom entered the vestry, which, owing to the absence of guests, was almost empty. Then they passed out again. At the door of the church a loud crash startled the bride and made the Baroness scream: the peasants were firing a salute with their guns, and the reports continued until *Les Peuples* was reached.

At the wedding breakfast were present the family, their own parish priest and the priest from Yport, the bridegroom, and the witnesses, who had been selected from the principal farmers in the neighbourhood.

Afterwards the party went for a turn in the garden till dinner-time. The Baron, the Baroness, Aunt Lison, the mayor, and Abbé Picot strolled in the Baroness's avenue, while the Yport priest strode up and down the other avenue, reading his breviary. From the other side of the house, where the peasants were drinking cider under the apple trees, came loud sounds of revelry. The courtyard was full of country-folk in their best, and the boys and girls were chasing one another.

Jeanne and Julian went through the wood, climbed on to the bank, and silently gazed at the sea. Although it was the middle of August, it was cool. The wind blew from the north, but a strong sun beat down fiercely from a cloudless sky. The young couple crossed the moor, and turned to the right to find shelter in the wooded valley which wound down towards Yport. In the copse no breath of wind reached them. They left the road, and struck off down a narrow path, where the branches hung so low that they could scarcely walk upright. She felt his arm glide slowly round her waist. She remained silent; but her heart was beating, and there was a catch in her breath. The trailing boughs caressed their hair as they bent their heads to pass. Jeanne plucked a leaf and found a pair of ladybirds, like two frail red shells, concealed on the under side. Jeanne was feeling more at ease now, and said innocently, "Look, they're keeping house together."

Julian lightly kissed her ear.

"This evening you will be my wife."

Although she had learned a good deal since she had lived in the country, her dreams had as yet touched only upon the poetry of love. She was taken by surprise. His wife? Was she not already his wife? He began to shower little quick kisses upon her temples and neck, where the short curly hairs began. Confused by this succession of unaccustomed and masculine kisses, she turned her head aside to evade his caresses, which, none the less, filled her with ecstasy. Suddenly they found themselves on the outskirts of the wood. She halted, dismayed at having come so far. What would everyone think?

"Let us go back," she said.

He withdrew his arm from her waist. But, as they turned, they came face to face, so close that each could feel the other's breath. Their eyes met. Each cast upon the other one of those steady, piercing glances in which two souls are fain to mingle. They sought in the depths of each other's eyes the personality that lurks there; deeper still they sought, in the unknown and impenetrable fastnesses of being. Silently, persistently questioning, they plumbed the depths of each other's souls. What part would each play in the other's destiny? How would this life, that they were beginning together, shape itself? What joy and happiness, or what disillusions, awaited each at the other's hands, in that long, indissoluble partnership of matrimony? And it seemed to both of them as if they had never seen each other before.

Suddenly Julian placed both his hands on his wife's shoulders, and kissed her full on the lips. It was such a kiss as she had never before received. It sank into her, penetrating to her veins and the marrow of her bones. It gave her such a mysterious shock that she pushed Julian frantically away with both hands, and almost fell backwards.

"Let us go, let us go," she faltered.

He made no reply, but took her hands and kept them in his own. They returned home in silence. The rest of the afternoon went slowly.

At nightfall they sat down to dinner.

Contrary to Norman custom, it was a simple meal. The guests seemed to be suffering from a certain constraint. Only the two priests, the mayor, and the four farmers mustered something of the ponderous jocularity proper to a wedding. Laughter seemed extinct, till a word from the mayor revived it. It was about nine o'clock; coffee was served. Outside, under the apple trees in the outer courtyard, a rustic ball was beginning. The open window commanded a view of the festivities. The candles hanging on the branches lent to the leaves the tints of verdigris. Peasants of both sexes were dancing in a round, shouting a primitive dance tune to the feeble accompaniment of two violins and a clarionet. The musicians were perched on a kitchen table, which served as a stage. Sometimes the clamorous singing entirely drowned the instruments; but now and then broken snatches of music, a few disconnected notes, seemed to float down from the sky, amid the unrestrained uproar. Two huge casks, surrounded by flaming torches, had been broached, and two maids were kept busy rinsing glasses and bowls in a tub, and holding them, still dripping with water, under the taps, one of which dispensed red wine and the other pure golden cider. Thirsty dancers, placid old men, and perspiring girls crowded round the casks, holding out their hands to seize the wine-cups, throwing back their heads and pouring down their throats great draughts of whichever liquid they preferred.

46

There was a table laden with bread, butter, cheese and sausages, to which, from time to time, everyone helped himself. The spectacle of this wholesome and riotous revelry beneath the illuminated canopy of leaves inspired the gloomy party in the dining-room with a longing to join in the dance, to drink from the round-bellied barrels, and to eat a slice of bread-and-butter and a raw onion.

The mayor, who was keeping time with his knife, exclaimed, "By Jove, it's going splendidly; it reminds one of the marriage of Ganache."

There was a ripple of suppressed laughter. But Abbé Picot, the natural enemy of civil authority, rejoined, "You mean the marriage of Cana."

The mayor, however, did not accept this rebuke. "No, sir; I know what I'm talking about. When I say Ganache I mean Ganache."

The party rose from table and entered the drawing-room. Then they looked in for a little at the peasant's ball. Soon afterwards the guests went away.

The Baron and the Baroness were disputing in low tones, and Madame Adelaide, more than usually breathless, seemed to be refusing some request of her husband's. At last she protested, almost out loud, "No, my dear, I simply can't. I shouldn't in the least know how to set about it."

The Baron broke away from her and turned to Jeanne, "Will you come for a little stroll, my child?"

She replied with emotion, "If you like, Papa," and they went out together.

Outside the door, facing the sea, they felt a light wind, one of those cool summer breezes in which there is already a touch of autumn. Clouds were racing across the sky, now veiling, now revealing, the stars. The Baron pressed his daughter's arm to his side and clasped her hand tenderly. They walked up and down for some minutes. He seemed irresolute and perplexed. At last, however, he made up his mind.

"Darling, I have a difficult part to play, which is really your mother's; but, as she refuses, it devolves on me. I do not know to what extent you are aware of the facts of life. There are mysteries which are kept carefully hidden from children, and especially from girls. For girls should preserve their purity of mind, their spotless purity, until the moment when we surrender them to the arms of

47

the man to whom their happiness is committed. It is for him to raise the veil. But if no whisper of these things has reached them, they recoil sometimes from the somewhat crude reality behind their dreams. Hurt and wounded, they refuse their husbands the absolute rights that are his by human and natural law. I cannot tell you more, my love. But do not forget this: you belong to your husband entirely."

What did she actually know? What did she surmise? She began to tremble in a mood of oppressive and painful melancholy, which weighed on her mind like a presentiment. They returned to the house. On the threshold of the drawing-room they halted in surprise. Madame Adelaide was weeping on Julian's bosom. As if actuated by a blacksmith's bellows, she emitted blasts of lamentation from nose, eyes and mouth simultaneously, and Julian, in confusion and embarrassment, was supporting her massive weight. She had flung herself in the Viscount's arms, commending to his care her darling, her precious, her beloved daughter.

The Baron darted forward.

"Oh, no scene, no emotion, I beg you."

He led his wife to an armchair, and she began to dry her tears. Then he turned to Jeanne, "Come, child. Kiss your mother quickly and go to bed."

On the verge of tears, Jeanne embraced her parents hurriedly and fled.

Aunt Lison had already retired to her room. The Baron and his wife remained alone with Julian. All three were so profoundly embarrassed that they could think of nothing to say. The two men in evening dress stood about aimlessly, while Madame Adelaide had collapsed in her chair, and was still choking with her sobs. The situation became intolerable, and at last the Baron began to speak of the journey on which the young people were to set out in a few days' time.

Jeanne was in her room, and Rosalie, in floods of tears, was undressing her. The maid's hands fumbled blindly with ribbons and pins, and she showed far more emotion than her mistress. But Jeanne paid no heed to her tears. She felt that she had entered another world, had departed to a different earth, remote from all she had known and loved. Everything in her existence, everything in her mind, seemed to have suffered an upheaval. And this curious idea haunted her. Was she in love with her husband? Suddenly he seemed to her like a stranger whom she hardly knew. Three months ago she had not been aware of his existence, and now she was his wife. Why? Why should one precipitate oneself into marriage, as into a pit gaping at one's feet?

When she was in her nightgown, she slipped into bed. The cold sheets made her shudder, and deepened the sensation of chill, loneliness and sadness which had oppressed her soul for the last two hours.

Still sobbing, Rosalie fled from the room, and Jeanne waited. She waited anxiously, with thrilling heart, for this unknown thing that she divined, and for which her father's confused words had prepared her, this mysterious revelation of the great secret of love. She had heard no sound of footsteps on the stairs, yet someone knocked lightly three times on her door. She trembled, and made no reply. There was another knock; then she heard the fastening of the door grate. She hid her head under the sheets, as if a thief had entered her room. Shoes creaked softly on the floor, and suddenly someone touched her bed.

She gave a nervous start, uttered a low cry, and, uncovering her head, she saw Julian standing before her, smiling at her.

"Oh, how you frightened me," she said.

"Weren't you expecting me?" he asked.

She made no reply.

He looked well in evening dress, with his serious, handsome face, and she felt horribly ashamed of being in bed in the presence of this immaculate propriety. Both felt at a loss. They hardly dared to glance at each other in that solemn and decisive hour, on which depends the intimate happiness of married life. He had, perhaps, some vague idea of the dangers of that conflict, of the need for tact and self-control and subtle tenderness, lest a wound be dealt to the shrinking delicacy, the infinite refinements, of a virgin's soul, nurtured on dreams.

Gently he took her hand and kissed it, and, kneeling beside the bed, as if before an altar, he whispered in a voice low as a breath, "Will you love me a little?"

Suddenly reassured, she lifted her head in its filmy lace cap from the pillow, and smiled, "I love you already, dear."

He put her little slim fingers between his lips, and, in a voice

muffled by this impediment, he murmured, "Will you prove to me
that you love me?"

Her agitation returned. Hardly conscious of what she was saying,
but mindful of her father's words, she replied, "I am yours, dear."

He covered her wrists with fervent kisses. Then, slowly raising
her, he bent towards her face, which she hid again. Suddenly he
threw one arm across the bed, clasping her through the clothes,
while he slipped the other arm beneath the pillow and raised her
head. In a low voice, he asked, "Then will you make a little room
for me beside you?"

She felt an instinctive thrill of fear, and gasped, "Oh, please,
not yet."

He seemed disappointed and hurt, and he replied, still plead-
ingly but less gently, "Why later, since we must come to it in the
end?"

Although she resented this remark, she repeated submissively
and resignedly, "I am yours, dear."

He withdrew hastily into the dressing-room, and she could distinctly hear his movements, the rustling of his clothes as he took
them off, the jingling of money in his pockets, and the fall of his
boots one after the other on the floor. Suddenly he crossed her room
in his underclothes and laid his watch on the mantelpiece. Then he
ran back to the dressing-room, and moved about there a little
longer. When Jeanne heard him approaching, she turned hastily on
her other side and closed her eyes.

She jumped as if to throw herself out of bed when she felt a cold,
hairy leg pressing against hers. Suppressing a cry of terror, she
covered her face with her hands, and huddled down in bed. Although
her back was turned to him, he took her in his arms, and eagerly
kissed her neck, the floating laces of her cap and the embroidered
collar of her nightgown. She lay still, panting, rigid with fear, feeling a strong hand searching for her breast, guarded as it was by
her arms. She panted in affright under the rough handling; she
longed to escape, to run away through the house, and to lock herself in some place out of this man's reach. He was no longer moving.
She felt the warmth of him against her back. Presently her fears
subsided, and it suddenly occurred to her that she had only to turn
round to embrace him. At last he grew impatient, and said in a
pained voice, "Then you won't be my little wife?"

She murmured through her fingers, "But I am."

With a shade of annoyance, he replied, "Come, my dear, don't make fun of me."

Distressed by his displeasure, she suddenly turned to him and asked his pardon. He seized her madly in his arms, as if he were hungry for her, and covered her face and neck with swift, poignant, passionate kisses, smothering her with caresses. She had unclenched her hands, and lay unresistingly, scarcely realising what was happening, in utter bewilderment. Suddenly a keen pang ran through her, and she began to moan, twisted up in his arms, while he eagerly took possession of her. What happened next? Of subsequent events she had no clear recollection, for she had completely lost her head. But it seemed to her that Julian showered little grateful kisses upon her lips. Then he must have spoken, and doubtless she had replied. He made further advances, which she repulsed fearfully; and as she struggled, she felt on her bosom the thick growth of hair that she had already noticed against her leg, and drew back at the shock. At last, weary of unsuccessful pleading, he lay on his back without moving.

Then she began to think. Distressed to her inmost soul, disillusioned by a reality so different from the transports she had imagined, her cherished hopes shattered, her happiness in ruins, she said to herself, "So this is what he calls being his wife! Just this! Just this!"

Thus she remained a long time, her eyes roaming over the tapestries on the wall, with their ancient tale of love. As Julian neither spoke nor moved, she slowly turned her eyes towards him, and saw that he was asleep. He was asleep, with his mouth half open and his face calm. He was actually asleep!

She could hardly believe her eyes. She was indignant, even more deeply insulted by his slumber than by his roughness. He was treating her like any casual woman. How could he sleep on such a night? Was it that this experience had for him no element of surprise? She would have minded less if he had beaten her, mishandled her, stunned her into insensibility with his odious caresses.

She remained motionless, leaning on one elbow, bent over towards him, listening to the light breathing which issued from his lips, and at times became almost a snore. Day dawned. The pale sky grew light, and a rosy glow gave place to a dazzling brightness. Julian opened his eyes, stretched out his arms, and yawned. Then he looked at his wife and smiled, "Did you sleep well, my dear?"

She noticed the familiarity of his address, and answered in surprise, "Yes. Did you?"

"Yes, very well."

He turned and kissed her, and then calmly began to talk. He sketched his plans for the future, and dwelt upon his notions of economy. To Jeanne's surprise, he repeated the word economy several times. She listened to him, scarcely grasping the sense of his words, and, as she gazed at him, a thousand swift thoughts brushed lightly across her mind.

Eight o'clock struck.

"We must get up," he said, "they will laugh at us if we stay late in bed." He rose first. When he had finished dressing, he skilfully assisted his wife in all the trifling details of her toilet, and would not let her call Rosalie. As they were leaving the room, he paused.

"You know, we can talk to each other without any constraint now, but when your parents are present we had better wait a little. It will seem quite natural when we come back from our honeymoon."

She did not make her appearance till luncheon. The day passed like any other day, as if nothing new had occurred. There was merely another man in the house.

5

FOUR days later the travelling coach arrived which was to convey them to Marseilles.

After her first distress, Jeanne had already grown accustomed to Julian's proximity, to his kisses and caresses, though she still felt the same repugnance for their more intimate relations. She admired and loved him, and she soon recovered her natural gaiety. She bade her parents a brief and cheerful farewell. The Baroness alone displayed emotion. Just as the carriage was starting, she placed a purse, well filled and heavy as lead, in her daughter's hands.

"That's for pocket-money," she said.

Jeanne put it away, and the horses set off. Towards evening Julian asked, "How much money did your mother give you?"

She had forgotten about the purse, but now she emptied it into her lap. From it issued a stream of gold, amounting to two thousand francs. She clapped her hands. "How extravagant I shall be!" and she put the money away again.

After a week's appalling heat, they arrived at Marseilles. On the following day they sailed for Corsica on a little packet boat, the *Roi-Louis*, that touched at Ajaccio on its way to Naples.

Corsica! The bush! Bandits! Mountains! Napoleon's birth-place! Jeanne felt that she was leaving prosaic reality and entering, wide awake, a land of dreams. Side by side on the deck of the ship, they watched the cliffs of Provence glide past. The sea, intensely azure, lay like a painted ocean. It had an appearance of solidity in the blazing sunshine, beneath the infinite and almost unnaturally blue sky.

"Do you remember our sail with old Lastique?" asked Jeanne.

For answer he lightly kissed her ear.

The paddles of the steamer churned up the water, disturbing its deep repose, and in their wake a long straight furrow, foamy and white, like the froth of champagne, stretched away out of sight. Suddenly in front of the bows, only a few fathoms away, a dolphin leaped out of the water, then dived head first and disappeared. With a cry of alarm, Jeanne threw herself into Julian's arms. Then she

53

laughed at her fears, and watched eagerly for the dolphin's re-
appearance. In a few moments it bobbed up again, like a huge
mechanical toy. Then it dived, and rose again to the surface. Soon
there were two, then three, then six dolphins gambolling around the
clumsy ship, as if they were escorting a gigantic brother, a wooden
fish with iron fins. They appeared now on the port, now on the star-
board side, sometimes all together, sometimes singly, chasing one
another as if in merry sport. They described great curves as they
leaped into the air, then they plunged again into the sea one after
the other. Quivering with delight, Jeanne clapped her hands in
ecstasy at each appearance of these great creatures which swam so
gracefully. Her heart leaped with them in simple and childlike joy.
All at once they vanished. She caught one more glimpse of them
in the far distance, out to sea. Then they were lost to sight, and
Jeanne had a momentary sensation of sadness at their departure.

Evening came, tranquil, radiant, full of light and quiet happiness.
There was no motion either in the air or in the sea. And the infinite
calm of ocean and sky communicated itself to the spellbound souls
that seemed no less untroubled. The great sun was sinking slowly

towards invisible Africa, that burning land of Africa which seemed already to project something of its heat. But, when the sun had set, the lovers felt upon their faces a cool caress, too slight to be called a breeze.

They did not go down to their cabin, which reeked of all the vile odours that are characteristic of packet boats. Wrapped in their cloaks, they lay side by side on the deck. Julian fell asleep at once. But Jeanne, thrilled by the wonder of the voyage, remained open-eyed. The monotonous sound of the paddles lulled her, and she gazed at the myriad stars shining overhead, piercingly bright, sparkling as with liquid fire in the clear southern sky. But towards morning she dropped off to sleep. Sounds and voices awakened her. The sailors were singing as they washed down the decks. She roused her husband, who was fast asleep, and they both rose. She drew in rapturously the salt air, tingling with it to her finger-tips. There was sea all round them. On the bow, however, something that looked grey and blurred in the early dawn—something that resembled a bank of curious, pointed, jagged clouds—loomed above the waves.

Presently it grew more distinct, and as the sky brightened the outlines were more sharply defined, and a long chain of peaked, fantastic mountains stood forth. Corsica lay before them, veiled in a thin haze. Behind the mountains the sun was rising, throwing into relief the jutting peaks. Then all the heights were flooded with light, while the rest of the island remained enveloped in mist.

The captain, a little wizened old man, tanned, wrinkled, and shrivelled by salt gales, came on deck. He addressed Jeanne in a voice grown hoarse under the strain of thirty years of shouting orders above the din of storms. "Do you catch the scent of her, the witch?" he asked.

Jeanne became aware of a strong, strange odour of wild, aromatic plants.

"That is the scent of Corsica, Madame. She is a pretty woman, and that is her perfume. If I had been away for twenty years, I should know it again from five miles off. Corsica is my home. And our Emperor away over there on St. Helena, they say he is always talking about this perfume of his country. He is a kinsman of mine."

Taking off his hat, the captain saluted Corsica, and saluted too, far away across the ocean, the captive, the great Emperor, his kinsman. Jeanne was moved almost to tears. The seaman pointed with his arm towards the horizon. "There are the Sanguinaires," he said.

Julian was standing by his wife, with his arm round her waist, and both tried to make out the islands he had indicated. At last they caught sight of some pyramidal rocks, which the ship presently skirted, entering into a large sheltered bay, surrounded by high mountains, whose lower slopes looked as if covered with moss.

The captain pointed to this expanse of verdure. "The bush," he exclaimed.

As the ship proceeded, sailing slowly on an azure lake of such transparency that sometimes the bottom was visible, the ring of mountains seemed to close in behind it. Presently at the end of the bay, close to the water's edge, at the foot of the mountains, the dazzlingly white town came in sight. A few small Italian vessels lay at anchor in the harbour. Four or five boats circled around the *Roi-Louis* to take off passengers. Julian, who was putting the baggage together, said to his wife in an undertone, "I suppose it will be enough if I give the steward a franc?"

For the last week he had continually vexed his wife by asking her this sort of question. She replied, with a shade of impatience, "It's better to give too much than too little."

He had endless disputes with waiters, cabmen, and shopkeepers, and when by some quibble he had succeeded in obtaining a reduction, he would rub his hands and say to Jeanne, "I hate being done."

She shuddered when she saw a bill presented, foreseeing that Julian would raise objections to every item. Humiliated by his haggling, she blushed to the roots of her hair under the contemptuous glances of the servants, whose eyes followed her husband, while they held in their open hands his inadequate tips. He had another altercation with the boatman who put them ashore.

The first tree she saw was a palm.

They went to a great empty hotel at the corner of a large square and had luncheon. Just as Jeanne was preparing to go for a stroll round the town, Julian took her arm, and murmured tenderly, "Let's go and lie down for a little, puss."

She was surprised. "Lie down? But I don't feel tired."

He clasped her to him. "I want you. Do you understand? It's two days now! . . ."

She blushed with shame, and stammered: "What? Now? But

what would people think? However could you ask for a bedroom in the daytime? Oh, Julian, please. . . ."

But he interrupted her. "What do I care what the hotel people say or think? You'll see what that matters to me!"

He rang the bell.

She said no more. She lowered her eyes, revolted in body and soul before her husband's overmastering desire, obedient but revolted, resigned but humiliated, feeling that she was being asked to share in something animal and degrading, a loathsome thing.

Her sensual feelings were still unroused, and her husband treated her now as if she shared his own passion.

When the waiter came, Julian ordered him to take them to their room. The man, a typical Corsican, covered with hair to the very eyes, failed to understand, and said that the room would be ready in the evening.

Julian explained impatiently: "No, at once. We are tired after our journey, and want to rest."

A smile glided over the waiter's face, and Jeanne yearned to make her escape.

When they came down again, an hour later, she dared not face the people she met, for she was convinced that they would grin and giggle as soon as her back was turned. She was angry in her heart with Julian for not understanding what she felt, for his lack of the finer feelings, of instinctive delicacy; she felt that between him and her there was a kind of veil, an obstacle of some kind. She realised for the first time that two people can never reach each other's deepest feelings and instincts, that they spend their lives side by side, linked it may be, but not mingled, and that each one's inmost being must go through life eternally alone.

They stayed three days in that little town, which lies hidden away at the far end of its blue bay, and is as hot as a furnace behind its screen of mountains, which intercept every breath of wind. Then they made out an itinerary for their journey. To avoid being held up by any difficult part of the road, they decided to hire saddle horses, and chose two small, fiery-eyed Corsican stallions, lean and untiring. They set out one morning at daybreak. Their guide rode a mule, and carried provisions, for that wild country boasted of no hostelries.

At first the road followed the line of the coast. Then it plunged into a shallow valley leading towards the high mountains. It was continually crossing dried-up beds of torrents, where, like a lurking animal, a thread of water still trickled and gurgled faintly beneath the rocks. Destitute of cultivation, the country had an utterly barren aspect. The hillsides were covered with a growth of tall grass, burnt brown by the scorching heat. Sometimes the travellers met a mountaineer, either on foot, or riding a small pony, or astride a donkey no bigger than a dog. Each of these wayfarers carried on his back a loaded gun, old and rusty, but a formidable weapon in such hands. The air was heavy with the pungent perfume of the aromatic plants which cover the island. The road wound its way upward gradually, following the long flanks of the mountainsides. Peaks of pink or blue granite lent fairy hues to the wide landscape, and the undulations of the ground were on so mighty a scale that the immense forests of chestnut trees on the lower slopes dwindled to thickets.

Now and then the guide pointed towards the jagged peaks and mentioned a name. Jeanne and Julian gazed, but could see nothing. At last they would distinguish a grey object, resembling a pile of stones which had slipped down from the summit. This was a village, a small hamlet of granite, clinging there, perched like a bird's nest, and almost invisible on the vast mountainside. Presently Jeanne grew weary of riding at a pace which never exceeded a walk.

"Let us go a little faster," she said, and urged on her horse. As she did not hear her husband galloping behind her, she turned round, and burst out laughing when she saw him, pale, clutching his horse's mane, and bumping ludicrously in the saddle. His lack of skill and his terror were rendered more absurd by their contrast with his handsome person and his air of a dashing cavalier.

After that they trotted gently. On either side of the road lay a never-ending growth of bushes and trees, which covered the hillsides like a cloak. This was the bush, the impenetrable bush. It consisted of holm oak, juniper, arbutus, mastic, buckthorn, heather, laurustinus, myrtle and box, interlaced, like a tangled head of hair, with twining clematis, bracken of enormous size, honeysuckle, cistus, rosemary, lavender, briar — a tangled fleece flung upon the backs of the mountains.

They felt hungry. The guide joined them, and led them to one of those delightful springs common in craggy country. A slender jet of icy water issued from a crevice in the rock and trickled over the edge of a chestnut leaf, placed there by some passer-by to guide the slender stream to his lips.

Jeanne felt such keen delight that she could scarcely suppress her cries of joy. They set out again, and began to go downhill, skirting the gulf of Sagone. Towards evening they passed through Cargèse, a Greek village founded in bygone times by refugees exiled from their country. Tall, handsome girls of singularly graceful bearing, with finely moulded hips, long hands and slender waists, were grouped around a fountain. Julian called out good-evening to them, and they replied in musical tones and in the harmonious language of the country from which they had fled.

At Piana they had to beg for hospitality, as in ancient days and in uncivilised countries. Trembling with joy, Jeanne awaited the opening of the door at which Julian had knocked. Oh, this was real travelling, with all the unforeseen incidents that arise far from the beaten track. It so happened that they had come to the house of a young married couple, who welcomed them as the patriarchs of old must have welcomed the guests sent by God. They slept on a maize paillasse, in an old worm-eaten house. Its woodwork, full of worm-holes, infested by the long teredo which eats away rafters, creaked and sighed like a living thing.

They left at sunrise, and shortly afterwards halted in full view of a forest — a veritable forest — of purple granite, with peaks, columns, steeples, all moulded into weird shapes by the age-long erosion of winds and mists. Rising to the height of a thousand feet, slender, rounded, twisted, crooked, contorted, startling and fantastic, these amazing rocks had the appearance of trees, plants, beasts, monuments, men, robed monks, horned devils, giant birds, an assemblage of prodigies, a nightmare menagerie, petrified at the will of some eccentric deity.

Jeanne's heart was too full for speech. She took Julian's hand and pressed it; the sight of so much beauty inspired in her a yearning for love. Suddenly emerging from that scene of chaos, they came upon another bay, girt with a glowing wall of red granite. The flaming rocks were reflected in the blue water.

"Oh, Julian!" gasped Jeanne, too deeply moved to utter another word. She had a lump in her throat, and the teardrops welled from her eyes. Julian looked at her in amazement.

"What is the matter, puss?"

Smiling, she dried her eyes, and said in a somewhat tremulous voice, "It's nothing. Simply nerves. I don't know why, but I was a little upset. I am so happy that the least thing moves me to the heart."

Julian could make nothing of these womanish vapours, of these tremors that thrill those sensitive beings who are transported by a trifle, moved to the depths alike by an ecstasy or by a catastrophe, convulsed by incomprehensible emotions, thrown off their balance with equal readiness by joy and by despair. Her tears seemed to him absurd. The roughness of the road completely engrossed his own attention.

"It would be better," he said, "if you were to look after your horse."

By an almost impracticable track they reached the level of the bay, and then turned to the right in order to ascend the gloomy vale of Ota. The path proved appalling.

"Suppose we walk up on foot?" suggested Julian.

Jeanne asked nothing better. She was delighted to walk and to be alone with him after her recent emotion. While the guide went on ahead with the mule and the horses, they followed slowly. The mountain was cleft from summit to base with a deep fissure, and the path plunged into this breach. It lay far down between two mighty walls, and down this crevasse foamed a raging torrent. The air was glacial, and against the black granite a glimpse of blue sky high above dizzied and startled the eye. Jeanne was alarmed by a sudden noise. Raising her eyes, she saw a great bird fly out of a cleft. It was an eagle. It seemed as if his outstretched wings would span the two walls of the chasm. He soared towards the blue ether, and vanished from sight. After a while the fault in the mountain divided into two branches. The path climbed upwards in sharp zigzags, with a ravine on either side. Light of foot and light of heart, Jeanne went first. Pebbles rolled away under her step, and she leaned boldly over the precipices. Her husband followed her. He was a little out of breath, and kept his eyes on the ground for fear of dizziness.

The next moment they were bathed in sunlight, and they felt as if they had emerged from an inferno. They were thirsty. They followed a trail of moisture, which led them over chaotic heaps of stones to a tiny spring, trained to flow through a hollow stick for the con-

venience of the goat herds. The ground all around was carpeted
with moss. Jeanne knelt down to drink, and Julian followed her example. As she tasted the cool water, he seized her by the waist and
tried to usurp her place at the end of the wooden pipe. She resisted.
Their lips brushed together, met, and repulsed each other. In the
varying fortunes of the struggle both in turn caught the thin end of
the pipe, seizing it in their teeth, and held it fast. And the thread of
cold water, continually recaptured only to be abandoned, broke and
joined again, and splashed their faces, necks, hands and clothes.
Little pearly drops glistened in their hair, and their kisses were mingled with the stream.

Suddenly Jeanne had an amorous fancy. She filled her mouth with
the crystal fluid, until her cheeks were swollen like goatskin water-
bottles. Then she signed to Julian that with her lips on his she wished
to quench his thirst. Smiling and with outstretched arms, he threw
back his head and leaned towards her with open mouth. And as he
drank at one draught from this living fountain, his veins were filled
with feverish desire. Jeanne leaned against him with unwonted tenderness. Her heart was beating and her bosom heaved. With languorous, glistening eyes, she murmured in a low voice, "Julian, I
love you," and this time it was she who wooed. She threw herself
down on the moss, hiding her blushing face in her hands. He threw
himself on her and embraced her passionately. She panted in nerveless expectation. Suddenly she uttered a cry, smitten as by a flash
of lightning by the sensation she had evoked.

It was long before they reached the top of the ascent, so trembling
and stiff had she become. They did not arrive at Evisa till the evening. They put up at the house of Paoli Palabretti, a relation of their
guide. He was a tall man, somewhat bent, with the melancholy air
of a consumptive. He showed them their room, a dreary chamber of
bare stone, but good accommodation by the standards of Corsica,
where luxury is unknown. In his Corsican dialect, a hotch-potch of
French and Italian, he expressed his pleasure at their arrival. He was
interrupted by a clear voice. A small dark woman, with large black
eyes, sun-browned skin and slender waist, her teeth flashing in a continual smile, darted into the room. She kissed Jeanne and shook
hands with Julian, exclaiming, "Good-evening, Madame; good-evening, Sir. How are you?"

She took their hats and wraps, using one arm only, for the other she carried in a sling. Then she sent everyone out, bidding her husband take the guests for a walk till dinner-time.

Monsieur Palabretti hastened to obey. Walking between the young couple, he showed them round the village. He moved and talked with a languid air, coughing frequently, and observing after each paroxysm, "It's the cold air of the valley; it has gone to my chest."

He led them along an out-of-the-way path shaded by gigantic chestnut trees. Suddenly he stopped short.

"Just here," he said in his monotonous voice, "my cousin Jean Rinaldi was killed by Mathieu Lori. Look. I was standing there, quite close to Jean, when Mathieu appeared, ten paces away from us. 'Jean,' he cried, 'don't you go to Albertacce. If you do I'll kill you, I swear I will.' I took Jean by the arm. 'Don't go, Jean. He'll kill you.' It was all because of a girl called Paulina Sinacoupi, whom they were both courting. But Jean began shouting, 'I'm going, Mathieu; I shan't stay away for you.' Then, before I could take aim, Mathieu lowered his gun and fired. Jean jumped up in the air with both feet together, like a child skipping, and then fell right back on top of me, so that I dropped my gun and it rolled away down to that big chestnut tree over there. Jean's mouth was wide open. But he never said another word. He was quite dead."

The young people stared aghast at the tranquil witness of this crime.

"And the murderer?" asked Jeanne.

Paoli Palabretti had a prolonged fit of coughing. Then he replied, "He got away to the mountains. But my brother killed him the following year—my brother Philippi Palabretti, you know, the bandit."

Jeanne shuddered. "Your brother a bandit?"

The eyes of the placid Corsican flashed proudly.

"Yes, Madame, and a famous one he was. He accounted for six gendarmes. He and Nicolas Morali were surrounded in the Niolo and fell after six days' fighting, when they were dying of hunger."

Then he added in tones of resignation, "It's the way of the country"; just as he would have said, "It's the cold air of the valley."

They went home to dinner, and the little Corsican woman treated them as if she had known them twenty years.

Jeanne was haunted by an uneasy doubt. Would she recapture in Julian's arms those strange and violent emotions which she had experienced as she lay on the moss by the fountain? When they were alone in their room, she dreaded lest his kisses should once more leave her cold. But her fears were soon allayed. It was her first night of love.

The next day, at the hour of departure, she could hardly tear herself away from the lonely cottage where, it seemed, a new bliss had come into her life. She drew her little hostess into her room, and, while she declared that she had no intention of offering her a present, she insisted with vehemence on sending her a souvenir from Paris, an idea to which she attached an almost superstitious importance. The young Corsican woman was unwilling to accept it, and held out for a long time. In the end, she yielded. "Very well," she said, "send me a small pistol, quite a little one."

Jeanne opened her eyes wide. The other woman added softly in her ear, as if communicating some exquisite and intimate secret, "It's to kill my brother-in-law."

Smiling, she briskly unwound the bandages from her disabled arm, and showed the round white flesh. Right across it ran a stiletto wound, now almost healed.

"If I had not been as strong as he, he would have killed me," she said. "My husband is not jealous, because he knows me, and he is ill, you see, and that calms his blood. Besides, I am an honest woman, Madame. But my brother-in-law always believes everything he is told. He is jealous on my husband's behalf, and he will certainly be at it again. But if I had a small pistol, I should have an easy mind and could depend on revenging myself."

Jeanne promised to send the weapon, kissed her new friend tenderly, and went her way.

The rest of the journey passed like a dream, composed of endless embraces and intoxicating caresses. Jeanne noticed nothing, neither landscapes, people, nor places where she stayed. She had eyes only for Julian. There sprang up between them a childish and charming intimacy, made up of all the absurdities of love, of fond, foolish prattle, of pet names for all the curves and corners of their bodies on which their lips rested.

Jeanne used to sleep on her right side, and her left nipple was in consequence often uncovered when they woke. Julian had noticed this, and called it "Mr. Sleep-out," and the other one, "Mr. Lover," for its rosy, flower-like tip seemed more ready for his kisses.

The deep cleft between the two became "Mother's walk," since he used to pass up and down it incessantly; and another cleft, in a still more recondite place, was "the road to Damascus," in memory of the Vale of Ota.

When they arrived at Bastia, the guide had to be paid. Julian fumbled in his pockets, unable to find what he wanted. He said to Jeanne, "As you are not using your mother's two thousand francs, give them to me to keep. They will be safer in my belt, and it will save me the trouble of getting change."

She handed over her purse.

They went to Leghorn, Florence, Genoa, and drove the whole length of the Corniche. One morning they arrived at Marseilles in a mistral.

Two months had elapsed since their departure from *Les Peuples*, and it was now the fifteenth of October. Jeanne's spirits were affected by the high, cold wind which seemed to come from far-away Normandy, and she felt depressed. Of late, Julian had seemed changed, as if weary and indifferent, and she had a fear that she could not define. She delayed their return journey for four more days, reluctant to leave that pleasant land of sunshine. It seemed to her that she had accomplished the whole circuit of happiness. At last they resumed their journey.

In Paris they were to make all the purchases necessary for their permanent installation at *Les Peuples*. On the strength of her mother's present, Jeanne was looking forward to bringing home many treasures. But her first thought was for the pistol she had promised the young Corsican woman at Evisa. The day after their arrival, she said to Julian, "Please, dear, will you give me Mamma's money? I want to do my shopping."

He turned a frowning face towards her. "How much do you want?"

She was taken aback. "Why, whatever you like," she faltered.

"I'll give you a hundred francs," he replied; "but be careful not to waste it."

Disconcerted and bewildered, she hardly knew what to say. At last she began hesitatingly, "But I gave you that money to . . ."

He interrupted her. "Exactly. From the moment that we share a common purse, what does it matter whether it's in your pocket or mine? I'm not refusing it to you, am I, as I'm giving you a hundred francs?"

Without another word, she took the five gold coins, but she did not venture to ask for more, and she bought nothing but the pistol. A week later they set out for *Les Peuples*.

6

THE entire household was waiting outside the white gate with its brick pillars. The post chaise drew up, and there was much kissing and embracing. The Baroness wept. Jeanne herself wiped away two tears, while her father came and went, in nervous agitation. While the luggage was being unloaded, the travellers related their experiences in front of the drawing-room fire. A torrent of words flowed from Jeanne's lips, and in half an hour, except for a few trifling details omitted in her rapid narrative, the whole story was told.

Then Jeanne went away to unpack, with the assistance of Rosalie, who was in a similar state of excitement. When the unpacking was finished, and the underlinen, gowns and toilet accessories had been put away, the maid left her mistress. Somewhat weary, Jeanne sat down. She wondered what she should do next, to occupy her mind and hands. She had no inclination to go down to the drawing-room, where her mother was dozing. She thought of taking a walk, but the mere view of the dreary landscape through the window weighed upon her spirits.

All at once she realised that there was nothing more for her to do, that there would never be anything more. Her youthful days in the convent had been fully taken up with dreams of the future, and the hours had slipped away imperceptibly in a perpetual ferment of anticipation. Scarcely had she emerged from the austere walls, in whose shelter her illusions had blossomed, when her hopes of love had been immediately fulfilled. In the space of a few weeks she had met the man of her dreams, fallen in love with him, and married him on the spur of the moment, and he had carried her off in his arms without giving her time to think.

But now that the poetic reality of the honeymoon was to relapse into the prosaic reality of every day, the door was closed upon those vague hopes, those blissful questionings of the unknown. No, there was nothing left to wait for.

Accordingly, neither to-day nor to-morrow, nor ever again, would there be anything for her to do. A certain feeling of disillusion brought all this vaguely home to her. Her visions were losing power.

She rose and leaned her forehead against the cold window-panes. For some time she watched the heavy clouds drifting across the sky. At last she decided to go out.

Could these be the same trees, the same landscape, the same grass, as in the month of May? Whither had vanished the sun-steeped, dancing leaves, the glamour of the green lawns with their flaming dandelions, blood-red poppies and shining marguerites, where fantastic yellow butterflies fluttered, as if at the end of invisible threads? And that intoxicating quality in the air, fraught with life, with vital essences, with teeming atoms, had likewise departed.

Thickly carpeted with dead leaves, the paths lay dripping with incessant autumn showers beneath the lean, shivering, almost naked poplars. The lank branches shuddered in the wind, and shook the last lingering leaves, ready to drift away into space. All day long, like ceaseless rain, depressing to the point of tears, these yellow leaves, like large gold coins, detached themselves, fluttering and whirling to the ground.

She went as far as the copse, which was as mournful as a death-chamber. The leafy screens, which had separated and lent privacy to the charming little winding paths, were stripped bare. Tangled shrubs, their twigs like a network of lace, rubbed against one another their puny branches. The rustling of dry fallen leaves, swept and whirled, and heaped together here and there by the wind, resembled the mournful sigh of the expiring year. Tiny birds, with a faint shivering twitter fluttered from tree to tree, seeking shelter. Protected by the dense ranks of the elms, which were like an advance-guard thrown out against the sea gales, the lime tree and the plane still retained their summer garb, and appeared to be clad respectively in red velvet and orange silk, hues with which the first frost had invested them, according to the nature of their sap.

Jeanne walked slowly up and down the Baroness's avenue, which lay alongside the Couillards' farm. She was oppressed by her anticipation of the long-drawn-out tedium of the monotonous existence that lay before her. She seated herself on the bank, where Julian had first made love to her. She lingered there dreamily, her mind almost a blank, in a languor that pervaded her very heart. She had a longing to lie down and to take refuge in sleep from the melancholy of the day. Suddenly she caught sight of a sea gull flying across the sky, borne along by a squall of wind. It reminded her of the eagle she had seen in Corsica in the gloomy Vale of Ota. She felt the sharp pang provoked by the memory of some vanished happiness. In a flash she beheld once more the radiant island. She smelt its wild perfume, saw again its sun ripening the oranges and the citrons, its rose-peaked mountains, azure bays, and ravines with their rushing torrents. Then the sodden and barren landscape around her, with its dismal falling of leaves, its grey clouds swept along by the winds, overwhelmed her with such a profound sense of desolation that she returned to the house, lest she should burst into sobs.

Her mother was dozing lethargically by the fire. She was accustomed to the dreariness of her existence, and it no longer affected her spirits. The Baron and Julian had gone for a walk, and were talking business. Night came on, diffusing its mournful shade throughout the large drawing-room, which was fitfully illuminated by the firelight. Through the window the waning light still revealed the dingy landscape, typical of the expiring year, and the greyish sky, which seemed itself as if daubed with mud.

Soon Monsieur Le Perthuis appeared, followed by Julian. As soon as the Baron entered the gloomy room, he rang the bell, exclaiming, "Bring the lights at once. How dismal it is in here!"

He took a chair by the fire. His wet boots, close to the flame, were steaming, and the mud, dried by the heat, fell off in flakes from his soles. He rubbed his hands gaily.

"I really think it is going to freeze," he said. "The sky is clearing in the north. It's full moon this evening. There will be a sharp frost to-night."

He turned to his daughter. "Well, child, are you glad to be back in your own country, in your own home, with the old people?"

This simple question moved Jeanne deeply. With tears in her eyes, she threw herself into her father's arms, and kissed him passionately, as if seeking pardon. In spite of all her efforts at cheerfulness, she felt almost faint with sadness. When she remembered the joy with which she had looked forward to seeing her parents again, she wondered at the coldness which now paralysed her affection. Absent from those one loves, however much they may have been in one's thoughts, one loses the habit of constant intercourse, and on one's return a certain constraint is felt, until the broken threads of common existence have been joined again.

Dinner was a lengthy meal, and there was no conversation. Julian seemed to have forgotten his wife's existence. Afterwards, in the drawing-room, Jeanne yielded to the drowsy influence of the fire. Opposite her sat her mother, frankly asleep. Disturbed for a moment by the voices of the two men, who were engaged in some discussion, Jeanne endeavoured to rouse herself, and wondered whether she too would fall a prey to that mournful lethargy which is born of an uninterrupted routine.

The fire, which had glowed dully throughout the day, now burned with a clear, crackling flame. It cast bright and flickering lights on the faded tapestry of the chairs, on the fox and the stork, the melancholy heron, the cricket and the ant. The Baron drew close to the blaze, and stretched out his hands to the cheerful logs.

"It's burning well to-night. It's freezing, children; it's freezing." Then he laid his hand on Jeanne's shoulder, and, pointing to the fire, said, "My dear, this is the best thing in the world: one's own fireside, with those one loves around one. Nothing can equal that. But it is time to go to bed. You two children must be worn out."

Alone in her room, Jeanne wondered how it was possible that there could be such a complete contrast between her first homecoming and that of to-day, to this very same place, which she believed that she loved. How was it that she felt so utterly crushed? Why did this dear homeland, and all that had hitherto thrilled her soul, now affect her with such an intense depression? Then her eyes lighted on her clock. The little bee still swung from left to right and from right to left, with the same brisk, regular movement, above the silver-gilt flowers. She was seized with a sudden burst of affection, and was moved to tears at the sight of this little piece of mechanism, which seemed to be alive, which chimed the hour to her, and throbbed like a human bosom. Certainly she had not felt such keen emotion when she had embraced her father and mother. The heart has its mysteries, which no logic can fathom.

For the first time since her marriage, she slept alone. Pleading weariness, Julian was occupying another room. In any case, it had been arranged that they should have separate rooms. It was a long time before she fell asleep. She felt strange without his companionship, for she was no longer accustomed to sleeping alone, and she was disturbed by the sullen north wind raging against the roof. The next morning she was awakened by a bright light, which dyed her bed crimson, while her frosted window-panes were as red as if the sky were on fire.

Wrapping herself in a thick dressing-gown, she ran to the window and opened it. There was an inrush of icy wind, bracing and keen; the piercing cold made her skin tingle and her eyes water. A great flaming sun, like the bloated face of a drunkard, rose behind the trees in a crimson sky. The earth, white with frost, and hard and dry, rang out under the farm labourers' feet. In a single night the poplars had been stripped of their remaining leaves, and beyond the moor was visible the long greenish line of waves, all flecked with white foam.

The plane tree and the lime were rapidly shedding their leaves in the gusts of wind. Each time the icy breeze blew through the branches, eddies of leaves, which the sharp frost had loosened, were whirled into the air like flights of birds. Jeanne dressed and went out, and, having nothing better to do, paid a visit to the farmers.

The Martins threw up their hands. The wife kissed Jeanne on both cheeks and obliged her to drink a glass of noyau. Then she went on to the other farm. The Couillards threw up their hands. Madame Couillard kissed Jeanne lightly on each ear, and made her drink a small glass of black-currant brandy. After these visits, she returned home to luncheon. This day passed like the preceding day, except that it was cold instead of wet. And the remaining days of the week were exactly like the first two days, and all the succeeding weeks of the month resembled the first week.

Gradually, however, her yearning for distant lands subsided. Habit superimposed upon her existence a veneer of resignation, like the chalk coating which is deposited on things by certain waters. She began to take a certain interest in the thousand insignificant trifles, the simple, commonplace, regular occupations of daily life. Vaguely disillusioned with life, she fell into a mood of pensive melancholy. What was lacking in her life? What did she really want? She herself hardly knew. She had no social ambitions, no thirst for pleasure, no yearning even for such joys as were within her reach. And, indeed, what were these? Like the old drawing-room arm-chairs that time had faded, all things seemed to her eyes gradually to be losing colour, growing fainter, and assuming wan and cheerless hues.

Her relations with Julian had changed completely. Since their return from the honeymoon he seemed a different person, like an actor who has played his part and now resumes his everyday character. He scarcely noticed her or spoke to her. Every sign of love had suddenly vanished, and he seldom came to her room.

He had taken over the management of the money and the property, and was revising leases, tyrannising over the peasants, and cutting down expenses. Adopting the ways of a gentleman farmer, he had lost the polished elegance that had distinguished him during his engagement. The only coat he ever wore was a spotted old velvet shooting-jacket with copper buttons, which he had routed out from his bachelor wardrobe. He fell into the slovenly habits of a person who no longer cares to make a favourable impression; he gave up shaving; his appearance was incredibly coarsened by his long, ill-trimmed beard; and he neglected his hands. After every meal he drank four or five little glasses of brandy.

When Jeanne remonstrated gently with him, he replied so roughly, "Can't you leave me in peace?" that she did not venture to offer him further advice.

She adapted herself to these changes with an indifference that amazed her. She came to look upon him as a stranger, alien in heart and soul. She often puzzled over this, and wondered how it was that they could meet, love and marry in one passionate impulse, and then suddenly find that each knew almost as little of the other as if they had never slept side by side. And how was it that she did not suffer more from his neglect? Was life like this? Had they made a mistake? Did the future hold nothing but this for her? If Julian had remained handsome, well groomed, well dressed and seductive, would she perhaps have suffered more?

It was arranged that after New Year's Day the young couple should be left to themselves, while the Baron and his wife returned to their house in Rouen for several months. Julian and Jeanne were to spend the whole winter at *Les Peuples*, to enable them to settle down completely and to adapt themselves and become attached to the place where they were to spend their lives.

There were some neighbouring families, the Brisevilles, the Couteliers, and the Fourvilles, to whom Julian was to present his wife. But hitherto they had been unable to begin their round of calls, because it had been impossible to secure the services of a painter capable of altering the armorial bearings on the carriage.

The Baron had actually made over the old family coach to his son-in-law. But no power on earth would have induced Julian to show himself at the neighbouring country houses until the arms of de Lamare had been quartered with those of Le Perthuis des Vauds. There was only one man in that part of the country who specialised in heraldic insignia. He was a painter of the name of Bataille, who lived at Bolbec, and went the round of all the great houses in Normandy to paint the precious insignia on the carriage doors.

At last, one morning in December, towards the end of luncheon, a man was seen to open the gate and walk up the straight drive. He had a box on his back. It was Bataille.

He was shown into the dining-room, and was served at table like a gentleman. His special calling, his continual relations with the entire aristocracy of the Department, his knowledge of heraldry, of esoteric phraseology and of emblems, had invested him with a kind of honorary nobility, and all his aristocratic clients shook hands with him.

Pencil and paper were brought, and, while Bataille finished his meal, the Baron and Julian made sketches of their quarterings. The Baroness, thoroughly aroused by this important subject, contributed her opinion, and even Jeanne took part in the discussion, as if some mysterious interest had been suddenly awakened in her. While Bataille lunched, he expressed his own views. Sometimes he would take the pencil and make a rough sketch. He quoted precedents and described all the carriages of the nobility throughout the Department. His ideas, his very voice, seemed to diffuse an aristocratic atmosphere. He was a small, clean-shaven, grey-haired man; his hands were stained with paint, and he smelt of scent. There had been some ugly scandal about him, but the general esteem of all the titled families had long ago effaced this blot.

As soon as he had had his coffee, he was taken to the coach-house, and the tarpaulin was removed from the carriage. Bataille made his examination, and then gravely gave his opinion as to the dimensions he considered suitable to his design. After further discussion, he set to work. In spite of the cold, the Baroness had a chair brought, so that she could watch him, and presently she had to send for a foot-warmer. She had a quiet chat with the painter, eliciting from him new information about marriages, deaths and births, and thus supplementing her own recollection of the details of family-trees. Julian had remained with his mother-in-law. He sat astride his chair, smoking his pipe, spitting on the ground, listening, and watching closely the blazoning of his arms. Presently old Simon, spade on shoulder, stopped on his way to the kitchen garden, and looked on. The news of Bataille's arrival had reached both the farms, and before long the two farmer's wives put in an appearance. Standing one on either side of the Baroness, they went into raptures, exclaiming, "It takes a skilful hand to do niggling work like that!"

The coats-of-arms on the two doors were not finished till nearly eleven o'clock the next morning. The entire household assembled, and the carriage was taken into the open for a better view. The work was admirably done. After receiving congratulations, Bataille went away with his box strapped on to his back. The Baron, his wife, and Jeanne and Julian all agreed that the painter was a fellow of great gifts, and that in favourable circumstances he would doubtless have been an artist.

In the interests of economy, Julian carried out certain reforms, which involved some new arrangements. The old coachman had been made gardener, while the Viscount had undertaken to do the driving himself; and he had sold the carriage-horses to save the cost of feeding them. But, as it was necessary to have someone to hold the horses while the carriage was waiting, he turned a young cowherd, called Marius, into a little footman. Finally, in order to secure horses, he introduced into Couillard's and Martin's leases a special clause, obliging each of them to supply a horse one day a month, on a date fixed by himself. In consideration of this, they were exempted from supplying poultry.

Couillard produced a gaunt chestnut, and Martin a small white pony with a shaggy coat. The two animals were harnessed to the carriage, and Marius, smothered in old Simon's discarded livery, brought the turnout round to the front of the house.

Correctly dressed, with his shoulders thrown back, Julian had recaptured something of his former polish. But he still retained his long beard, and with it a certain bucolic air. He surveyed his pair of horses, the carriage, and the small servant, and was favourably impressed. The fresh coat-of-arms was the only thing to which he attached any importance. The Baroness came down from her room on her husband's arm, climbed laboriously into the carriage and sat down, leaning back against the cushions. Then Jeanne appeared.

She began by laughing at the ill-assorted pair of horses, and said that the white one was the grandson of the chestnut. Then she caught sight of Marius, his face buried in the cockaded hat, which only the bridge of his nose kept from slipping further down; his hands hidden in his vast sleeves; the skirts of his coat winding like a petticoat about his legs; his feet, in enormous shoes, protruding grotesquely beneath. When she saw how he had to throw back his head in order to see anything, and to lift his legs from the knee, as if stepping across a stream, while he bestirred himself blindly to carry out his orders, lost and floundering in the amplitude of his garments, she burst into uncontrollable laughter. The Baron turned round to look at the bewildered little fellow, and, catching the infection joined in Jeanne's mirth. His speech broken with laughter, he called to his wife, "Look at Marius! Isn't he funny? Oh Lord, isn't he funny?"

The Baroness leaned out of the carriage and looked at Marius, and was seized with such a paroxysm of mirth that the carriage rocked on its springs, as if jolting on a rough road.

Julian turned pale.

"What are you laughing at?" he demanded; "you must be mad."

Convulsed with hysterical laughter, Jeanne collapsed on a step of the perron. The Baron followed her example. Convulsive snorts, like the continual clucking of a hen, issued from the carriage, and indicated that the Baroness was choking. At last even Marius's long coat began to heave. Doubtless he had grasped the situation, for he, too, was laughing unrestrainedly in the depths of his hat. In a fury, Julian sprang at him and boxed the boy's ears, knocking off the huge hat, which rolled away on to the lawn. Then, turning to his father-in-law, he exclaimed in a voice trembling with rage, "It seems to me that it's not your place to laugh. We shouldn't be in this state, if you hadn't squandered your fortune and eaten up your property. Whose fault is it, if you are ruined?"

All the merriment was crushed, and ceased abruptly. Not another word was said. Now on the verge of tears, Jeanne quietly took her place beside her mother, while the Baron, speechless with surprise, seated himself opposite the ladies. Julian climbed on to the box, and hoisted up beside him the tearful boy, whose cheek was swelling. It was a dismal drive, and seemed to last a long time. Inside the carriage no one spoke. All three were gloomy and embarrassed. They would not openly avow what was in their minds, yet they felt that it was impossible to converse on other matters. Obsessed by these distressing thoughts, they preferred to maintain a mournful silence, rather than touch upon the painful subject.

The carriage, with its pair of unequally trotting horses, drove past the farmyards, scattering the startled black fowls, which dived out of sight into the hedges. Sometimes a wolf-dog would follow howling; then return bristling to its home, turning round to bark at the vehicle. A long-legged boy in muddy sabots, sauntering casually along with his hands in his pockets, the wind puffing out his blue smock, stood back to let the carriage pass, and raised his cap awkwardly from his plastered-down hair. Between the roadside farms lay stretches of flat country, and other farms were dotted here and there in the distance. Presently the carriage turned into a long avenue of pine trees, opening off the road. The carriage tilted from side to side in the deep, muddy ruts, evoking cries of alarm from the Baroness. At the end of the avenue there was a closed white gate. Marius ran to open it. The circular drive skirted a great lawn, and the carriage drew up in front of a tall, massive, gloomy house with closed shutters.

The central door suddenly opened. An old, paralytic servant, in a red waistcoat with black stripes, which was partly covered by his working apron, came slowly sideways down the flight of steps in front of the house. He took the visitors' names and showed them into a large drawing-room and laboriously drew back the venetian blinds which were usually kept closed. The furniture was covered over with dust cloths, and the pendulum clock and candelabra were swathed in white linen. The damp, stale, chilly air affected the visitors with a sense of mental and physical depression.

They sat down and waited. Steps were heard in the corridor above, moving with unwonted haste. The master and mistress of the house had been taken by surprise and were hurriedly making themselves presentable. This was a slow process. A bell was rung several times. Again footsteps were heard, first descending, then ascending, a staircase. Affected by the penetrating cold, the Baroness sneezed repeatedly. Julian strode up and down the room; Jeanne sat mournfully beside her mother, while the Baron stood with bent head, leaning against the marble mantelpiece.

At last one of the tall doors was thrown open and the Viscount and Viscountess de Briseville appeared. Both were small and lean, and might have been any age. They had a mincing gait, and their manners were stiff and formal. The wife wore a gown of flowered silk and a little, beribboned dowager's cap; she talked rapidly in a peevish voice. The husband was imposingly dressed in a close-fitting tail coat. He bowed to his visitors, bending at the knees. Everything about him, his nose, his eyes, his teeth, whence the gums had receded, his hair, which was plastered down as if with wax, and his fine, ceremonial attire, had the shiny appearance of things that are carefully preserved.

After the first neighbourly courtesies no one could think of anything to say. Then, for no reason at all, they began to congratulate one another, and both parties expressed a hope that their cordial relations would continue. Such meetings, they said, were a great resource when one lived all the year round in the country. The icy atmosphere of the drawing-room chilled them to the bone and made them hoarse. The Baroness was now coughing, as well as sneezing. The Baron gave the signal for departure. The Brisevilles protested. "What, so soon? Do wait a little longer." But in spite of signs from Julian, who considered that the visit had been too short, Jeanne had risen from her seat. An attempt was made to ring for the servant to have the carriage brought round, but the bell was out of order. The master of the house darted from the room, and presently returned with the information that the horses had been put into the stable. There was nothing for it but to wait. All four racked their brains for something to say, and they discussed the rainy winter. With an involuntary shudder of horror, Jeanne asked their hosts what they found to do all by themselves the whole year round. The Brisevilles were surprised at her question. They were fully occupied in keeping up a correspondence with their aristocratic kinsmen who were scattered all over France, and they spent their days in trifling occupations, never relaxing the ceremonious politeness usually reserved for strangers, and majestically conversing on the most insignificant subjects. In the huge disused, linen-swathed drawing-room, with its lofty, dingy ceiling, these two, man and woman, so tiny, so neat, so correct, seemed to Jeanne like aristocratic mummies.

At last the carriage passed the windows, with its two oddly assorted steeds. But there was no sign of Marius. Believing himself free till the evening, he had doubtless gone for a stroll in the neigh-

bourhood. Julian was furious, and asked that he might be sent home
on foot. After an effusive exchange of compliments, the visitors took
the road to *Les Peuples*.

As soon as they were in the carriage, although Julian's outrageous
behaviour still oppressed their spirits, Jeanne and her father began to
make fun of the Brisevilles and to imitate their mannerisms and way
of speech. The Baron mimicked the husband and Jeanne the wife.
But the Baroness, somewhat affronted, reproved them.

"You shouldn't make fun of them. They are quite the right sort
of people, and very well connected."

They were silent out of regard for the Baroness's feelings, but
from time to time, in spite of themselves, the Baron would catch his
daughter's eye and they would begin again. He would bow ceremoniously and say in solemn tones:

"Your country house, *Les Peuples*, must be very cold, Madame de
Lamare, with that strong sea wind blowing upon it every day."

She assumed a mincing air, and said simperingly, with a dip of
the head, like a duck taking a bath:

"Oh, yes, Baron, I have enough to keep me busy all the year
round. And then we have so many relations to write to, and it all
devolves on me, for Monsieur de Briseville is engaged with Abbé
Pelle in research work. They are collaborating in a religious history
of Normandy."

The Baroness could not suppress a smile, half-resentful, half-in-
dulgent, but she repeated:

"No, it's not right to make fun of people of our own class."

Suddenly the carriage halted, and Julian shouted to someone
who was coming up behind. Jeanne and the Baron leaned out of the
windows and saw a curious apparition trundling towards them. It
was Marius. His legs were encumbered by the flowing skirts of his
livery coat, and his eyes were blinded by his hat, which was continually toppling forward, while his sleeves fluttered like the sails of
a windmill. Covered with mud, splashing desperately through pud-
dles, and stumbling over all the stones in the road, he dashed after
the carriage as fast as his legs could carry him. As soon as he had
caught up with it, Julian leaned down, seized him by the collar and
dragged him up on to the seat beside him. Letting go the reins, he
battered the hat with his fists as if it were a drum, forcing it right

down on the urchin's shoulders. The boy inside howled, tried to jump off the box and escape, while his master, holding him with one hand, kept on beating him with the other.

"Father, oh, Father!" gasped Jeanne distractedly. The Baroness, roused to indignation, grasped her husband's arm.

"Why don't you stop him, Jacques?"

The Baron hurriedly lowered the front window and seizing his son-in-law by the sleeve, exclaimed in a voice trembling with indignation:

"Have you nearly finished beating the child?"

Julian turned round in amazement:

"Don't you see in what a state the young rascal has got his clothes?"

The Baron, with his head between the two, said: "What do I care? You needn't be such a brute."

Julian lost his temper again. "Please leave me alone. It's not your business," and he raised his hand once more. But his father-in-law promptly seized it and flung it down so violently that it struck against the wood of the seat.

"If you don't stop I shall get out and make you," he exclaimed, in such fierce tones that Julian suddenly calmed down. Shrugging his shoulders, and without another word, he whipped up the horses into a fast trot. The two women sat pale and motionless, and the violent palpitations of the Baroness's heart were distinctly audible.

At dinner Julian made himself unusually pleasant, as if nothing had occurred. Thanks to their even and kindly tempers, Jeanne and her parents soon forgave him. They melted when they saw him in such an amiable mood, and were as happy as a convalescent rejoicing in his recovery. When Jeanne referred again to the Brisevilles, her husband actually made some jesting remarks, but he was quick to qualify them: "All the same, they have an air of distinction."

No other visits were paid, for none of them was anxious to revive the difficulty about Marius. They decided to send cards to their neighbours on New Year's Day, and to defer their visits until the first warm days of spring.

On Christmas Day the priest and the mayor and his wife came to dinner, and they were invited again for New Year's Day. These were the only distractions which broke the monotonous sequence of days.

The Baron and his wife were to leave *Les Peuples* on the 9th of January. Jeanne pressed them to stay, but Julian did not second her invitation. In view of his son-in-law's increasing coldness, the Baron ordered a post chaise from Rouen.

The evening before their departure was clear and frosty, and as the packing was finished, Jeanne and her father decided to walk to Yport, which they had not visited since her return from Corsica. They passed through the wood, where she had wandered on her wedding day, one in heart with him whose life-long companion she was to be. In this wood she had received his first kiss, and had felt the first quivering presentment of that passion which she was not destined fully to experience till that day in the wild Vale of Ota, by the spring at which they had drunk, mingling their kisses in its waters. Gone were the leaves and tall grasses. There was no sound but the creaking of the branches and the dry rustling of bare wintry thickets.

They entered the little village. The quiet, empty streets still retained their smell of ocean, seaweed and fish. The huge, tanned nets were still left outside to dry, either before the doors or on the shingle. The cold grey sea with its perpetually moaning line of foam, was beginning to ebb, leaving bare the greenish rocks at the foot of the cliffs towards Fécamp. All along the beach the clumsy boats lay over on their flanks, like huge dead fish. Dusk was falling. Groups of fishermen were on their way to the quay, walking heavily in their great sea boots. They had woollen mufflers round their necks, and each carried a litre of brandy in one hand and a ship's lantern in the other. They spent a long time busying themselves with the beached vessels. With Norman deliberation they stowed away on board nets, floats, a large loaf of bread, a jar of butter, a tumbler, and the usual bottle of spirits. Righting each boat, they pushed it down to the sea and it slid over the shingle with a loud noise. It cut through the line of foam, hung a moment on the crest of a wave, then spread its brown wings and disappeared into the night, its little lantern shining at the mast-head. The sailors' buxom wives, their hardy bodies bulging beneath their thin dresses, waited till the last fisherman had gone out, then returned to the drowsy village, their shrill voices disturbing the heavy slumber of the dark streets.

The Baron and Jeanne stood motionless, watching the disappearance into the gloom of these men, who nightly ran the risk of death to save themselves from starvation, and yet were so poor as not to know the taste of meat.

Roused to enthusiasm by the sight of the ocean, the Baron exclaimed: "Jeannette, how stupendous, how superb is this sea, in the gathering darkness, with so many lives in danger on its waters."

With a smile of indifference, she rejoined: "It's not nearly so good as the Mediterranean."

"The Mediterranean," cried her father, with indignation. "The Mediterranean! Oil and sugar and water! Its very blue is the colour of the water in a wash-tub! Look at this, how terrifying are its crests of foam! And think of all these men, who have launched out upon the deep, and are lost to sight."

"Yes, I daresay," agreed Jeanne, with a sigh. But that word which had sprung to her lips, "the Mediterranean," had pierced her heart with a fresh pang, bringing back to memory those far-off countries, where her dreams still lingered.

Instead of returning through the woods, father and daughter went by the highroad and climbed the slope with slow steps. Saddened by the prospect of parting, they scarcely spoke. At times, as they skirted the farm dykes, there came to them the perfume of heaped-up apples, that scent of fresh cider, which at this season hovers over the Norman countryside, or again the rich stable odour, that pleasant, warm reek exhaled by the middens of cowsheds. At the far end of the courtyard a small lighted window revealed the dwelling house.

It seemed to Jeanne that her soul expanded with realisation of things invisible; and those tiny spots of light gleaming here and there in the fields gave her a sudden and vivid sense of the isolation of all living beings, destined to be torn apart, to be separated from one another, and dragged away from those they love.

In a tone of resignation she said: "Life's not always too cheerful."

The Baron sighed: "Well, my child, we can't help that."

The next day her father and mother left for Rouen, and Jeanne remained alone with Julian.

7

PRESENTLY Jeanne and Julian began to take an interest in cards. Every day, after luncheon, Julian, smoking his pipe, and sipping brandy of which he contrived to drink six or eight glasses, would play several *partis* of bezique with his wife.

After this she would go up to her room, take a chair by the window, while the rain beat against the panes, or the wind shook them, and conscientiously work away at the embroidered trimming of a petticoat. Sometimes she would wearily raise her eyes and watch far off the white horses on the leaden sea. After some minutes of this vague contemplation, she would resume her work.

For, after all, she had nothing else to do. Julian had undertaken the entire management of the household in order to assert his authority, and to satisfy his mania for economy. His thrift was absolutely ferocious; no tips were allowed; and food was reduced to the barest necessaries. On coming to live at *Les Peuples* Jeanne had ordered a little Norman cake from the baker every morning, but Julian suppressed this extravagance, and restricted her to toast. To avoid explanations, arguments and wrangles, she made no protests, but each new example of her husband's avarice stung her like a pinprick. Brought up, as she had been, in a family where money was of so little account, this seemed to her a sordid and ignoble trait. How often had she heard the Baron say to her mother, "Money is meant to be spent"! Julian, on the other hand, would say again and again, "Is it quite impossible for you to learn not to throw money out of the window?" And whenever he managed to cut a few sous from wages, or a bill, he would observe with a smile as he slipped the small change into his pocket, "Little streams make big rivers."

But there were still times when Jeanne fell a-dreaming. She would quietly leave off working, and, with listless hands and vacant look, renewing one of the romances of her childhood, set out on delightful adventures. But all too quickly the voice of Julian, giving an order to old Simon, would snatch her back from this realm of soothing fancy. She would patiently resume her work, sighing, "That's all over," and a tear would fall on the fingers which plied the needle.

Rosalie, too, once so gay and full of little songs, was a changed girl. Her once round cheeks had lost their rosy bloom, and were now sunken and hollow, and her complexion was muddy.

Jeanne often asked her, "Are you ill, child?" And the maid always answered, "No, Ma'am," a faint blush rising to her cheeks, as she hurried away. Instead of tripping lightly as of old, she dragged her feet wearily, she had no longer any coquettish airs, and never made any purchases from the pedlars, who in vain displayed to her their silk ribbons, corsets, and many varieties of scent.

The great house seemed to ring hollow; it was a dismal place, its exterior stained with long grey streaks of rain. At the end of January came the snow. From afar, great clouds could be seen coming from the north over the sombre sea; and the white flakes began to fall. In a single night the whole plain was covered with a white shroud, and at daybreak every tree appeared clad with icy foam.

Julian, all unshaven, and wearing top-boots, spent his time on the edge of the little wood, ambushed behind the ditch which skirted the moor, and lying in wait for the migrant birds. From time to time a gunshot broke the frozen silence of the fields; and flocks of startled crows flew circling round the high trees. Jeanne, unable to endure her boredom, went out from time to time on to the steps in front of the house. From very far away came sounds of life echoing over the slumbering quietude of that blank and desolate waste.

Again, she would hear nothing but the roar of waves in the distance, and the vague monotonous whisper of fine powdered snow falling, falling forever. And the drifts rose higher and ever higher with the unceasing fall of fleecy snow, dense yet feathery.

On the morning of one of these colourless days, Jeanne was warming her feet at the fire in her room, while Rosalie, looking less like herself from day to day, was languidly making the bed. Suddenly she heard behind her a grievous sigh. Without turning her head she asked, "What is the matter with you now?" As usual the maid replied, "Nothing, Ma'am," but her voice sounded broken and faint.

Jeanne was already thinking of something else, when she noticed that she no longer heard the girl moving about. "Rosalie, Rosalie," she called, but nothing stirred.

Thinking that she had quietly slipped out of the room Jeanne cried in louder tones, "Rosalie," and was about to stretch out her hand to ring the bell, when a deep groan, uttered close by, made her leap to her feet with a shudder of dismay. The little maid, livid and haggard-eyed, was sitting on the ground with her legs stretched out, and her back resting against the wood of the bedstead.

Jeanne started towards her crying: "What's the matter with you? Tell me."

Rosalie neither spoke nor moved; she fixed on her mistress a frenzied look and gasped for breath as if torn by some frightful spasm of pain. Then all at once, she slid to the floor, stretched out at full length, stifling between her clenched teeth a cry of anguish. Beneath her dress something was moving. Jeanne heard a strange noise, a murmur, a gasp as from the throat of one strangled and suffocating; and suddenly a long-drawn sound like the mew of a cat, a plaintive and doleful wail, the first sad call of a child coming into the world.

In a moment Jeanne understood. In great distress she rushed to the stairs, crying, "Julian, Julian."

"What do you want?" he answered from below.

She could scarcely speak: "It's—it's—Rosalie. She . . ."

Julian darted up the steps two at a time, and rushing into the room, pulled up the girl's clothes with a single movement and discovered a hideous little atom of a baby, crumpled, whining, shrivelled, moving between the naked legs. He rose with a face of fury, and pushed his distracted wife from the room, exclaiming: "This is none of your business. Be off. Send up Ludivine and old Simon."

Trembling in every limb, Jeanne went down to the kitchen, and then, not daring to go upstairs again, found her way to the drawing-room, where no fire had been lighted since her parents' departure. There she stayed and anxiously waited for news. Very soon she saw a servant run out. Five minutes afterwards he came back with the Widow Dentu, the local midwife. There was a bustling on the staircase as if a wounded man was being carried along; and then Julian came to tell Jeanne that she could go back to her room. She was shaking from head to foot as if she had just witnessed some shocking accident. Resuming her seat before the fire she asked: "How is she?"

Nervous and perturbed, Julian was walking up and down the room, and seemed to be in a bad temper. He did not answer at once, but after a few moments he said: "What are you going to do about the girl?"

She did not understand. Looking at her husband, she said: "What do you mean? How should I know?"

At that, as if beside himself, he cried out: "Anyhow, we can't keep a bastard in the house."

Jeanne hesitated in much perplexity, and there was a long silence. "Well, dear, perhaps we could put him out to nurse."

"And who's going to pay for that?" he broke in. "You, no doubt?"

She thought for a long time, seeking a solution of the problem. Then she said: "Surely the father will look after the child; and if he marries Rosalie, there will be no further difficulty."

Julian lost all patience, and flew into a rage: "The father! The father! Do you know who is the father? No, of course not. Well, then?"

Jeanne was much moved, and exclaimed vehemently: "But surely he will not desert the girl in her trouble. He would be a coward. We will ask her his name, and we will find him, and he will just have to speak up."

Julian grew calmer, and began to walk up and down. "My dear, she will never tell you the man's name; she will not confess it to you any more than to me. And, even so, suppose the man will have nothing to do with her? In any case, we could not possibly keep this girl with her illegitimate child; you must see that yourself."

Jeanne repeated obstinately: "Then the man's a wretch; but we must really find out who he is, then he will have to deal with us."

Julian turned very red and said irritably: "And in the meantime?"

She could not make up her mind, and said: "What do you propose to do yourself?"

He promptly gave his opinion.

"Why, it's perfectly simple. I should give her some money and send her to the devil with her brat."

But Jeanne protested indignantly.

"Never! That girl is my foster sister; we grew up together. She has made a slip; so much the worse; but I will never turn her out of doors for that, and if necessary I myself will bring up the child."

Then Julian burst out: "A nice reputation we shall have! We have our name and family to consider. Every one will say that we are protecting vice and harbouring hussies; and respectable people will not set foot in our house. Come, come, what are you thinking of? You must be mad."

She remained unmoved: "I will never let Rosalie be turned out of doors. And if you will not keep her here, my mother will take her back; and sooner or later we must find out the name of the child's father."

He flung out of the room in a rage, slamming the door and shouting: "What idiots women are with their notions!"

In the afternoon Jeanne went up to see Rosalie. The girl, who was under the care of the Widow Dentu, was lying in bed, motionless and with open eyes, while the nurse cradled in her arms the newborn infant. As soon as she saw her mistress, Rosalie began to sob, hiding her face in the sheet, in a paroxysm of despair. Jeanne tried to kiss her, but she resisted and covered her face. The nurse intervened and drew away the sheet. She did not resist again, but went on weeping softly. There was a miserable fire on the hearth; the room was cold, and the baby was crying. Jeanne was afraid to speak of the little one for fear of bringing on another attack of nerves.

Taking Rosalie's hand, she repeated mechanically:

"Never mind; never mind." The poor girl looked surreptitiously towards the nurse and shuddered at the infant's wailing. Half stifled with grief, which burst forth in an occasional convulsive sob, she forced back her tears.

Jeanne kissed her once more, and murmured very softly in her ear:

"We will take great care of him, my child." Then, as a fresh burst of tears threatened, she hastily left the room.

She paid a daily visit to Rosalie, who invariably broke into sobs as soon as she saw her mistress.

The baby was put out to nurse with a neighbour.

All this time Julian hardly spoke to his wife, as if deeply offended by her refusal to send Rosalie away. One day he re-opened the subject, but Jeanne drew from her pocket a letter from the Baroness asking her to send Rosalie to her at once if she was not staying on at *Les Peuples*.

"Your mother is as big a fool as you are," cried Julian, furiously; but he raised no further objections. A fortnight later the young mother was able to get up and resume her household duties.

One morning Jeanne made her sit down, took her hands, and looking steadfastly at her, said: "Come, my child, tell me all about it."

Rosalie began to tremble and faltered:

"What, Ma'am?"

"Whose is the baby?"

Once more the poor girl was convulsed with anguish. She tried frantically to draw her hands away so that she might hide her face. But Jeanne kissed her in spite of her reluctance, and tried to comfort her.

"You have had bad luck, to be sure, Rosalie. You were weak, as many others have been. But if the father marries you, no one will think any more of your slip; and we could take him into our service with you."

Rosalie moaned as if she were on the rack, and every now and then she made an effort to free herself and escape.

Jeanne resumed:

"I quite understand that you are feeling ashamed of yourself; but you can see that I am not angry with you, and that I am speaking gently to you. I am asking you for the man's name, but it is for your own good. I can see from your distress that he has deserted you, and that is what I wish to prevent. My husband shall find him, and we will make him marry you; and as we shall keep you both with us, we will see to it that he makes you happy."

At this Rosalie, with a desperate effort, snatched her hands from her mistress's clasp, and fled like one beside herself.

That evening at dinner Jeanne said to Julian:

"I have been trying to persuade Rosalie to tell me the name of her seducer, but I did not succeed. Will you please try, too, so that we may make the wretch marry her?"

But Julian at once lost his temper.

"I tell you I do not want to hear any more about it. You decided to keep the girl. Very well, you can, but do not worry me about her."

Since the birth of Rosalie's child, he seemed to be unusually irritable. He had got into the habit of never speaking to his wife without shouting as if he were in a furious rage. Jeanne, on the contrary, spoke in a low voice, and was gentle and conciliatory, so as to avoid argument. But often she wept in bed at night. Notwithstanding his constant ill-humour, her husband had resumed his amorous attentions, which he had neglected since their return, and seldom let three days pass without coming to her room.

Rosalie was soon quite well and her spirits improved, though she still seemed terrified, as if haunted by some unknown fear. And twice she again managed to escape when Jeanne tried to renew her enquiries.

Julian also began to make himself more agreeable; and the young wife nursed vague hopes, and once more recovered her former gaiety, although she sometimes experienced curious feelings of uneasiness, which she mentioned to no one. The thaw had not yet set in and for five whole weeks the clear sky, crystal blue by day and at night all sown with stars that glittered like hoar-frost in the vast frozen firmament, brooded over the unbroken expanse of sparkling snow.

Solitary farms, with their square courtyards behind their screens of lofty trees, frosted with rime, seemed as if asleep in their snowy vesture. Neither man nor beast stirred abroad; the only sign of the concealed life within the cottages was the slender thread of smoke which rose from the chimneys straight up into the wintry air.

The moor, the hedges, the rows of elms, all seemed dead, killed by the cold. From time to time a tree would crack, as if one of its wooden limbs had snapped beneath the bark; and now and then a big branch detached itself and fell, its sap congealed and its fibres burst by the all-conquering frost.

Jeanne eagerly looked forward to the coming of spring, attributing to the terrible rigour of the weather all the vague discomfort which she was experiencing. Sometimes she was seized with distaste for all food and could eat nothing, sometimes her pulse beat frantically, and the lightest meal gave her indigestion. Her nerves were highly strung and all on edge, and she lived in a constant and intolerable state of agitation.

One evening the thermometer dropped lower than ever. Julian, shivering as he rose from table (for the dining-room was never properly warm because of his niggardliness with regard to fire-wood), rubbed his hands and whispered:

"It will be cosy sleeping together to-night, won't it, little puss?"

He laughed the jolly laugh of old times. Jeanne threw her arms round his neck; but really she felt so ill at ease that evening, so full of aches and pains, so strangely nervous, that as she kissed him on the lips, she begged him to let her sleep alone. Briefly she told him of her indisposition:

"I am sorry, dearest, but really I am not feeling at all well. I expect I shall be better to-morrow."

87

He did not insist.

"Just as you like, darling; if you are ill, you must take care of yourself."

They changed the subject. She went to bed early and Julian, for once, had a fire lighted in his own room. When he was told that the fire was burning up he kissed his wife's forehead and went off.

The whole house seemed to be labouring under the frost. The walls were frozen through and through and emitted low sounds, as if shuddering, and Jeanne shivered in bed with cold. Twice she got up, heaped logs on the hearth, and looked for gowns, skirts, and old clothes to pile upon the bed. In vain. Nothing seemed to make her warm; her feet grew numb; and tremors ran along her legs. Throwing herself from side to side, she tossed about restlessly till all her nerves were tingling. Presently her teeth began to chatter; her hands trembled; her chest grew tight, her heart beat slowly with great heavy throbs and sometimes seemed to stop entirely. She gasped as though she could not breathe. Deadly anguish clutched her soul while the all-conquering cold penetrated the very marrow of her bones. Never had she felt anything like this, as if she were losing her hold on life, and were about to breathe her last. She thought: "I'm going to die . . . I'm dying." Horror-struck she jumped out of bed, rang for Rosalie, waited, rang again, waited once more, shuddering and cold as ice. But the maid did not come. No doubt she was sleeping that deep first impenetrable slumber. In desperation, Jeanne darted barefooted to the staircase. She groped her way noiselessly up the steps, found the door she was seeking, opened it, and called: "Rosalie, Rosalie." She advanced into the room and stumbled against the bed, felt it with her hands, and found it empty. It was empty and quite cold as if no one had slept there.

In surprise she exclaimed: "What! Can she have gone gadding about in weather like this?"

The tumultuous throbbing of her heart suddenly seemed to stifle her. She went downstairs again with tottering steps, intending to wake Julian.

She burst into his room, impelled by the conviction that she was dying and by her desire to see him once more before losing consciousness. By the light of the expiring fire she saw on the pillow two heads, her husband's and Rosalie's.

At the cry which she uttered both started up. For a moment she

stood motionless, appalled by her discovery. Then she fled back to her room. But when Julian, in dismay, cried "Jeanne," she was seized by a sickening dread of seeing him, of hearing his voice, of listening to his lying explanations, of looking him in the face, and she dashed again to the staircase and sped down in the dark at the risk of rolling down the whole flight, and of breaking her limbs on the stone steps.

She went straight down, driven by an overmastering necessity to escape, to learn no more, and never to see any one again. When she reached the bottom, she sat down on the lowest step, barefooted and in her nightdress, and remained there in desperation.

Julian had jumped out of bed and was hastily dressing. She sprang to her feet to escape him. He was already coming down the stairs crying: "Do listen, Jeanne."

No, she would not listen nor let him touch her as much as with the tips of his fingers; and she flung herself into the dining-room, fleeing as if before a murderer. She sought a way out, a hiding place, a dark corner, any means of escape. She hid under the table. Now he was opening the door, with a light in his hand, and calling repeatedly, "Jeanne, Jeanne." She started off like a hare, darted into the kitchen, running round it twice like a beast at bay; and as he still followed her, she hastily threw open the door into the garden and darted out into the open. The icy contact with the snow, into which her bare legs plunged knee-deep, endowed her suddenly with desperate energy. Lightly clad though she was, she did not feel the cold; she had no sensation of anything, so utterly had the convulsions of her mind benumbed her body. She ran on and on, white as the snow-covered ground. She went down the long avenue, through the copse, crossed the ditch, and made for the moor.

It was a moonless night; the stars glistened like points of fire, scattered broadcast on the blackness of the sky. But the moor was clearly visible, of a dull and toneless white, without movement of any living thing; and over all brooded the silence of the void.

Breathless, reckless, and at random, Jeanne sped onwards. Suddenly she found herself on the edge of the cliff. She stopped instinctively and crouched down, divested of all power of thought and will. From the dark chasm at her feet rose from the invisible and silent sea the briny odour of seaweed left stranded by the tide.

She stayed there a long time, mind and body alike insensible.

Suddenly she began to tremble, to tremble violently like a sail quivering in the wind. Arms, hands, and feet seemed shaken by some invincible power, and shuddered convulsively. With a start, consciousness returned to her, only too clear and piercing. Before her eyes passed visions of other days, the sail with Julian in old Lastique's boat, their talk, the dawning of love, the christening of the vessel, and so back to that night of happy dreams, when she had first come home to *Les Peuples*. And now! Now! Oh, her life was ruined; never any prospect of joy or happiness again, only a dreadful vista of coming years full of tortures, treasons, and despair. Better to die and so make an end of all.

But a distant shout reached her:

"This way; here are the tracks; hurry up."

It was Julian searching for her. Oh, she never wished to see him again. From the chasm at her feet rose a gentle murmur, the lapping of the sea upon the rocks. She started up, ready to take the fatal leap; and flinging to life a despairing farewell, she sighed the last word of the dying, the last word on the lips of young soldiers in the agony of death in battle: "Mother!" At this word, the thought of her dear mother pierced her heart; she heard her mother's sobs, she saw her father kneeling beside her dripping corpse; in a moment she realised all the anguish of their despair. Softly she sank back in the snow, and made no effort to escape when Julian and old Simon, lighted by Marius's lantern, caught her by the arm and drew her back, so near was she to the brink. They did what was necessary for her, for she could not move. She was aware that she was carried home, put to bed, and rubbed with hot towels; then everything was blotted out and she lost consciousness.

But a nightmare — was it really a nightmare? — haunted her. She was in bed in her own room. It was broad daylight but she could not rise; why, she knew not. Then she heard a little noise on the floor, a scratching and rustling, and all of a sudden a mouse — a small grey mouse — darted across the sheet. Another followed, then a third, boldly advancing towards her bosom, with brisk, tiny steps. Jeanne was not afraid. She put out her hand to catch it, but without success. Other mice, in scores, and hundreds, and thousands, swarmed on all sides. They clambered up the bed-posts, trooped over the curtains, and took possession of the whole bed. Presently they made their way under the clothes, and Jeanne felt them rub against her skin, tickle her legs, and run up and down all over her body. She saw them advancing from the foot of the bed to creep in and nestle in her breast. She struggled and threw out her hands to catch one, but they always closed on emptiness. In a frenzy she tried to escape and cried out; but though she could see no one, she felt that somebody held her down, that strong arms enfolded her and kept her powerless. She had no idea of time; but all this must have lasted a very long while.

At last she awoke, weary and stiff, yet with a feeling of content. She felt unutterably weak. Opening her eyes, she saw without surprise that her mother was sitting in the room, with a burly man whom she did not recognise. How old was she? She had no idea, but felt as if she were still a little girl. Her memory was a blank.

The burly man said:

"Ah! She has regained consciousness." Her mother burst into tears. The burly man resumed:

"Come, be calm, Baroness; I'll answer for her now. But do not say a single word to her. Let her sleep."

It seemed to Jeanne that she spent another long spell in a drowsy condition, which turned to deep slumber as soon as she tried to think. So she gave up all efforts of memory, as if, in some vague way, she dreaded the sense of reality which her mind was recovering. But once, when she awoke, she saw Julian standing alone by her bedside, and, in a flash, everything came back to her as if the curtain veiling her past life had been withdrawn. A pang of anguish pierced her heart, and once more she tried to escape. Flinging off the bedclothes, she leaped on to the floor, but her legs gave way and she fell. Julian sprang towards her; but she screamed to him not to touch her. She writhed and rolled about on the ground. The door opened and her Aunt Lison ran in with the Widow Dentu, followed by the Baron and last of all her mother, panting and distraught. They put her back to bed and she at once cunningly closed her eyes so as not to have to talk and to be able to think in peace. Her mother and aunt busied themselves about her, asking:

"Can't you hear us, Jeanne, dear little Jeanne?"

She would not answer, and pretended not to hear them, but she was perfectly aware that the day had come to an end and that it was night. The nurse took her place by the bedside, and from time to time gave her something to drink. She drank, but never spoke a word. Nor did she sleep. Laboriously she thought matters out, seeking to recapture incidents which eluded her, as if there were gaps in her memory, great, white, vacant spaces, where events had left no impression. Little by little, after prolonged efforts, all the facts came back to her. And she brooded over them with fixed determination. Her mother, Aunt Lison, and the Baron had come, so she must have been very ill. But what about Julian? What had he told them? Did her parents know all? And Rosalie, where was she? What was to be done? What, indeed? One idea pierced the gloom. She would go back and live with her father and mother at Rouen as before. She would be a widow; that was all. Thus she waited, with patient cunning, hearing everything that was said around her, understanding perfectly but not letting the others know, and rejoicing in her recovered reason.

At last, one evening, she found herself alone with the Baroness, and called to her, very softly:

"Mother, dear." Her own voice surprised her; it seemed changed. The Baroness seized her hands.

"My little one, my darling Jeanne, my own child, do you really know me?"

"Yes, Mother, darling, but you mustn't cry. We have much to say to each other. Has Julian told you why I ran away in the snow?"

"Yes, darling; you had very high fever and were dangerously ill."

"That was not the reason, Mamma. I had fever afterwards. But has he told you what gave me fever and why I ran away?"

"No, dear."

"It was because I found Rosalie in bed with him."

The Baroness soothed her, thinking her mind was still wandering: "Go to sleep, darling. Calm yourself and try to sleep."

But Jeanne persisted.

"I am quite rational now, Mamma; I am not talking nonsense, as I must have done the last few days. One night I felt ill and I went to find Julian. Rosalie was sleeping with him. I went out of my mind with the shock and I ran off in the snow, meaning to throw myself from the cliff."

But the Baroness only said:

"Yes, my pet, you were very ill."

"That's not the point, Mamma. I really did find Rosalie in bed with Julian and I will not live with him any more. You must take me back with you to Rouen, as in the old days."

The Baroness, who had been warned by the doctor not to cross Jeanne in anything, replied:

"Certainly, my pet."

At this the sick girl lost patience.

"I am quite sure that you do not believe me. Go and bring papa. I shall be able to make him understand."

Painfully rising from her chair, her mother hobbled out of the room with her two sticks, returning a few minutes later leaning on the Baron's arm. They sat down by the bedside, and Jeanne at once began again. She told them everything, in a weak voice, but quietly and clearly; dwelling upon Julian's extraordinary character, his harshness, his meanness, and, last of all, his unfaithfulness. When she had finished, the Baron was convinced that she was not wandering, but he did not know what to think, what course to take, what answer to give. He took her hand tenderly, as in old days, when he had lulled her to sleep with fairy stories.

"Listen to me, dearest, we must not be rash. Don't let us be hasty; try to put up with your husband till we have come to some decision. Will you promise me?"

She murmured:

"Yes, I promise, but I will not stay here when I get well."

Then in a whisper, she asked: "Where is Rosalie now?"

"You won't see her any more," replied the Baron.

But she persisted: "Where is she? I insist on knowing."

He was obliged to admit that she was still in the house, but declared that she was about to leave.

The Baron came out of the sick room blazing with wrath, his father's heart deeply wounded. He went to find Julian, and addressed him abruptly:

"Sir, I have come to ask you for an explanation of your conduct towards my daughter. You have been unfaithful to her, and with your own maid-servant, an added insult."

Julian played the injured innocent; passionately denied the charge, with oaths and appeals to God. Besides, what evidence was there? Was it not clear that Jeanne was out of her mind? Was she not just recovering from brain fever? Had she not run out into the snow, at night, in a fit of delirium, at the onset of her illness? And it was just at this crisis, when she was running half naked through the house, that she claimed to have seen her maid in bed with her husband. He lashed himself into a fury, threatened an action for slander, and professed himself grossly insulted. The bewildered Baron apologised, begged his pardon, and frankly held out his hand, but Julian refused to take it.

When Jeanne heard of her husband's answer, she showed no concern, but merely said: "He is not telling the truth, Papa; sooner or later we shall make him admit it."

For two days she remained silent, self-absorbed and brooding. On the third morning she expressed a wish to see Rosalie. The Baron declined to bring the maid to her room, saying that she had gone away. Jeanne repeated obstinately: "Very well; send someone to her to fetch her here."

And just as she was working herself up the doctor arrived. He was told the whole story, and was asked to advise. But Jeanne, beside herself with nervous agitation, suddenly burst into tears, almost screaming:

"I must see Rosalie, I must see her."

The doctor took her hand and said in a low voice:

"Keep calm, Madame; any excitement may have serious consequences, for you are about to become a mother."

She was overwhelmed, as if she had had a blow, and all at once something seemed to quicken within her. She lay silent, deep in thought, not even hearing what was said. She could not sleep that night, kept awake by this new and singular idea that her body sheltered a living child. She felt sad and troubled to think that it was Julian's son, and was rendered restless by a fear that he might resemble his father. The next morning she sent for the Baron.

"Papa, I have quite made up my mind; I must know all, now more than ever. I absolutely insist, and you know that you must not cross me in my present state. Now, listen to me. Go and bring the priest. I want him to prevent Rosalie from telling lies; then, as soon as he comes, send up Rosalie, and you and mother are to be present. Above all, take care not to rouse Julian's suspicions."

An hour later the priest entered the room. He was fatter than ever, puffing quite as much as the Baroness. He took an armchair beside the Baroness, his belly bulging between his knees, and mopping his forehead, as usual, with his handkerchief, he began to chaff her.

"Well, Baroness, we don't seem to get any thinner; I think we make a very good pair." Then, turning to the sick bed:

"Aha! What do they tell me, young lady? We are soon going to have another christening, but it won't be a ship this time, ha! ha!" He added more seriously: "It will be a soldier to fight for his country." Then, after a little thought: "Unless it's a good mother of a family, like you, Baroness."

The door at the far end of the room opened. Rosalie distracted and in tears, was refusing to enter, clinging like grim death to the doorpost, while the Baron attempted to push her forward. At last, losing patience, he thrust her violently into the room. She covered her face with her hands and stood there sobbing.

As soon as she saw her, Jeanne started up in bed, paler than the sheets; her thin clinging nightdress rose and fell with the passionate throbs of her heart. She could not speak; she could hardly breathe and was nearly suffocated. At length, in a voice broken by emotion, she stammered:

"I—I—need not question you. I have only—to look at you—to see your—your shame at the sight of me." She stopped for want of breath; but after a pause she resumed:

"But I insist on knowing the whole story—everything. And I have sent for the priest so that it may be like a confession, you understand."

Rosalie stood motionless, uttering half-stifled cries through her quivering fingers. The Baron, whose temper was rising, seized her arms and roughly tore her hands from her face, and flinging her on her knees beside the bed, cried: "Speak up. Answer."

She remained on the floor, in the attitude of a repentant Magdalene, her cap awry, her apron on the floor, her face hidden again in her hands.

Then the priest spoke to her:

"Come, my daughter, listen to what is said to you and answer. No one wants to hurt you; but we wish to know what happened."

Leaning to the side of the bed, Jeanne looked steadily at her and said: "It is true that you were in bed with my husband when I caught you."

"Yes, Ma'am," moaned Rosalie through her clasped hands.

At this the Baroness likewise burst into tears, with a loud choking noise, and mingled her convulsive sobs with Rosalie's. Jeanne, her eyes fixed steadily on her servant, asked: "How long has this been going on?"

"Ever since he came," stammered Rosalie.

Jeanne failed to understand: "Ever since he came? What, since the spring?"

"Yes, Ma'am."

"Ever since he came to this house?"

"Yes, Ma'am."

A flood of questions rose to Jeanne's lips: "But how did it happen? How did he seduce you? How did he get hold of you? What did he say? When and how did you yield to him? How could you give yourself to him?"

This time Rosalie removed her hands of her own accord, and now she, too, seemed in a fever to speak, and to answer everything.

"How can I tell? The first day he dined here he came to my room. He had hidden in the attic. I didn't dare to cry out for fear of a scandal. He came to my bed. I didn't know a bit what I was doing. He did just as he liked. I didn't tell on him because I liked him so much."

A cry burst from Jeanne's lips:

"Then—your—your child is—his?"

"Yes, Ma'am," sobbed Rosalie.

Both were silent. Nothing was heard but the noisy weeping of Rosalie and the Baroness.

Overwhelmed with grief, Jeanne felt her own tears begin to flow; the drops trickled noiselessly down her cheeks. Her maid's son had the same father as her own child! Her anger had subsided. Now she felt only steeped in gloomy, dull, profound, and hopeless despair. When she spoke again her voice was changed and tearful:

"And after we came back from our—from our honeymoon—when did it begin again?"

Collapsing on the floor, the poor girl faltered: "The—the first night, he came again."

Every word wrung Jeanne's heart. To think that, the very first night, the night of their return to *Les Peuples*, he had left her for this girl! That was why he had let her sleep by herself. She knew enough now; she wished to learn no more.

"Go away, go away," she cried. And as Rosalie, stupefied, did not move, Jeanne called to her father:

"Take her away; take her away."

But the priest, who had not yet spoken, thought the moment opportune for delivering a little homily.

"What you have done, my daughter, is very wicked, very wicked, indeed. God will not readily pardon you for it. Remember that hell awaits you, if you do not behave well in future. Now that you have a child, you must reform. No doubt the Baroness will do something for you, and we will find you a husband . . ."

He would have gone on talking, but the Baron once more seized Rosalie by the shoulders, raised her to her feet, dragged her to the door and bundled her out into the passage.

When he came back he was paler even than his daughter. The priest took up his parable again:

"What can you expect? They are all the same in this part of the country. It's deplorable, but one cannot mend it, and one must have a little indulgence for the weakness of human nature. They never marry until they have to, never. One might almost call it a local custom," he added, smiling. Then in scandalised tones: "Even the children! Last year, in the cemetery, didn't I catch two youngsters together, who were being prepared for confirmation, a boy and a girl? I told their parents. What do you think they answered? 'What can you expect, Father? We did not teach them these dirty tricks; we can't do anything.' There it is, Baron; your servant has only done like the rest."

But the Baron, trembling with impotent rage, interrupted him:

"That girl? What do I care about the girl? It's Julian who infuriates me. His conduct has been infamous, and I shall take my daughter away."

He strode up and down, lashing himself into a fury.

"It is infamous to have wronged my daughter in this way, infamous. The fellow is a scoundrel, a blackguard, a low wretch; I shall tell him so. I shall box his ears. I shall give him a sound thrashing."

But the priest, sitting beside the tearful Baroness, calmly took a pinch of snuff. Anxious to complete his task of pacification, he resumed:

"Come, come, Baron; between ourselves, he has been no worse than anyone else. Do you know many husbands who are faithful to their wives? Why, I bet that even you have played your little games," he added with sly good humour. "Come, your hand upon your heart, isn't that true?"

The Baron was completely nonplussed, and the priest went on. "Yes, yes, you have done like the rest. Who knows even whether you have never amused yourself with a little baggage like that? I tell you all the world does as much. And your wife has been none the less happy, none the less loved for all that, has she?"

The Baron was so overcome that he did not stir. It was true that he had done as much, often enough; in fact, as often as he could; he, too, had not respected the conjugal roof; and, when they were pretty, he had had no scruples in regard to his wife's servants. Was he, therefore, a scoundrel? Why, then, should he condemn so severely the conduct of Julian, when he had never dreamed that his own conduct was blamable?

On the lips of the Baroness, still out of breath with sobbing, hovered the shadow of a smile at the memory of her husband's frolics; for she was of that class, sentimental, readily moved, kind-hearted, for whom love affairs are an essential element of life.

Jeanne, worn out, her open eyes gazing into vacancy, lay on her back with listless arms, her mind full of dismal thoughts. One of Rosalie's remarks recurred to her and wounded her to the very soul, boring its way into her heart like a gimlet: "As for me, I did not tell anyone because I liked him so much." She, too, had "liked him so much." And it was solely on this account that she had given herself to him, had tied herself for life, had surrendered every other hope, every half-formed project, all the unknown future. She had fallen into this marriage, into this unfenced pit, merely to emerge into this life of misery, grief and despair, because, like Rosalie, she had liked him so much!

The door was pushed violently open. Julian appeared on the threshold with a savage look on his face. On the stairs he had found Rosalie, groaning and moaning, and he came to find out what was happening. He guessed that Rosalie must have confessed, and that some plot was being hatched. But the sight of the priest rooted him to the spot.

In a subdued but shaking voice, he asked, "Well, what's the matter?"

The Baron, lately so violent, did not venture to say anything, fearing the priest's arguments and his son-in-law's possible appeal to his own example. The Baroness's tears became even more profuse; but Jeanne, raising herself on her hands, her bosom rising and falling, gazed at the man who had made her suffer so cruelly. "The matter is that everything is clear to us now," she faltered. "We know all your infamous conduct since—since the first day when you came to this house. The child of that servant girl is yours, just as mine is. They are brothers."

Overwhelmed by intolerable grief at this thought, she sank back in bed and burst into frenzied weeping. Julian stood open-mouthed, not knowing what to say or do.

Once more the priest came to the rescue. "Come, come, young lady; we must not take things so hardly. Be reasonable."

He rose, approached the bed, and placed a soothing hand on the unhappy girl's forehead. Strangely enough, the mere contact brought relief. A delicious feeling of languor stole over her, as if that strong peasant's hand, practised in the gestures of absolution and the offices of consolation, had brought with its touch mysterious solace.

Standing erect, the good man went on: "Madame Jeanne, one must always forgive. A great sorrow has come upon you, but God in His mercy has compensated it with a great happiness, for you are about to become a mother. Your child will be your consolation. In his name, I implore you, I adjure you, to forgive your husband's fault. The infant will be a new bond between you, a pledge of his future fidelity. Can you live estranged from the heart of him whose child you bear in your bosom?"

Crushed with grief, utterly worn out, with no strength even for anger or resentment, she made no answer. Her nerves were all unstrung, and there seemed little life left in her. The Baroness, who seemed unable to cherish rancour, and whose mind was incapable of sustained effort, murmured, "Come, Jeanne."

Drawing Julian to the bed, the priest took his hand and placed it in his wife's. Giving their joined hands a little pat, as though to confirm their union, he threw off his professional manner, and said complacently, "Well, well, there's an end to that. Believe me, that is much the best way."

Their two hands, joined for a moment, fell asunder immediately. Julian did not venture to kiss Jeanne; but he kissed his mother-in-law's forehead, turned on his heel, and took the arm of the Baron, who made no objection, glad at heart that matters had been thus settled. They went off together to smoke a cigar. Utterly worn out, the invalid fell into a doze, while the priest and her mother talked quietly in subdued tones.

The Abbé continued to expound his plans, and the Baroness nodded her consent to everything. To sum up the matter, he said: "Well, then, that is settled. You give the girl Barville Farm, and I will find her a husband, some good fellow, who has sown his wild oats. With a property worth twenty thousand francs, we shall have plenty of aspirants. The only difficulty will be to choose."

The Baroness was now smiling happily; and, though she still had a tear on each cheek, the traces they had left were already dry. "I quite agree," she replied. "Barville is worth at least twenty thousand francs. We will settle the property on the child, and the parents shall have the use of it for their lives."

The priest rose, and shook hands with the Baroness. "Do not disturb yourself, Baroness; do not disturb yourself. I know what a bother it is to move."

As he went out, he met Aunt Lison coming to see the invalid. She noticed nothing; was told nothing; and, as usual, knew nothing.

8

ROSALIE had left the house, and Jeanne's months of waiting were dragging wearily along. So many troubles had been heaped on her that no joy thrilled her heart at the thought of becoming a mother. Still depressed with the vague apprehension of some misfortune, she awaited without interest the arrival of her child.

Spring stole over the land. The bare branches of the trees shivered in breezes that were still wintry. But in the ditches, among the damp herbage and decaying autumn leaves, peeped out the first yellow cowslips. From moor, farmyards, and water-logged fields arose a moist odour, a savour of fermentation. And multitudes of little green points shot out from the brown earth and glittered in the sunlight.

A stout woman, solid as a fortress, took Rosalie's place and accompanied the Baroness on her monotonous strolls up and down the avenue, where her dragging foot left a wet and muddy track. Jeanne, depressed and out of sorts, leaned on her father's arm, while Aunt Lison, who was restless and flurried at the thought of the coming event, held her other hand. The old maid felt aghast at this mystery, which it would never be her lot to understand. So they walked up and down for hours, hardly ever speaking; while Julian suddenly seized by a passion for riding, galloped all over the country.

Nothing ever occurred to disturb the dreary monotony of their existence. The Baron and his wife and Julian paid a visit to the Fourvilles, whom Julian seemed to know rather well already, though no one could explain exactly why. Formal calls were also exchanged with the Brisevilles, forever buried in their sleepy old manor-house.

One afternoon, about four o'clock, two riders, a man and a woman, trotted into the front courtyard of the house. Julian ran excitedly into Jeanne's room.

"Go down as quickly as you can. The Fourvilles are here. They have dropped in in a neighbourly way, without ceremony, as they know that you are not going out just now. Say that I am out, but will soon be back. I am just going to tidy myself up a bit."

Somewhat surprised, Jeanne went downstairs. She found a pale, pretty young woman, with a sad face, feverish eyes and fair hair, which had a lustreless look, as if it had never been touched by a ray of sunshine. She introduced her husband, a gigantic sort of bogey man, with big red moustaches. She added:

"We have met Monsieur de Lamare several times. He told us that you were not well, and we did not like to put off any longer coming to see you, in an informal, neighbourly way. As you see, we have ridden over. The other day I had the pleasure of a visit from your mother and the Baron."

Her manner of speaking was easy, familiar and distinguished. Jeanne fell a victim to her charm, and adored her on the spot. "Here," she thought, "is a friend."

Count de Fourville, on the other hand, was like a bear in a drawing-room. When he sat down, he put his hat on the nearest chair, and could not for a long time decide what to do with his hands. He rested them first on his knees, then on the arm of the chair, and at last clasped them as if in prayer.

Julian burst into the room. Jeanne was so much surprised that she hardly knew him. He had shaved. He looked as handsome, as well groomed and attractive, as in the days of their engagement. He shook the hairy paw of the Count, who seemed to wake up when he came, and kissed the hand of the Countess, whose ivory cheek flushed delicately and whose eyelids flickered.

He spoke with all his former amiability. His great eyes, in which love was reflected, once more grew soft and melting, and his hair, but a moment ago dull and dry, had become soft and shining and wavy by dint of brushing and much scented pomade.

As the Fourvilles rode off, the Countess turned to him. "Would you care to come for a ride on Thursday, my dear Viscount?"

He bowed and murmured, "I shall be delighted, Countess."

She took Jeanne's hand, saying, with a charming smile, in soft but impressive tones, "Oh, when you are all right again, we will all three gallop over the country. That will be delicious. You will, won't you?"

With a graceful gesture, she lifted the skirt of her riding-habit, and sprang into her saddle as light as a bird, while her husband, after an awkward bow, mounted his great Norman horse, sitting it with the ease of a centaur.

When they had turned into the roadway, and were out of sight,

Julian exclaimed enthusiastically, "What delightful people! They will be very pleasant acquaintances."

Jeanne, who was equally charmed without quite knowing why, answered, "The little Countess is perfectly fascinating; I am sure I shall be very fond of her. But the husband seems rather a boor. Where did you meet them?"

"I met them casually at the Brisevilles," said he, rubbing his hands together gaily. "The husband is a bit rough, but quite a gentleman. He is mad on hunting."

Dinner that night was almost festive, as if some secret happiness had come to the house.

Nothing more happened till the last days of July.

One Tuesday evening, as they were sitting under the plane tree round a wooden table, with two little glasses and a small decanter of brandy in front of them, Jeanne suddenly uttered a cry, grew pale as death, and pressed her hands to her side. A quick, sharp, momentary pang had shot through her. A few minutes afterwards she felt another pang, more prolonged, but less acute. She got back to the house with difficulty, supported by her father and her husband. The short journey from the plane tree to her room seemed endless; she moaned involuntarily, and had to stop and rest now and then, as if weighed down by an intolerably heavy burden.

Her confinement was not expected before September; but, fearing some mishap, the Baron ordered the trap, and old Simon galloped off for the doctor, who reached the house by midnight, and at a glance diagnosed the symptoms of a premature delivery. Once in bed, the pains were easier, but Jeanne was convulsed with a frightful agony of spirit, a feeling of utter hopelessness, a touch, as it were, of the mysterious finger of death—death, which at such moments brushes by us, so near that its breath freezes our very heart.

The room was full of people. The Baroness lay back in an armchair, panting for breath. The Baron, with trembling hands, ran hither and thither, bringing things, asking questions of the doctor, and generally losing his head. Julian strode up and down with a preoccupied expression, but inwardly quite calm; and the Widow Dentu stood at the foot of the bed with an appropriate expression of countenance, the self-possessed air of a woman of experience. Sick-nurse, midwife, and watcher of the dead, she received the newly born, heard their first cry, washed for the first time their tender bodies, wrapped them in their swaddling-clothes. With the same tranquillity, she listened to the last words, the last death-rattle, the last shudder of the dying, made their last toilet, sprinkling the empty shell with vinegar and folding it in the winding-sheet. She had developed an imperturbable indifference to all the incidents of birth or of death. Ludivine, the cook, and Aunt Lison remained discreetly hidden behind the door opening into the hall.

From time to time the invalid uttered a feeble groan. For two hours it was thought that the event would be protracted; but just before daybreak the pangs returned suddenly and violently, and soon became excruciating. Jeanne clenched her teeth, but could not suppress her cries of anguish. She kept on thinking of Rosalie, who had not suffered at all, who had hardly uttered a groan, whose child—whose base-born child—had come into the world without trouble or anguish. In her wretched, harassed soul, she drew a comparison between the two cases. And she murmured against God, in whose justice she had hitherto believed; she inveighed against the shameful preference shown by fate, and the wicked falsehoods of those who preached that all was rightly and duly ordered. Sometimes the agony became so unbearable that all power of thought was obliterated. She had life, strength, consciousness, solely that she might suffer.

In moments of respite she could not keep her eyes from Julian, and she was convulsed by another pang—a pang that pierced her very soul—as she called to mind the day when her servant had fallen down at the foot of this very bed, giving birth to her child, the brother of the tiny being who so cruelly tore and rent her. With lucid memory, she recalled the gestures, looks, and words of her husband as he stood looking down on the girl at his feet. Now, as if his movements revealed his thoughts, she discerned in him the same boredom, the same indifference, the same uninterested attitude of the egoist, who resents paternity. Then a frightful convulsion overcame her, a spasm so agonising that she cried out, "I am dying; I am dying."

In a rebellious fury, she had an impulse to utter imprecations; her soul was filled with bitter hatred of the man who had brought this fate upon her, and of this unknown infant who was killing her. She strained herself in a supreme effort to be rid of her burden. Sud-

denly her womb seemed to empty itself, and her sufferings abated. The nurse and the doctor leant over her and picked up something. Then that stifled sound, which she had heard once before, thrilled her: the little plaintive cry, the feeble voice, as of a cat mewing, of the new-born baby, penetrated her heart and soul and all her poor, exhausted body. Unconsciously she stretched out her arms, in a glowing transport of joy, towards the new bliss that had come into her life. In a moment she found herself free from pain, and happy — happy as she had never been before. Soul and body revived, for she knew that she was a mother.

She insisted on seeing the child. Born too soon, he had no hair or finger-nails; but when she saw the little, undeveloped creature move, when she saw him open his mouth to utter a wail, when she touched the wretched little atom of humanity, crumpled and grimacing, yet alive, a flood of unutterable joy overwhelmed her. She knew that she was saved, insured against despair, that she now owned something which she would love to the exclusion of all else.

From that moment she had but one thought: her child. She became suddenly the fanatical mother; so much the more enthusiastic, as she had been deceived in her love and duped by her hopes. The cradle must always be by her bedside, and, when she was well enough to get up, she spent whole days sitting at the window, rocking the cradle. She was jealous of the nurse, and when the little thirsty creature stretched its arms towards the swelling, blue-veined bosom, and pressed the button of brown wrinkled flesh to its greedy lips, she would watch, pale and trembling, the tranquil, robust peasant woman, dying to snatch away her son and to beat and scratch that breast at which he was drinking so eagerly.

With her own hands she embroidered elaborately trimmed baby clothes for his adornment. He was smothered in clouds of lace, and decked with ravishing bonnets. She could not talk of anything else, interrupting conversation to hold up for admiration a swath of linen, a bib, or some finely worked scrap of ribbon. She did not listen to a word of what anyone said, but went into ecstasies over odds and ends of lawn, which she turned and turned about and held up to examine, and she would suddenly exclaim, "Won't he look perfectly sweet in this?"

The Baron and Baroness smiled at these frenzied outbursts of affection. But Julian, whose customary habits were disarranged, and whose dominant importance was diminished, by the arrival of this squalling and all-powerful tyrant, became unconsciously jealous of this scrap of humanity, who had robbed him of his place as master of the house, and kept saying irritably, "Isn't she too sickening over her brat?"

Very soon she became so completely obsessed by this passion that she spent her nights sitting near the cradle, watching her little one asleep. She wore herself out by these passionate and morbid vigils, depriving herself of sleep, till she grew weak and thin, and was racked by a cough; and in the end the doctor ordered her to be parted from her child. She wept bitterly, flew into a rage, begged and entreated. But her prayers fell on deaf ears. The baby was put to sleep in the nurse's room; and every night his mother used to get up and steal away with bare feet and put her ear to the keyhole, to make sure that he was sleeping peacefully and not in want of anything. One night Julian, returning home late after dining with the Fourvilles, found her there. After that she was locked in her room, so that she should have to stay in bed.

The child was baptised towards the end of August. The Baron was godfather, and Aunt Lison godmother. He was named Pierre Simon Paul, and called Paul for short. Early in September, Aunt Lison quietly took her departure, and her absence was noticed as little as her presence.

One evening, after dinner, the Abbé came in. He seemed ill at ease, as if he had a secret on his mind, and after a little commonplace talk he asked the Baroness and her husband to give him a few minutes of private conversation. The three of them strolled slowly to the end of the avenue, engaged in animated talk, to the surprise and irritation of Julian, who stayed behind with Jeanne. When the priest went away, Julian insisted on accompanying him, and they walked off together towards the church, where the Angelus was being rung. The night was fresh, almost cold, and the Baron and Baroness and Jeanne returned to the drawing-room. They were all having a little nap, when Julian came in abruptly, his face flushed with indignation. As soon as he entered, regardless of Jeanne's presence, he shouted at her parents, "Good heavens, you must be mad to think of throwing away twenty thousand francs on that girl!"

They were all struck dumb with surprise. Beside himself with anger, he continued: "How can you be such fools? You want to leave us without a farthing."

Recovering his self-possession, the Baron tried to stop him: "Hold your tongue. Remember your wife is here."

Julian stamped with rage. "What the devil do I care! She knows all about it. Besides, it is her interests that will suffer from this robbery."

Jeanne was startled, and looked from one to the other without grasping the situation. "What is it all about?" she stammered.

Julian turned to her, treating her as his witness, as a partner cheated out of anticipated profits. He explained to her the plan for marrying Rosalie and giving her as a dowry Barville Farm, which was worth at least twenty thousand francs.

"Your parents are out of their senses, my dear. They ought to be under restraint. Twenty thousand francs! Oh, they're mad! Twenty thousand francs for an illegitimate brat!"

Surprised at her own tranquillity, Jeanne listened quite unmoved and not at all annoyed, indifferent to all that did not concern her own child. The Baron gasped for breath, struggling to speak. At last he broke out, stamping his foot, "For Heaven's sake, think what you are saying. It's perfectly disgusting. Whose fault is it that we have to give this poor girl a dowry? Whose child is it? Yours, and now you want to disown it."

Taken aback by the Baron's violence, Julian looked steadily at him. In more composed tones, he replied, "Fifteen hundred francs would be quite enough. All these girls have babies before they marry. Whether it's this man's or the other's, what earthly difference does it make? Besides, when you give this girl a farm worth twenty thousand francs, you not only rob us, but you publish the facts to all the world. You might at least think of our name and position."

He spoke in a solemn voice, like a man thoroughly satisfied that he was in the right and that his reasoning was logical. Bewildered by this unexpected argument, the Baron stood open-mouthed.

Perceiving that he had made an impression, Julian pushed the matter home. "Luckily, nothing is settled yet. I know the lad who is going to marry her; he's a capital fellow, and I shall be able to arrange matters with him. Leave it to me."

And he went off at once, fearing, no doubt, to continue the discussion, and well pleased at their silence, which he took for consent.

As soon as he had gone, the Baron, quivering with surprise and indignation, exclaimed, "Oh, this is too much; it is indeed."

But Jeanne, catching sight of her father's bewildered expression, burst out laughing, with the frank laugh of her girlhood at anything amusing. "Oh, Father, did you hear how he said 'twenty thousand francs'?"

The Baroness was as ready for laughter as for tears. At the recollection of her son-in-law's enraged air and vehement protestations, his indignant refusal to let them give his victim money which did not belong to him, and pleased also with Jeanne's mirth, she chuckled convulsively, till the tears came into her eyes. Catching the contagion, the Baron went off in his turn, and all three, as in the happy days of the past, laughed till they felt quite ill.

When they quieted down a little, Jeanne said, in some surprise, "It is curious that this does not distress me at all. He seems quite a stranger to me nowadays. I hardly realise that I am his wife. You see for yourselves, I am amused at his—his want of delicacy."

And, without knowing why, they all embraced one another, still smiling and in a softened mood.

But two days later, after luncheon, as soon as Julian had gone off for his usual ride, a tall young man, between twenty-two and twenty-five years of age, wearing a brand new blue smock, which hung in stiff folds, with sleeves buttoned at the wrist and puffed out like balloons, slunk through the gateway, as if he had been lying in wait all the morning. He skirted the Couillards' dyke, and came round the corner of the house. With stealthy steps he approached the Baron and the two ladies, who were occupying their usual seat under the plane tree. When he came in sight he took off his cap, and shuffled towards them with an embarrassed air. As soon as he was near enough for them to hear, he blurted out, "Your servant, Baron and ladies."

And, as no one answered, he introduced himself: "I am Désiré Lecoq."

As they were none the wiser for this information, the Baron asked, "Well, what can I do for you?"

The young man was quite upset at the idea of having to explain his business. Now lowering his eyes to the cap in his hand, now lifting them to the roof of the house, he stammered, "The fact is—the priest has spoken a word or two about that business——" Then he stopped, afraid of letting out too much, and compromising his case.

Still in the dark, the Baron said, "What business? I do not know what you mean."

The peasant decided to speak out, and lowered his voice: "That business of your servant-girl—Rosalie——"

Jeanne guessed what was coming; she rose and moved away, with her child in her arms. The Baron bade him come nearer, and pointed to the chair which his daughter had just left.

The young man sat down, muttering, "You are very kind." Then he waited, as if he had nothing more to say. After a long pause, he plucked up courage again and, gazing at the blue sky, he observed: "Fine weather for the time of year. But it's not good for what's already sown." And he relapsed into silence.

The Baron lost patience. He came briefly to the point and said drily, "So you are the man who is going to marry Rosalie?"

The other at once grew restless, his characteristic Norman cunning aroused. In a more assured voice, but mistrustfully, he replied, "That's as may be; perhaps yes, perhaps no."

Annoyed by these evasions, the Baron cried out, "Hang it all! Answer straight out. Is this what you came about: yes or no? Are you going to take her? Yes or no?"

The man stared at his boots in perplexity. "If it's as the priest said, I'll take her; if it's as Monsieur Julian said, I won't."

"What did Monsieur Julian say?"

"Monsieur Julian said I was to have fifteen hundred francs; the priest talked of twenty thousand. I'm willing to do it for twenty thousand, but not for fifteen hundred."

At the peasant's anxious face, the Baroness, who was leaning back in her easy-chair, gave her little giggling laugh. Lecoq glanced at her askance and dissatisfied, and, seeing no occasion for laughter, he kept silence.

Tired of this bargaining, the Baron cut it short. "I told the priest that you should have Barville Farm for your life, with reversion to the child. It's worth twenty thousand francs. I am a man of my word. Is it a bargain; yes or no?"

The peasant, with a respectful smile of satisfaction, now became garrulous. "Oh, if that's how it is, I won't say no. That was my only objection. When the priest spoke to me, I jumped at it, to be sure, and was only too glad to oblige the Baron, who won't let me lose by it. Isn't it true that when people do each other a good turn, it comes back to them again some day? But Monsieur Julian comes along with his fifteen hundred francs. Says I to myself, 'I must get to the bottom of this,' and here I am. Not that I didn't trust the Baron, but I wanted to know for certain. Short reckonings make good friends, don't they, sir?——"

To put an end to this talk, the Baron said, "When do you propose to marry her?"

At this the man's timidity and embarrassment returned, and after a pause he said, "Can I have just a line in writing?"

This time the Baron was really angry. "Damn it all, won't you have the marriage contract? That's the best writing of all."

The peasant tried to hold out: "All the same, I really should like a scrap of writing to go on with. That can't do any harm."

The Baron rose to put an end to the scene. "Answer yes or no, and at once. If you won't, say so; I have another candidate."

The fear of a competitor upset the cunning Norman. He made up his mind, and held out his hand, as if he had bought a cow. "Shake hands, sir; it's a bargain. He's a rogue who cries off."

The Baron shook him by the hand, and ordered the cook, who put her head out of the window, to bring some wine. They drank to wet the compact, and the young man went off with a lighter foot.

Nothing was said to Julian about this visit. The marriage contract was drawn up with great secrecy; and, after publication of the banns, the wedding took place one Monday morning.

A neighbour brought the baby to the church, behind the newly married couple, just for luck. And no one in the place was surprised. They all envied Désiré Lecoq. "He was born with a silver spoon in his mouth," they said, with a sly smile quite free from malice.

Julian made a terrible scene, in consequence of which the Baron and his wife cut short their visit to *Les Peuples*. Jeanne felt no deep distress at their departure, for in Paul she had an inexhaustible well-spring of happiness.

9

WHEN Jeanne had recovered from her confinement, they decided
to return the Fourvilles' visit, and also to call on the Marquis de
Coutelier. Julian had just bought at an auction a new carriage, a
phaeton which took only one horse, so that they might be able to
drive out twice a month. One bright December day the horse was
put in, and, after a two hours' drive over the Norman moors, they
began to drop down into a little valley with wooded banks on either
side and ploughed fields at the bottom. After the fields came pasturage, and after the pasturage a marsh full of tall reeds, dry at
this time of the year, with long leaves, like yellow streamers, rustling
in the wind. The valley described a sudden curve, and they came
in sight of the manor-house of *La Vrillette*. Behind it rose a wooded
slope, and the whole length of the front wall was washed by a large
lake, whose farther bank was fringed by a wood of lofty fir trees
climbing the opposite incline of the valley.

Crossing an ancient drawbridge, they passed through a great
Louis XIII gateway into the main courtyard, which lay in front of
a stately manor-house of the same period, of panelled brickwork,
and having at each end a slate-roofed turret.

Julian pointed out to Jeanne the different parts of the building,
speaking as one who knew it thoroughly. He did the honours of the
house, and expatiated on its beauties.

"Pray observe that gateway. Don't you think it's a fine house?
The whole length of the other façade abuts on the lake, and there
is a stately flight of steps down to the water. At the foot of the steps
four boats are moored, two for the Count and two for the Countess.
Down there on the right, just where you see the screen of poplars,
is the end of the lake. There the river starts which flows down to
Fécamp. The country is full of waterfowl, and the Count is desperately keen on shooting. This is what I call a lordly mansion."

The door was opened, and the Countess, pale, but smiling, appeared and welcomed her visitors. She was clad in a flowing robe,
like a châtelaine of old times. Indeed, she might have been the
lovely Lady of the Lake, born for this noble manor-house.

115

Four of the eight windows of the drawing-room opened on the lake and the dark pine wood which climbed the slope beyond. The sombre foliage of the pines lent an appearance of depth and gloomy austerity to the lake; and the wind, sighing through the branches, was like a voice from the marsh.

The Countess took both Jeanne's hands, as if they had been friends from childhood, and seated herself beside her on a low chair, while Julian, all smiles, joined in the pleasant small-talk, with all the grace of manner which he had lost for a time, but had recaptured in the last five months. The Countess and he talked of their rides together. She laughed a little at his horsemanship, calling him "the Knight of the Unstable Balance," and he laughed back and called her "Queen of the Amazons."

Jeanne jumped at the sound of a shot close by. It was the Count, shooting teal. His wife called to him. There was a sound of oars and the bump of a boat against the stone steps, and in came the Count, looking gigantic in his waders, while his two dogs, tawny like himself, threw themselves, dripping wet, on the doormat. He seemed more at ease in his own house, and was delighted to welcome his

116

guests. He had more logs put on the fire, and called for Madeira and biscuits. Then, with a sudden inspiration, he exclaimed: "But of course you will stay to dinner!" Jeanne, whose thoughts at once flew to her baby, would have refused the Count's pressing invitation, but Julian showed signs of displeasure at her obstinacy. Afraid of rousing his quarrelsome temper, she gave way, though it went to her heart to think that she would not see Paul till next day.

They spent a delightful afternoon. First they went to see the spring, which gushed out at the foot of a mossy rock into a boiling and bubbling pool, clear as crystal. Then they rowed along open channels, cut through forests of withered reeds. The Count took the oars, sitting between his dogs, who held their noses up to the wind, scenting for game. The boat leaped forward at every stroke. Jeanne dipped her hands in the cool water, and a delicious sensation of refreshing coldness coursed from her fingers to her heart. In the stern of the boat sat Julian and the Countess, who was wrapped in shawls, and they smiled the placid, unchanging smile of people whose happiness is complete. Twilight came, bringing with it the chill, long-drawn sighing of the north wind in the withered rushes. The sun had set behind the pine wood, and the mere sight of the red sky, sprinkled with scarlet cloudlets, grotesque in shape, gave an impression of cold.

They returned to the great drawing-room, where there was a roaring fire, which welcomed them, as they entered, with a pleasant sense of warmth.

In an exuberance of gaiety, the Count caught up his wife in his brawny arms, raised her like a child to the level of his lips, and printed two smacking kisses on her cheeks, like a good fellow thoroughly pleased with the world. Jeanne smiled as she looked at this genial giant, whom she had set down as an ogre, merely because of his ferocious moustaches. How often one misjudges people, she thought to herself. Almost involuntarily she turned her eyes towards Julian, and saw him standing rigid in the doorway, horribly pale, with his gaze fixed on the Count. She went up to her husband, and whispered anxiously, "Are you ill? What is the matter?"

He answered roughly, "Nothing; let me alone. I am only chilly."

When they went in to dinner, the Count asked to be allowed to let in his dogs; and they at once took up their position, sitting on their haunches, one on either side of their master. He kept throwing tidbits to them and stroking their long, silky ears. They thrust forward their heads, wagged their tails, and shivered ecstatically.

After dinner, when Jeanne and Julian were ready to set out for home, nothing would do but the Count must show them fishing by torchlight. He posted them with the Countess on the steps leading down to the lake, while he went off in the boat, with a man holding a casting-net and a lighted torch. The night was clear and keen, and the sky was sown with stars. The torch cast on the water strange ripples of fire, threw dancing gleams on the reeds, and lit up the screen of pines. Then, as the boat turned, a colossal, fantastic shadow—the shadow of a man—reared itself up on the illuminated border of the wood. The head towered above the trees, and was lost in the sky, while its feet remained standing in the lake. Then this enormous apparition raised its arms, as if to seize the stars. The huge limbs were raised for a moment and then sank downwards, and a slight sound was heard, as of someone beating the water. While the boat veered slowly round, the mighty shadow seemed to run along by the wood, which stood out clear as the light was turned upon it. Then the shadow was lost in the distant darkness, to re-appear again on the front of the house, smaller but more distinct, and still moving grotesquely. The Count's hearty voice rang out: "Gilberte, I have caught eight."

The oars plashed in the ripples. The gigantic shadow was now thrown on the wall, and remained there, upright and motionless, its proportions gradually dwindling. Its head came lower, and its body shrank. And when Monsieur de Fourville came up the steps, fol-lowed by his man with the torch, the shadow, which mimicked all his movements, was only life-size. In his net he carried eight large, wriggling fish.

When Jeanne and Julian were on their way home, covered with wraps and rugs lent by their hosts, Jeanne said, almost involun-tarily, "What a good sort that giant is!"

Julian, who was driving, agreed: "Yes, but he oughtn't to be so demonstrative in company."

Next week they called on the Couteliers, who were considered the leading people in the province. Their estate, Reminil, extended as far as the large market-town of Cany. The new mansion, built in the time of Louis XIV, lay hidden in a magnificent walled park. On an eminence were seen the ruins of the older house. Footmen in livery ushered the visitors into an imposing apartment. In the middle of the room, on a pillar, stood an immense Sèvres cup, beneath which, protected by a crystal plaque, was an autograph letter from the King, bidding the Marquis Leopold Hervé Joseph Germer de Varneville de Rollebosc de Coutelier accept this gift from his sovereign.

As Jeanne and Julian were examining this royal gift, the Marquis and Marchioness entered. The lady wore powdered hair. She was amiable as a matter of duty, and had an affected air of condescension. Her husband, a corpulent personage, his white hair brushed straight up on the crown of his head, assumed in his manner, his voice and his whole attitude a lofty mien, which betrayed his sense of his own importance. They were people who attached great importance to ceremony, and whose conversation, whose very thoughts and sentiments, seemed stilted.

They spoke in a sort of monologue, without waiting for a reply, and smiled with a detached air, suggesting that they were merely discharging the duty, imposed upon them by their birth, of showing politeness to the petty gentry of the neighbourhood.

Jeanne and Julian felt discomfited, though they did their best to be agreeable. They were bored at having to prolong the visit, but did not know how to get away. The Marchioness, however, herself put an end to it, quite naturally and simply, by stopping the conversation dead, like a queen politely dismissing her courtiers.

On the way back Julian said, "If you don't mind, we will make this call do. As far as I am concerned, the Fourvilles are enough for me." Jeanne agreed with him.

December gradually slipped away, that month of gloomy days, the dark void that ends the year. Another year of secluded life began. Jeanne was fully occupied with Paul, and was no longer bored; but Julian disliked the child and looked askance at him, with uneasy, dissatisfied glances. Often when she held him in her arms, covering him with passionate kisses, as women do, Jeanne would lift him up to his father and say, "Do kiss him; one would think you disliked him." Bending stiffly from the hips, as if to avoid the tiny quivering hands, Julian would just brush the little creature's smooth forehead with a perfunctory kiss. Then he would go away abruptly, as if in disgust. Occasionally the mayor, the doctor and the priest came to dinner, and sometimes the Fourvilles, with whom they became more and more intimate. The Count made much of Paul. He would have him on his knees all through a call, or even for a whole afternoon. He would fondle him very gently with his gigantic hands, tickle the tip of his nose with the end of his long moustaches, or suddenly cover him with passionate kisses, just like a mother. The grief of his life was that he had no children.

March was bright, dry and mild. Countess Gilberte again proposed that the four of them should go for rides together. Somewhat tired of the monotony and sameness of the long days and nights, Jeanne joyfully agreed. For a week she amused herself with making a riding-habit.

They explored the countryside, riding in pairs — the Countess and Julian on ahead, the others a few yards behind. The Count and Jeanne chatted away quietly like two friends — for they had become friends, in the loyal and innocent fellowship of kindred souls. The other pair often spoke in subdued tones, bursting now and then into shouts of laughter, and exchanging quick glances, as if their eyes said things which their lips dared not utter. Then they would set off at a round gallop, as if impelled to speed onwards, farther and ever farther away. Sometimes Gilberte showed signs of vexation. Her penetrating voice, borne on the breeze, came back to the riders who were bringing up the rear. The Count would say, with a smile, "You see my wife does not always get out of bed the right side."

One evening, as they were riding home, the Countess was teasing her mare, now touching her with the spur, now jerking her mouth, and they heard Julian say more than once, "Take care, do take care; she will run away with you."

"Who cares? It's none of your business," she called back, in tones so hard and penetrating that the words rang out clearly, and seemed to linger in the air. The mare reared and kicked, and champed her foaming bit. The Count shouted anxiously, at the top of his voice, "Do look what you are about, Gilberte."

At that, as if stung to defiance, with one of those hysterical impulses which women cannot resist, she fiercely struck the animal between the ears with her whip. The mare reared violently, pawing the air, then bounded forward and bolted at full gallop across the moor. She first crossed a stretch of grass, then dashed over ploughed fields, scattering clods of heavy clay, and galloped away with such speed that horse and rider were almost out of sight. Julian seemed paralysed. All he could do was to call out in agonised tones, "Countess! Countess!"

The Count uttered a growl, and, bending over the neck of his great lumbering steed, he flung it forward with the impetus of his whole frame, urging it on, pressing it, stimulating it with voice, hand and spur, with such energy that it seemed as if the gigantic rider actually lifted the horse between his thighs and flew with him over the fields. They covered the ground with inconceivable speed, swerving neither to right nor left. And Jeanne watched the two silhouettes of husband and wife steadily receding, shrinking, fading in the distance, and at last vanishing from sight, like two birds chasing each other until lost on the horizon.

Julian rode up slowly to his wife, muttering angrily: "She is quite mad to-day." They set out in pursuit of their friends, who were now hidden from them by rising ground. Some minutes later they saw them coming back, and very soon they rejoined them. The Count, who was flushed and streaming with perspiration, but laughing and elated, grasped with a strong hand the reins of his wife's still trembling mare. The Countess was pale, her face was quivering as if with pain, and she leant a hand on her husband's shoulder as if she were ready to faint. Jeanne realised for the first time that the Count's love was a consuming passion.

All the next month the Countess had never seemed so gay. She came more frequently to *Les Peuples*, was always laughing, and would kiss Jeanne with gushes of affection. She seemed as if possessed by some secret and ravishing joy. Her husband, who was equally happy, could not keep his eyes off her and kept touching her hand, or her gown. His passion for her was more intense than ever.

One evening he said to Jeanne: "We are very happy together nowadays. Gilberte has never been so charming. She has got over her fits of sulks and peevishness. I am now convinced that she loves me. Until now I have not been sure."

Julian, too, seemed changed; he was livelier, less petulant, as if the friendship between the two families had brought peace and happiness to both.

The spring was unusually early and warm. All day long from the mild morning until the quiet, balmy evening, the earth, quickened by the sun's genial warmth, put forth tender shoots. It was one of

those rare and wonderful years when all the seeds spring up at once;
when the gush of vital sap is irresistible; and in an ardour of resur-
rection the world seems to renew its youth. Jeanne's emotions were
vaguely stirred by this fermentation of life. The sight of a little
flower in the grass inspired her with sudden languor, lulled her to
delicious melancholy, to hours of tender reverie. She recalled sweet
memories of the early days of her love. Not that her affection for
Julian had revived; that was dead for ever and ever. But her whole
being, wooed by the soft breezes, stirred by the odours of spring,
was in a tumult, as though in response to an invisible and tender
summons. She delighted in solitude; she basked idly in the sun, penetrated by vague, serene feelings of delight, which awakened in her
mind no definite idea.

One morning, as she was indulging in these daydreams, there
rose before her a vision of that sun-kissed hollow in the midst of dark
foliage, in the little wood near Etretat. It was there that she had
felt the first thrill of passion by her lover's side; it was there that
for the first time he had, in faltering accents, timidly declared the
desire of his heart; it was there that she had seemed to realise, in a
flash, the radiant future of her hopes. She felt impelled to visit that
wood once more, to make thither a sentimental and superstitious
pilgrimage, as if the sight of this place would effect some change in
the course of her life.

Julian had gone off at daybreak, she knew not whither. So she
had the Martins' white pony saddled, which she rode now and then;
and started for her ride. It was one of those utterly peaceful days
when not a leaf stirs nor a blade of grass, and everything seems as
if it would remain motionless to the end of time, as if the wind
would never blow again. The very insects seemed to have vanished.
A warm and compelling calm was tranquilly diffused by the sun in
a golden haze. Happy and half asleep Jeanne rode her pony at a
foot pace. From time to time she raised her eyes to watch a tiny
cloudlet, like a handful of wool, a wreath of white vapour, floating
alone, as if forgotten, in the blue.

She rode along the valley which slopes down to the seashore, and
passing beneath the great arches of rock called the Gates of Etretat,
she reached the wood at a leisurely pace. The light streamed through
the young foliage. Jeanne wandered up and down the woodland
paths, but could not find the spot she was seeking.

All of a sudden, as she was crossing a long avenue, she saw two saddle horses tethered to a tree, and she recognised them as those of Gilberte and Julian. Already somewhat oppressed by a sense of loneliness, she welcomed this unexpected meeting, and put her pony to a trot. Coming up to the two horses, which were standing patiently as if used to long halts, she called out, but no one answered. A woman's glove and two riding-whips were lying on the grass, which she saw was crushed. So they had been sitting there and then had moved away from their horses.

She waited for a quarter of an hour or twenty minutes, surprised and wondering what they could be doing. She had dismounted and stood motionless leaning against the trunk of a tree. Unconscious of her presence two little birds dropped down on to the grass quite close to her. One of them fluttered and fussed around the other, with quivering flapping wings, chirping and moving its head; and suddenly they coupled.

Jeanne was taken aback, as if such a sight were new to her. Then she said: "After all, it's springtime." And with that a new idea shot through her mind. With sudden suspicion she looked again at the glove, the riding-whips, and tethered horses. And she jumped hastily into her saddle with an irresistible impulse of flight. She started for *Les Peuples* at a gallop. Then her mind began to work; she reasoned out the facts, putting two and two together, linking incident to incident. Why had she not guessed it all long ago? Why had she been so blind? Why had she not grasped the meaning of Julian's frequent absences, the reason of his renewed fastidiousness in dress, and the mitigation of his peevish humours? She called to mind also Gilberte's nervous irritability, the exaggerated warmth of her caresses, and her recent state of serene happiness, which had pleased her husband so much. She slowed her horse down to a walk, for she wanted to think seriously and the rapid pace was disturbing.

When the first shock had subsided she became inwardly calm, feeling neither jealousy nor hatred, but sick with contempt. It was not of Julian that she thought; nothing he did had power to surprise her now. But the double treachery of the Countess, her own friend, filled her with disgust. Everyone, it seemed, was treacherous, deceitful, and false. Tears came to her eyes. One may mourn vanished illusions as bitterly as one grieves for the dead.

Finally, she made up her mind to assume ignorance. She would shut out from her heart all casual affections, and would confine her love to her child and her parents; towards others she would show merely a tranquil toleration. As soon as she reached home she rushed to her baby, carried him off to her room, and kissed him passionately over and over again, for an hour without stopping.

Julian came home to dinner, smiling and charming, and anxious to make himself agreeable. "Aren't your people coming this year?" he asked.

Jeanne was so grateful to him for this kind thought that she almost forgave him for what she had found out in the wood. Seized by a violent longing to see those two whom she loved next to Paul, she spent the whole evening writing to them, pressing them to come soon. It was the 7th of May; they wrote to say that they would arrive in a fortnight. Jeanne awaited their visit with growing impatience, as if, apart from her affection for her parents, she yearned for contact with those loyal hearts. She longed to open her soul to guileless folk, innocent of dishonourable deeds, whose actions, thoughts, and desires had always been upright. Her feeling now was that her own integrity of conscience isolated her in the midst of all these sinful ones. And though she learnt quickly enough to dissemble, though she welcomed the Countess with outstretched hand and smiling lips, she felt an increasing sense of the hollowness of the world, and a growing contempt for mankind. The daily tittle-tattle of the parish disgusted her more and more, and rendered her fellow-creatures more despicable in her eyes. Couillard's daughter had had a baby and was going to be married presently. The Martins' orphan servant-girl was in trouble, as well as another little girl of fifteen. Even a squalid, crippled widow woman, who was so horribly filthy that she was known as the "Midden," was with child. There was a continual talk of new babies. Someone had gone wrong, some young girl, some peasant's wife, already a lawful mother, or some respectable and wealthy farmer.

The glowing springtime stirred the sap of men and women as it stirred that of the plants. Jeanne, whose senses were dulled and no longer troubled her, whose heart was bruised and broken, and whose spirit, all sentiment, alone seemed affected by these breaths of sensual emotion, whose dreamy raptures were of the mind, not of the body, was shocked at all this animalism, which filled her with a loathing amounting to hatred. The mating of living creatures enraged her, as if it were something unnatural, and her anger against Gilberte was not because she had taken Julian from her, but merely because she had fallen into the same mire as the rest. She herself was not of this low stock, with whom the baser instincts prevailed. How could she ever have allowed herself to be overcome by the same passions?

The very day on which her parents were to arrive, Julian gave fresh life to her disgust by narrating to her, as a good joke and the most natural thing in the world, a story about the baker. The night before, when there was no baking to be done, he had heard a noise in the bake-house, and, expecting to find a stray cat there, had discovered his wife, who was certainly not putting bread in the oven. "The baker shut the door to," Julian added, "and the two inside were almost suffocated, but his little boy, who had seen his mother go in with the blacksmith, alarmed the neighbours. They want to make us eat love-bread, these chaps. It's like one of La Fontaine's fables," he laughed. From that moment Jeanne shuddered at the sight of bread.

When the post chaise drew up at the door, and the Baron's cheerful face appeared at the window, his daughter's bosom was filled with deep emotion, with such a rush of passionate love as she had never before experienced. But when she saw her mother she was so horrified that she nearly fainted. In the past six months the Baroness had grown ten years older. Her great, flabby, pendulous cheeks were shot with purple, and looked as if swollen with blood; her eyes were lustreless; she could not move without an arm supporting her on either side; her breath was wheezy, and so laborious that she was an object of painful concern to those around her. The Baron, who saw her every day, had not observed these signs of breaking up. And when she complained of her constant fits of breathlessness and her increasing sense of oppression, he would say, "Why, my dear, you have been like that all the years I have known you."

Jeanne saw them to their room and then, shocked and overcome, retired to her own room to weep. Presently she went to her father and, her eyes still full of tears, threw herself into his arms:

"Oh, what a change in mother! Whatever is the matter with her?"

In surprise he answered: "You think she is changed? Not at all. Merely your fancy. I have been with her all this time, and I assure you I do not think she is looking ill; she is just the same as usual."

That evening Julian said to his wife, "Your mother is in a bad way. I don't like the look of her."

But when Jeanne burst into tears and sobs, he added peevishly, "Come, come, I did not say that she was done for. You exaggerate so insanely. She has altered; that is all. She is only growing old."

After a week, Jeanne had grown used to her mother's changed appearance and no longer noticed it. Perhaps, too, she repressed her fears as, with a sort of selfish instinct, with a natural desire for peace of mind, one is apt to repress and reject the apprehensions and anxieties with which one is threatened.

The Baroness could hardly walk at all, and went out only for half an hour a day. When she had dragged herself to the end of her favourite avenue once only she could go no further and insisted on seating herself on her bench. If she felt that even her usual walk was too much for her she would say: "I must stop now; my legs have no strength to-day. It is my hypertrophy."

She never laughed now, merely smiling at things which would have sent her into shrieks of laughter a year ago. But as her eyesight was still very good she spent her days reading over again *Corinne* or Lamartine's *Meditations*. Then she would send for her drawer of souvenirs. Emptying out on her lap piles of treasured old letters, she would put the drawer on a chair by her side, and, after fondly gazing at each souvenir in turn, would replace them, one by one. When she was quite alone she would kiss certain special treasures, as people kiss in secret a lock of hair of some loved one, who is no more.

Sometimes Jeanne, coming in unexpectedly, would find her weeping mournfully.

"What is the matter with you, Mother, dear?"

With a deep sigh the Baroness would answer: "My treasures have upset me. They bring back memories of the past, happy memories that are done with now. And people, almost forgotten, come back to me. You can see them, and hear them speak. It is terrible, terrible. You will understand this some day."

When the Baron came upon them in these melancholy moments he would murmur: "Jeanne, my darling, take my advice and burn all your old letters, your mother's and mine, every one. There is

126

nothing more heart-rending, when you are old, than this ferreting among the memories of your youth."

But Jeanne, too, kept her letters and made up her box of treasures. Though very different from her mother, she obeyed her hereditary instinct of dreamy sentimentality.

After a few days the Baron had to go away on business. It was perfect weather. To long peaceful evenings succeeded sweet nights, bright with a thousand stars; a brilliant day closed serenely; a gorgeous sunrise heralded a radiant day.

The Baroness was much better; and Jeanne, forgetting Julian's love affairs and Gilberte's treachery, was almost perfectly happy. The whole countryside was perfumed with flowers, and the mighty ocean lay without a ripple, glittering all day in the sunlight.

One afternoon Jeanne took Paul in her arms and went for a walk in the fields. She looked now at her child, now at the grass thick with flowers, and she was steeped in boundless felicity. Every minute she kissed her baby, pressing him passionately to her bosom. Then, as some sweet scent of the fields lightly touched her, she almost fainted with excess of joy. She dreamed of her boy's future. What should he be? Now she planned that he should be a great man, powerful and distinguished. Then she would have him without ambitions, content to stay at home with her, tenderly devoted to his mother and always ready to clasp her in his arms. When her selfish maternal love prevailed she wished him to be her son and nothing else; but at other times when the practical aspect of her passion predominated, she had an ambitious longing for him to make his mark in the world. Seated by the edge of a field, she gazed and gazed at him as if she had never seen him before. An astonishing thought flashed through her mind that this small mite would grow tall, would walk with a firm step, would have a beard, and speak in a deep voice.

In the distance some one was calling her. She looked up and saw Marius running towards her. Supposing that some unexpected visitor had arrived, she rose, vexed at being disturbed. But the boy came tearing along and, as soon as he was near enough, shouted, "Oh, Ma'am, the Baroness has been taken very ill."

Jeanne felt as if a drop of cold water was running down her spine. She hurried home, her head in a whirl. While still some way off she

127

saw a group of people under the plane tree. Darting forward through the crowd, she saw her mother lying on the ground, her head resting on two pillows. Her face was quite black, her eyes were closed, and her breast, which had laboured for a score of years, no longer moved. The nurse caught the baby from his mother's arms and took him away. Wild-eyed, Jeanne asked, "What has happened? How did she come to fall? Send for the doctor." Turning round she saw the priest, who had somehow heard of the calamity. He offered his services, tucked up the sleeves of his cassock, and exerted himself. But vinegar, eau de Cologne, and massage were of no avail.

"You must undress her and put her to bed," said the priest.

Joseph Couillard, the farmer, was there as well as old Simon and Ludivine. With Abbé Picot's help, they essayed to carry the Baroness. But when they lifted her, her head fell back, and her dress, by which they were raising her, began to tear under the strain of her great weight. Jeanne cried out in horror, and they replaced the huge, flaccid body on the ground. They had to bring an armchair from the drawing-room, and when they had seated her in it they succeeded in lifting her. Slowly they mounted the stone steps, then the staircase, and having reached her room, laid her on the bed. The cook had not succeeded in undressing her, but the Widow Dentu arrived at the appropriate moment, like the priest, just as if they had scented death, as the servants said.

Joseph Couillard set off at full gallop for the doctor; but as the priest was setting out to fetch the holy oil, the old nurse whispered in his ear, "Do not trouble yourself, sir. She is gone, I am quite sure."

Jeanne uttered distracted entreaties. She was at a loss what to do, what means to try, what remedy to use. The priest took it on himself to pronounce the Absolution. For two hours they watched by the discoloured and lifeless body. Jeanne was sobbing, on her knees, in a passion of grief and anguish. When the door opened and the doctor arrived it seemed to her that he brought with him help, hope, and consolation. Darting towards him, she faltered out as much as she knew of the circumstances.

"She took her daily walk as usual . . . she seemed well . . . very well, indeed . . . she had had her broth and two eggs for luncheon . . . she fell down all of a sudden . . . she became all discoloured as you see . . . and she never moved again . . . we have tried everything to bring her to life—everything." She stopped, arrested by a discreet sign which the nurse made to the doctor to indicate that all was over. Refusing to understand, she asked anxiously: "Is it serious? Do you think it is serious?"

"I am very much afraid that—that—it is all over. Be brave, be brave."

Flinging wide her arms, Jeanne threw herself on her mother's body.

When Julian returned he was dumfounded and taken aback. He uttered no cry of grief or regret, and looked as if he had been too suddenly surprised to assume at once a formal face of woe. But he murmured:

"I expected this. I was sure she could not last long."

Then he took out his handkerchief, wiped his eyes, knelt down, crossed himself, mumbled a few words; then he rose, and tried to lift his wife as well. But she clung to the corpse, kissing it and almost covering it with her body. She had to be removed; she seemed beside herself.

An hour afterwards she was allowed to return. No hope remained. The room was now arranged as a mortuary chamber. Julian and the priest were conversing in low tones near the window. The Widow Dentu, settled comfortably in an armchair, like a woman accustomed to vigils, and who felt at home in a house as soon as death had entered, seemed already to be dozing.

Night fell. The priest went up to Jeanne, took her hands, and spoke encouraging words, pouring on her inconsolable heart the unctuous flood of clerical consolation. He spoke of the dead, praising her in priestly language, and, with the hypocritical sorrow of priests, who benefit by a death, he offered to pass the night in prayer by the body.

Jeanne refused with floods of tears. She desired to be quite alone on that night of farewell. Julian stepped forward:

"Impossible; you and I will watch together." She shook her head, unable to utter another word. At last she gasped out: "She is my mother, my own mother. I insist on watching by her alone."

The doctor murmured: "Let her have her way. The nurse can be in the next room."

The priest and Julian consented, each thinking of his bed. Then Abbé Picot knelt in his turn, and after saying a prayer rose and went away, announcing: "She was a saint," in the tone in which he was wont to say *"Dominus vobiscum."*

Julian asked in his usual voice: "Won't you have something to eat?" Jeanne did not answer, not realising that he was speaking to her. He went on: "I think you had better eat a little to keep up your strength." With a bewildered expression, she replied: "Send at once for Papa." Julian went to despatch a man on horseback to Rouen.

Jeanne remained, plunged in a silent agony of sorrow, as if she had awaited the last hours alone with the dead to yield to the rising tide of grief and despair. Shadows crept into the room, veiling the dead in darkness. The Widow Dentu began to prowl about the room with noiseless footsteps, arranging things in the dark, with the silent movements of the sick nurse. She lighted two candles, which she placed gently on a table covered with a white cloth at the head of the bed. Jeanne seemed neither to see, to feel, nor to understand. She was longing to be alone. Julian came back after dinner, and asked again: "Won't you take anything?" His wife shook her head. He seated himself, with an appearance of resignation rather than of sorrow, and remained silent. The three watchers sat motionless and apart.

Every now and then the nurse snored and woke up with a start. At length Julian rose from his chair and coming over to Jeanne, said: "Would you like to be left alone now?"

"Oh, yes, please," she sighed, seizing his hand with a spontaneous impulse. He kissed her brow and murmuring, "I will come in and see you now and then," he went out with the Widow Dentu, who wheeled her armchair into the next room.

Jeanne closed the door and threw the two windows wide open. The warm evening air, mingled with the scent of the hay crop, caressed her face. The swaths of new mown hay lay out under her window in the bright moonlight. The very sweetness of the sensation hurt her and went to her heart like bitter irony.

Jeanne returned to the bed and looked long at her dead mother, clasping one cold and nerveless hand. The swelling noticeable at the time of her seizure had now subsided; she seemed as if sleeping more peacefully than ever in her life. In the wan flame of the candles, flickering in the breeze, the shadows on her face were continually shifting, lending to it a life-like appearance. Jeanne gazed at her intently, while a rush of memories swept over her from the far days of her early childhood. She recalled the convent parlour and her mother's visits and how she would hand the child paper bags full of cakes; a throng of petty details and trivial incidents, caresses, loving words, tricks of speech, familiar gestures, the wrinkles round her eyes when she laughed, the deep panting sigh of satisfaction as she sank into her chair. Jeanne stood there gazing at her in a kind of stupor, repeating, "She is dead," and she realised the full horror of that word. She, who was lying there, her Mamma, her dear little mother, Madame Adelaide, was she really dead? She would never stir again, never speak, never laugh, never sit at dinner opposite her husband, never wish Jeanne good-morning. Yes, she was dead. She would be nailed down in a coffin and hidden away in the ground and that would be the end of her. They would never see her again. Could this really be true? She would no longer have a mother? Gone into the void, that loved, familiar face, the first on which her eyes had looked, the first to which she had stretched out baby arms, gone that brimming stream of affection, that one unique being, more, far more, to one's heart than all the rest of the world, one's mother! Only a few more short hours in which she might gaze on that face, now so inanimate and still; then nothing, nothing but a memory.

Jeanne sank to her knees in a terrible paroxysm of despair; her quivering hands clutched the sheet, and with her lips pressed against the couch she uttered a heart-rending cry, half smothered in the coverings of the bed: "O Mamma, my poor Mamma, O Mamma!"

She felt as if she were going out of her mind, just as on that night when she had fled away across the snow. So she rose from her knees and ran to the window to revive herself, and to drink in the pure air, uncontaminated with that of the death chamber. The smooth lawns, the trees, the moor, the sea, lay all silent and peaceful, asleep in the magic moonlight. Something of that soothing sweetness stole into Jeanne's bosom, and set her quietly weeping. She returned to the bedside and sat down, clasping again her mother's hand, as if she were watching by a sick person. A large beetle had flown into the room, attracted by the candlelight. It blundered against the walls, flying from one end of the room to the other. Jeanne, her attention distracted by its droning, raised her eyes to look for it, but she could see only its shadow moving on the white ceiling. Presently the droning ceased. Then she noticed the soft ticking of the clock and then another small noise, like an almost imperceptible whisper. It was her mother's watch which had been left in the dress thrown over the chair at the foot of the bed and was still going. A vague comparison between that piece of mechanism which had not stopped, and its dead owner, awoke again the anguish in Jeanne's heart. She looked at the time. It was scarcely half-past ten and a horrible dread of passing the whole night in that vigil overcame her.

Other memories crowded upon her from her own past—Rosalie, Gilberte—the bitter disillusions of her heart. Was there then nothing but misery, grief, unhappiness, and death? Was everything a lying cheat, bringing only tears and suffering? Oh, where could some degree of peace and happiness be found? Doubtless in another world, when the soul was freed from its earthly probation. The soul! She began to muse upon that insoluble mystery the soul, plunging into fantastic imaginings, only to find them instantly refuted by other conjectures, no less vague.

At this moment where was her mother's soul, the soul of that cold, motionless body? Far, far away, perchance. Somewhere in space. But where? Utterly vanished like a bird escaped from its cage and lost to sight? Had God called it back to Him, or was it dispersed to the random chances of a new creation, mingled with vital germs awaiting birth?

Perhaps it was quite near her in that very room, hovering about the inanimate body which it had quitted! And at that thought Jeanne seemed to feel a soft breath, as if a spirit had touched her. At this, a panic terror seized her, so overwhelming that she was paralysed and could not breathe or look behind her. Her heart beat in a frenzy of fear. Just then the invisible beetle began to fly about again, colliding clumsily with the walls. Jeanne shuddered from head to foot; then she recognised the insect's droning, and felt suddenly reassured. She rose from her chair and turned round and her eyes fell on the writing table with the sphinx heads which enshrined the treasures. A tender yet somewhat fantastic idea occurred to her; it was to read, during that last vigil, as she might have read a holy book, the old letters that the dead woman had held so precious. She felt that she was about to perform an exquisite and sacred duty, a task of filial piety, which would please her mother in another world. There were old letters of her grandparents whom she had never

known. She yearned to stretch out her arms to them over their daughter's dead body, to go to them on that sorrowful night as if they, too, were mourning, and to link together, by a subtle chain of affection, those long since dead, her who had just departed, and herself still on earth. She let down the shelf of the writing table and took from the lowest drawer a dozen little packets of faded papers, carefully tied up and arranged in order. With a refinement of sentimentality, she placed them all on the bed between her mother's arms, and began to read them.

The first was a batch of old letters, such as one comes across in old family writing tables, with the faded fragrance of other days about them. The earliest began: "My pet"; another: "My sweet little granddaughter"; then came: "My dear little girl," "My darling," "My precious child"; then: "My dear child," "My dear Adelaide," "My dear daughter," according as they were addressed to the child, to the girl, and, later on, to the young married woman. All were filled with loving, childish endearments, a thousand petty, intimate details, all the incidents, great and small, of the domestic hearth, which are so trivial to outsiders: "Father has influenza"; "Hortense, the housemaid, has burnt her fingers"; "Mouser, the cat, is dead"; "The pine tree beside the hedge has been cut down"; "Mother lost her prayer book on her way back from church, she thinks someone stole it." Some of the letters mentioned people whom Jeanne had not known but whose names she vaguely remembered to have heard in her childhood. She melted over these details, which seemed to her like revelations, as if she had entered into all her dear mother's past life, the hidden life of her heart. She looked at the still body, and the fancy seized her to read aloud to the dead woman as if to entertain and comfort her.

The motionless corpse had an air of approval.

One by one she threw the letters to the foot of the bed, thinking that they might be put into the coffin like flowers.

She untied another packet. Here was a different hand-writing. It began: "I can no longer live without your caresses. I love you to distraction." That was all. There was no signature. Without understanding, she turned over the paper. There was the address, sure enough: "The Baroness Le Perthuis des Vauds." She opened the next: "Come this evening as soon as he goes out. We shall have a whole hour together. I adore you." In another: "I spent the night, mad with vain longing for you. I held you in my arms, with your lips, your eyes, pressed to mine. And then I felt frantic with rage, ready to throw myself out of the window, to think that at that very hour you were by his side, that you were his."

Jeanne was amazed, and still failed to understand. What was it all about? To whom, for whom, by whom, were written these ardent words? She went on, finding other passionate protestations, plans for meetings, and warnings to be careful; and always at the end these words: "Be sure to burn this letter." Finally, she opened a commonplace note in the same writing, merely accepting an invitation to dinner; it was signed "Paul d'Ennemare." This was the man whom the Baron always spoke of as "My poor old Paul," and whose wife had been the Baroness's dearest friend. All at once Jeanne flushed with a doubt, which grew immediately into a certainty. This man had been her mother's lover.

Distracted, she flung away these vile letters as she would have shaken off some poisonous creature crawling over her, and rushing to the window she began to weep frantically; cries that she could not suppress rent her bosom; then, with her whole world in ruins about her, she sank down by the wall, burying her face to stifle her groans, and gave way to a storm of sobs from the depths of her unfathomable despair.

She might have remained like this all night; but at the sound of a footstep in the next room she jumped up. Perhaps it was her father. And all those letters were lying about on the bed and on the floor. He had but to open one, and he, too, he would know.

Darting forward, she seized the old yellow papers by handfuls, those of her grandparents, those of her mother's lover, those which she had not untied, and others which she found still in packets in the drawers of the writing table, and she threw them all in a heap into the fireplace. Taking one of the candles burning on the table, she set fire to the pile of letters. The flames leaped up, lighting the whole room, the bed, and the corpse, with a vivid, flickering blaze, silhouetting on the white curtain at the foot of the bed her mother's rigid features and the contours of the enormous body under the sheet.

When only a heap of ashes was left on the hearth, she went back and sat by the open window as if she dared no longer remain near the dead woman; then she began to weep afresh, hiding her face in her hands, and sobbing in heart-broken tones, tones of desolation and despair: "Oh, my poor Mother! Oh, my poor Mother!"

A terrible idea appalled her. Suppose, by some miracle, her mother was not dead; suppose she was only in a trance; suppose she suddenly started up and began to speak? Would not her daughter's love be lessened by the knowledge of that guilty secret? Could she kiss her with her former filial devotion? Would she entertain the same pious affection for her? No. That was impossible. And the thought rent her heart.

The night wore away. The stars grew pale; it was the cool hour which precedes the dawn. The setting moon plunged into the sea, shedding a pearly lustre on the face of the waters. Jeanne remembered the night she had spent by the window on her arrival at *Les Peuples*. How far off it seemed; how all had changed; how different appeared the future!

And now the sky was all rosy red, with an exquisite flush of joy and love. As if surprised at some strange phenomenon Jeanne watched the radiant birth of day, asking herself if it were possible that, in a world over which such dawns arose, no delight or happiness existed.

She started at the sound of the door being opened. If was Julian, who came to ask if she was not worn out with fatigue.

"No," she faltered, relieved at being no longer alone.

"Now go and lie down," he said. She gently kissed her mother, a lingering, mournful, heart-broken kiss, and went to her own room.

The day slipped away fully occupied with those sorrowful duties demanded by the dead. The Baron arrived in the evening. He wept copiously.

Next day the funeral took place. When she had for the last time pressed her lips to the cold forehead, had given the last loving touches, and had seen the coffin nailed down, Jeanne withdrew from the death chamber. The guests were beginning to arrive.

Gilberte was the first; she threw herself sobbing into her friend's arms. From the window they watched the carriages turn into the iron gates and drive up to the house. Voices were heard in the great hall. Women, dressed in black, some of whom Jeanne did not know at all, came one by one to her room. The Marchioness de Coutelier and the Viscountess de Briseville kissed her. Suddenly she saw Aunt Lison gliding behind her. Jeanne embraced her tenderly, and at this attention the poor old lady nearly fainted.

Julian entered in deep mourning, well groomed, full of importance, much gratified by the crowd of mourners. He spoke to his wife in a low voice, asking her advice on some point. Then he added, confidentially: "All the best people have come; it will be a fine funeral."

Gravely bowing to the ladies, he went off. Aunt Lison and Countess Gilberte alone stayed with Jeanne till the funeral ceremony was over. The Countess kept on embracing her, murmuring, "My poor dear; my poor dear."

When Count de Fourville came to fetch his wife he cried as if he had lost his own mother.

10

THEN followed a procession of dreary days, those days of mourning when the house, from which the loved one has gone for ever, seems utterly desolate, days when the sight of every familiar object touched by the departed pierces the soul with grief. Every moment has its heart-breaking memory. Her armchair, her umbrella standing in the hall, her glass, which the maid has not put away; her scissors, her glove, her book still bearing the marks of her fumbling fingers, a thousand trifles, all these in our sorrow assume a mournful significance, calling to mind countless little incidents. Her voice is heard calling after you; you long to escape from this haunted house, no matter where. But you must stay, for besides yourself there are others who have to remain here and mourn. Moreover, Jeanne was overwhelmed by the memory of what she had discovered. The thought of it weighed her down; the wound in her heart could not be healed. That grim secret made her present solitude all the more oppressive; her last vestige of faith had vanished with the shattering of her last illusion. After a while her father went away, restless, and seeking change of air, and an escape from the dark sorrow which engulfed him ever more deeply. The great house which had seen its masters vanish thus one after another resumed its ordinary peaceful routine.

Then Paul fell ill. Jeanne was beside herself; for twelve days she hardly slept or ate. The child recovered. But Jeanne was aghast at the thought that she might lose him. What should she do then? What would become of her? Almost insensibly there stole into her mind a vague longing for another baby. Very soon her dreams were filled with this desire, which she had cherished in the old days, of seeing about her two little ones, a boy and a girl. This desire became an obsession.

But since the affair of Rosalie she had lived apart from Julian. Reconciliation seemed impossible in the circumstances. She knew that Julian was in love with another woman; and she had hitherto shuddered at the mere thought of submitting again to his caresses. Now, however, she felt that she could endure them in her vehement desire again to become a mother. But how to take the first step towards the renewal of their relations? She would rather die than let him guess her designs, and for his part he seemed to have forgotten her altogether. She would probably have given up the idea, but night after night she dreamed of a little daughter, and she saw her playing with Paul under the plane tree. And at this she felt a yearning to leave her bed and go, without a word, to her husband's room. Twice she actually stole as far as his door, but then rushed back to her own room, her heart throbbing with shame.

The Baron was away; her mother was dead; Jeanne had no one whom she could consult, to whom she could confide her inmost secrets. At last she made up her mind to go to Abbé Picot and disclose to him, under the seal of confession, the difficulties attending her design. She came upon the Abbé as he was reading his breviary in his little orchard.

After a few minutes' casual conversation she faltered blushing: "Will you hear my confession, Father?"

He was much surprised, and pushed up his glasses to look at her. Then he burst out laughing.

"I don't suppose you have any very serious sins on your conscience."

Greatly agitated she went on: "No, but I want to ask your advice . . . advice on such a delicate matter that I cannot speak about it off-hand."

He abandoned his jovial pose for his professional air: "Very well, my daughter, I will hear you in the confessional. Come along."

She hesitated and hung back, checked by a reluctance to speak of such intimate matters in the seclusion of an empty church.

"Well, after all . . . Father . . . I can . . . I can . . . if you would rather . . . tell you here why I have come. Let us go and sit in your little summer-house."

They strolled there slowly. She was trying to choose her words, to decide how she should begin. When they had sat down, she began, as if she were making her confession: "Father . . ." she stopped and said again: "Father . . ." and stopped again abashed.

He waited, his hands clasped over his paunch. Seeing her embarrassment he spoke encouragingly: "Come, come, my daughter; one would suppose that your heart failed you. Come, pluck up courage."

She took the plunge, like a coward who hurls himself headlong into danger. "Father, I am anxious to have another child."

He did not understand her, and made no reply. Then haltingly and in confusion she explained.

"I am a lonely woman now. My father and my husband do not get on well together. My mother is dead. And . . . and," she added, in low trembling tones, "only the other day I nearly lost my son. What would have become of me then?"

She was silent. The priest looked at her in perplexity.

"Come. Let's get to the point."

"I want another child," she repeated.

He smiled. He was accustomed to the coarse pleasantries of the peasants, who did not stand on ceremony with him. Shaking his head archly, he replied:

"Well, but it seems to me that that rests entirely with you."

She raised her ingenuous eyes to his. Then she faltered in confusion:

"Yes, but you must know that since . . . since that affair . . . with the maid . . . you know what I mean . . . my husband and I have been living . . . quite apart."

Accustomed to a rustic lack of restraint and dignity, the priest was surprised by this admission. He jumped to the conclusion that he had found the key to this young woman's real desires. He stole a sidelong glance at her, full of benevolent sympathy for her predicament.

"Quite so; I understand. Your . . . your widowed condition has become irksome. You are young and healthy. It's natural, perfectly natural."

He smiled again, misled by the somewhat gross habit of mind natural in a country priest. He patted Jeanne's hand gently.

"It is authorised, actually authorised, by the divine laws. Marriage alone sanctifies the desires of the flesh. You are married, aren't you? Then you need not worry your head about that."

Jeanne, on her part, had not immediately understood his insinuations. As soon as his meaning dawned upon her she turned scarlet with horror.

"Oh, Father," she exclaimed with tears in her eyes, "what do you mean? What are you thinking of? I swear to you . . . I swear . . ." her sobs choked her.

He was taken aback.

"Come, come," he said consolingly, "I did not mean to hurt you. I was only in fun; you mustn't mind a friendly joke. But count on me. You can count on me. I will go and see Monsieur Julian."

She did not know what to say. She now longed to reject his intervention as possibly awkward and dangerous. But she was afraid to do so. After faltering her thanks she made her escape.

A week went by, which she spent in an agony of uneasiness.

One evening at dinner Julian looked at her in a curious way, with a peculiar smile on his lips, which she had learned to associate with his moods of dalliance. He even treated her with a certain gallantry, which contained the merest hint of irony. Afterwards, when they were strolling up and down the Baroness's avenue, he whispered in her ear:

"It seems that we are to be friends again."

She made no reply. She was gazing down at the ground at a straight line, now almost invisible, and overgrown with new grass. It was the trail which her mother's foot had worn and which was now fading, like a memory. A pang went to Jeanne's heart, and she was plunged in sadness. She felt very forlorn, cut off from everyone in the world.

"Nothing would please me better," Julian continued, "but I was afraid of annoying you."

The sun had set and the air was balmy. Jeanne was on the verge of tears. She felt a yearning to pour out her heart, to whisper her sorrows, in the embrace of a friend. A sob rose to her throat. She flung out her arms and fell weeping on Julian's breast. He was surprised. Her face was hidden from him on his bosom, but he looked down at her hair, and supposing she still loved him, he planted a condescending kiss on the nape of her neck. Without a word they returned to the house. He followed her to her room and spent the night there. They resumed their former relations, which Julian regarded as a not unpleasant duty, but Jeanne as a distasteful and painful necessity. As soon as she attained her object she intended to put an end to this intimacy for ever.

But she soon noticed that her husband's caresses seemed different from of old. They were more subtle, perhaps, but less satisfying. He treated her no longer as a placid husband, but as a discreet lover.

142

Astonished, she took note, and soon realised that all his embraces stopped short before she could conceive.

Then, one night, her lips pressed on his, she murmured: "Why don't you give yourself to me wholly nowadays, as you used to do?"

"Why, so that you don't have a baby, to be sure," he said with a grin.

"But why don't you want any more children?" she asked in trepidation.

He was thunderstruck.

"What did you say? You must be crazy. Another child? Good Heavens, that would be the last straw. As if one squalling brat were not enough, occupying everyone's attention, and costing no end of money. Another child? No thank you."

She threw her arms round him, kissed him, fondled him, and whispered:

"Just one more child, Julian, I implore you."

He was as angry as if she had insulted him.

"Upon my soul, you must be off your head. Keep your silly ideas to yourself, please."

She was silent and resolved to resort to guile to obtain her heart's desire. She wooed him with lingering kisses and a semblance of ardent passion, holding him close to her with both arms in simulated outbursts of passion. She used every wile she could, but he retained his self-mastery, and never once let himself go.

At last, rendered more and more desperate by her frantic longing, at her wits' end, and ready to face and dare the uttermost, she paid another visit to Abbé Picot.

He was finishing his luncheon, and was very red in the face, as he suffered from palpitations after meals.

"Well?" he exclaimed as soon as she entered the room. He was eager to know the result of his intervention.

She was resolute now and cast aside her bashfulness. Without hesitation she replied:

"My husband does not want any more children."

Keenly interested, the Abbé turned to her. With the curiosity of a priest he was ever eager to pry into those mysteries which lightened for him the tedium of the confessional.

"How so?" he asked.

In spite of her determination she found it difficult to explain.

"Why, he . . . he refuses to make me a mother."

The worldly-wise old priest understood the situation. He went into minute details with all the avidity of a fasting man. After a few moments' thought, he suggested to her a cunning plan, and expounded it with as much calm as if he were discussing the prospects of the harvest.

"You have only one resource, my dear daughter. Make him believe that you are already with child. He will then become careless, and fancy will become fact."

She blushed up to the eyes, but persisted in her determination to go through with it.

"But—but supposing he doesn't believe me?"

The priest had at his finger ends every trick by which a man may be led to a point and held there.

"Make your condition known; speak about it to everyone. In the end he'll believe it, too."

Then, as to absolve himself from this strategy, he added, "You are within your rights. The Church does not tolerate relations between men and women, except with this one object in view."

She followed his subtle counsels, and a fortnight later told Julian that she was with child. He was startled.

"Impossible. It can't be true."

She gave reasons, but he soon comforted himself.

"Wait a little. You'll find you are mistaken."

Every morning he questioned her, and she replied:

"No. I shall be much surprised if it isn't so."

It was his turn now to be uneasy. He was angry and disgusted as well as surprised.

"I can't make it out at all," he kept saying. "Hanged if I know how it happened."

After a month she spread the news abroad, informing everyone, except Gilberte, with regard to whom she had a curious and complicated feeling of delicacy.

In his first mood of vexation, Julian kept away from Jeanne. Then, in disgust, he made up his mind to it, exclaiming, "Here's a brat that nobody wants." After this he returned to his wife's room again, and the priest's prognostications were fulfilled.

Jeanne was wild with joy. She locked her door now at night, vowing eternal chastity, in a burst of gratitude towards the shadowy divinity whom she adored. Once more she felt almost happy, and she was amazed at the rapidity with which her sorrow for her mother's death had been assuaged. She had believed herself inconsolable, and yet in less than two months the painful wound was already healing. All that remained was a gentle melancholy, shadowing her life, like a mournful veil. The future held no more for her. Her children would grow up; they would love her, and she would look forward to a tranquil and contented old age, without troubling about her husband.

Towards the end of September, Abbé Picot, in a new cassock, which had only a week's accumulation of spots, paid her a formal visit to present his successor, Abbé Tolbiac. The latter was quite a young man, lean and very small, with an emphatic way of talking, and black-rimmed, hollow eyes, which indicated a fanatical nature.

Abbé Picot had been appointed Superior at Goderville. Jeanne felt real grief at his departure. The genial old priest was associated with all the memories of her early wedded life. He had married her, christened Paul, and buried the Baroness. She could not picture Etouvent without seeing Abbé Picot's fair round belly passing along by the farms. She loved him for his merry and simple nature.

In spite of his promotion, he did not seem happy.

"It's a wrench, Countess; it's a wrench. I have been here eighteen years now. Oh, it's a poor parish, and doesn't bring in much. The men have no more religion than is good for them; and the women — the women, you know — have no discretion at all. The girls don't come to church to be married till it is high time, and orange blossom goes for very little in this part of the world. All the same, I have always liked the place."

The new priest blushed and fidgeted impatiently.

"I shall put a stop to all that sort of thing," he said abruptly. In his cassock, which was clean, though it had already lost its first freshness, he looked very thin and frail, and he spoke with the air of a petulant child.

Abbé Picot cast a sidelong glance at him, as was his wont when he was amused.

"You know, Abbé, if you want to do that, you will have to chain up all your parishioners, and even that won't do any good."

"We shall see," the little priest replied crushingly.

The old Abbé smiled and took a pinch of snuff.

"With age and experience you'll calm down. All you will succeed in doing will be to drive the faithful remnant away from your church. In this part of the country people are pious, but pig-headed. Be careful. Why, when I see a girl with a somewhat ample figure come to service, I say to myself, 'She is bringing me a new parishioner'—and I do my best to marry her. You will never prevent them from falling, believe me. But you can discover the lad, and see that he doesn't desert the mother. Marry them, my friend; marry them, and don't worry about anything else."

The new priest replied rudely, "Our ideas are different. It's no use arguing."

Abbé Picot continued his lament for his village, for the sea, which he could gaze at through his parsonage windows, the little funnel-shaped valleys where he used to read his breviary and watch the ships sailing away in the distance. The two priests took their leave. The old man kissed Jeanne, who could hardly restrain her tears.

A week later Abbé Tolbiac paid her another visit. He spoke of the reforms he intended to introduce, as if he were a prince entering upon his kingdom. He begged the Viscountess on no account to miss Mass on Sunday, and to communicate on all festivals of the Church.

"You and I," he observed, "are leaders of the community. We must govern it and always set it an example. We must unite to exercise authority and to win respect. If Church and manor-house are hand-in-glove, we shall be feared and obeyed in every cottage."

Jeanne's religion was based on sentiment, and she had that dreamy faith which a woman never loses. But if she was moderately punctilious in her observances, this was mainly due to the habits she had acquired in the convent, for the Baron's critical philosophy had long ago undermined her convictions.

Abbé Picot had always contented himself with her small concessions, and had never taken her to task. But, when she did not appear at Mass on the following Sunday, his successor hurried off to her in stern disapproval. She wished to avoid an open breach with the parsonage, and gave him her promise, with a mental reservation that she would only show zeal for the first few weeks, to oblige him.

Gradually, however, she formed a habit of going to church, and came under the influence of the frail, but single-hearted and masterful priest. His mysticism appealed to her, with its raptures and ec-

146

stasies. He played upon that chord of poetic devoutness which vibrates in every woman's soul. In his intractable austerity, his contempt for the world and things of the senses, his disgust with the vain ambitions of mankind, his love of God, his raw and youthful inexperience, his harsh speech, his inflexible will, Jeanne recognised the stuff of which martyrs are made. Unhappy and disillusioned, she fell under the spell of the rigid fanaticism of this mere boy, who was God's minister. He brought her to Christ, the Comforter, showing her how the holy joys of religion would assuage all her sorrows. So she knelt humbly in the confessional, feeling very small and feeble before this priest, who looked about fifteen years old.

But he was soon detested by the whole neighbourhood. Never sparing himself, he was implacable and intolerant towards others. Human love was the one thing which, above all, roused his wrath and indignation. In his sermons he spoke of it with transports of invective, using crude terms, according to clerical custom, and thundering against lust in the ears of his rustic congregation. He shook and stamped with fury, obsessed by images conjured up by his violent antipathy.

The big boys and girls exchanged sly glances across the church. The old peasants, always fond of making jokes on that particular subject, expressed disapproval of the little priest's bigotry as they returned to their farms after service, with their sons in blue smocks and their black-cloaked wives. The whole countryside was in a ferment. People whispered to one another stories of his severity in the confessional, and of the harsh penances which he imposed. And when he firmly refused absolution to girls who had yielded to temptation, people began to mock. At High Mass on Saints' days they laughed to see young people remaining in their pews, while the rest went to take the Communion.

Very soon he took to spying on lovers to prevent their meetings, like a keeper after poachers. On moonlight evenings he would pursue them along ditches, behind barns, and in clumps of rushes on the hillsides. Once he came upon a pair, who did not start away from each other at his approach; with their arms round each other's waist, they were walking along the stony bed of a dried-up torrent. The Abbé shouted out, "Stop that, you young scoundrels."

The boy turned round and called back, "Mind your own business, parson; this is nothing to do with you."

The Abbé picked up stones and threw them at the pair, as if he was stoning a dog. They ran off, laughing; and on the following Sunday the priest denounced them by name before the whole congregation. In consequence, all the boys of the countryside left off going to Mass.

The priest dined at *Les Peuples* every Thursday, and came often during the week to talk to his penitent. She was as enthusiastic as he, and discussed spiritual matters, wielding all the antique and complicated weapons of religious controversy.

Walking along the Baroness's avenue, they talked about Christ and his Apostles, the Virgin, and the Fathers as if they had known them personally. Sometimes they broke off to propound deep questions, digressing into mystic subtleties; she would lose herself in poetic rhapsodies, which soared into the sky like rockets, while he, more precise, would set forth his arguments like a monomaniac pleader, demonstrating the squaring of the circle.

Julian treated the new priest with great respect, constantly saying, "That fellow suits me; he's so uncompromising." He went freely to Confession and Communion, a very pattern of piety.

He paid daily visits to the Fourvilles, shooting with the husband, who could not do without him, and riding with the Countess in all weathers. The Count used to say, "They are mad about their riding; but it is good for my wife."

About the middle of November the Baron came back. He had changed greatly, grown old and spiritless, plunged in a gloomy melancholy which enveloped his soul. But the love which linked him to his daughter seemed to have increased, as if these months of mournful solitude had stimulated his need of affection and sympathy and kindness. Jeanne did not impart to him her new ideas, her intimacy with Abbé Tolbiac, and her religious ardour. But the first time the Baron saw the priest he conceived a violent antipathy to him. That evening, when Jeanne asked him what he thought of the Abbé, the Baron replied, "The fellow is a regular inquisitor. That sort of man is a positive danger."

Afterwards, when his friends the peasants told him of the young priest's severity and fulminations, and how he persecuted those who obeyed natural laws and instincts, his feelings turned to hatred.

The Baron's heart was ever touched by the love-making of any pair of living creatures. He belonged to the sect of ancient philosophers who worshipped Nature, and he bowed his knee to a kind of pantheistic deity. He revolted at the Catholic conception of a God whose designs were Philistine, who had the angry passions of a Jesuit, and exercised a tyrant's vengeance; a God who, to his thinking, disparaged Creation—Creation, half revealed, inevitable, boundless, almighty—Creation, which is life, light, earth, thought, plants, rocks, man, air, beast, star, God, and insect all in one, creating because it is itself Creation, a force stronger than Will, vaster than Intellect, producing without aim, without reason and without end, in all directions, in every form, subservient to chance and the juxtaposition of suns, by whose warmth the worlds are animated.

In the Baron's creed, Creation contained the germs from which spring life and thought, as naturally as flowers and fruit. For him, therefore, generation was the great universal law, a holy act, honourable and divine, accomplishing the mysterious but inflexible will of the Universal Being.

Going from farm to farm, he stirred up the country people to violent hostility against the intolerant priest, who made war on life itself. In deep concern, Jeanne prayed to the Lord and pleaded with her father. He answered invariably, "It is our right and our duty to fight against such men. They are not human." Shaking his long white hair, he repeated, "They are not human; they have no comprehension, none at all. Their actions are based on fatal delusions; they are contrary to nature." And he ejaculated "contrary to nature" as if uttering a malediction.

The priest recognised his enemy, but temporised. Sure of final victory, he counted on retaining his mastery over the manor-house and its young mistress. Moreover, he had become possessed of a fixed idea. He had by chance discovered Julian's relations with Gilberte, and he determined to break them off at any cost. One day he came to see Jeanne, and, after a long and mystical conversation, he begged her to join him in combating and slaying an evil in her own family, and in saving two souls from perdition. She did not understand, and asked him to explain. "The hour is not yet," he replied, "I will come again soon"; and he went away abruptly.

Winter was drawing to a close—a soft winter, as the farmers said, moist and warm. The Abbé came again a few days later, and made mysterious allusions to one of those vile liaisons between people who ought to be above reproach. It behooved those who knew the facts, he said, to put an end to the affair by all available means. Then he considered the matter from a loftier standpoint, and finally, taking Jeanne by the hand, he adjured her to open her eyes, to understand, and to help him. This time she had understood, but she kept silence, appalled at the thought of all the trouble that might ensue in her present peaceful house; and she pretended not to know what the Abbé meant.

He hesitated no longer, but spoke out plainly: "I have a very painful duty to perform, Countess; but there is no alternative. The office which I fill bids me not to leave you ignorant of an evil that you can hinder. Know, then, that your husband cherishes a guilty love for Madame de Fourville."

She bent her head, weakly submissive. The priest resumed: "Now, what do you propose to do?"

"What do you wish me to do, Father?" she faltered.

He replied vehemently, "You must throw yourself in the path of this guilty passion."

She began to cry, and in a heart-broken voice she sobbed, "But he has already been unfaithful with my maid-servant. He never listens to me. He no longer cares for me. As soon as I express a wish that does not suit him, he ill-treats me. What can I do?"

Avoiding a direct answer, the priest exclaimed, "Then you consent to this thing; you submit; you acquiesce? The adulterer lives under your roof and you tolerate him? The crime is enacted under your very eyes and you avert your glance? Do you call yourself a wife, a Christian, a mother?"

"What would you have me do?" she sobbed.

"Anything rather than suffer such infamy. Anything, I tell you. Leave him. Flee from this contaminated house."

"But I have no money," she replied, "and nowadays I haven't the courage. Besides, how can I leave him when I have no proofs? I haven't even a right to do so."

The priest rose. "You are actuated by your own cowardice, Madame de Lamare," he said in a quivering voice. "I thought you were different. You are unworthy of God's mercy."

She fell on her knees before him. "Oh, I implore you not to abandon me. Give me your counsel."

"Open Monsieur de Fourville's eyes," he said curtly. "It is his duty to put an end to this entanglement."

Terror-stricken at this suggestion, she exclaimed, "But he would kill them, Father, and I should be an informer. Never. Never."

In a passion of indignation, he raised his hand as if to curse her.

"Remain, then, sunk in your shame and sin, for you are more guilty than they: you are the complaisant wife. I have nothing further to do here."

And, shaking all over with rage, he went away. In despair, she followed him, ready to yield, to promise concessions. But, still trembling with indignation, he strode away, furiously brandishing a big blue umbrella, almost as tall as himself.

He caught sight of Julian, who was standing near the gate and superintending pruning operations. As he turned to the left, towards the Couillards' farm, he exclaimed once more, "Leave me alone, Madame de Lamare; I have nothing more to say to you."

In the middle of the yard he saw a crowd of children from both farms clustering round the kennel of Mirza, the dog, and watching something with a curiosity and attention that held them silent. In the middle of the group stood the Baron, with his hands behind his back, an interested spectator, with something of the air of a schoolmaster. But when he caught sight of the priest in the distance, he went away, to avoid meeting him and having to exchange civilities.

"Give me a few days, Abbé," Jeanne pleaded, "and then come and see me again. I will tell you what I have been able to do and what plans I have made, and we will consult."

By this time they were close to the group of children, and the priest drew near to see the object of their interest. Mirza was giving birth to young ones. In the front part of the kennel, five little puppies were already crawling round their mother, who, lying on her side and in pain, was licking them tenderly. Just as the priest stooped down to look, the crouching animal grew taut and a sixth little puppy made its appearance. All the urchins clapped their hands in glee and shouted, "Here's another! Here's another!"

To them it was an entertaining and perfectly natural spectacle, with no element of uncleanness in it. They watched the birth of the puppies as they would have watched apples falling.

At first Abbé Tolbiac was dumfounded. Then, in an uncon-

151

trollable rage, he raised his big umbrella and began to hit the children over the head with all his might. The startled youngsters ran away as fast as they could, and he found himself suddenly confronted with the labouring beast, which tried to rise. But he would not even suffer it to get on its feet, and he began to batter it madly with all the strength of his arms. As it was chained up, it could not escape, and it uttered frightful groans as it tottered beneath his blows. He broke his umbrella. Then, empty-handed, he stamped upon it, frenziedly trod it down, crushed it beneath his feet. It brought into the world another puppy, which burst forth beneath his attack; then, with a frenzied kick, he finished off the bleeding body, which still palpitated amid the crying puppies, as they already felt blindly for the teat.

Jeanne had fled. But suddenly someone seized the priest by the collar, and administered a box on the ear which sent his three-cornered hat flying. In a fury of indignation, the Baron dragged him to the gate and flung him out into the road. When Monsieur le Perthuis came back, he found his daughter sobbing on her knees among the puppies, which she was gathering up in her skirt. He strode up to her, gesticulating and exclaiming, "There you are; there you are. That's your friend in the cassock. Now do you know the sort of man he is?"

The farmer and his wife had hastened to the spot. Everyone looked at the mutilated dog, and old Mother Couillard exclaimed, "How can anyone be such a brute!"

Jeanne had picked up the puppies, and declared that she would rear them. An attempt was made to give them milk, but three died the next day. Old Simon scoured the country for a foster-mother; but, as he could not find a dog, he brought back a cat—which, he said, would answer the purpose. Three other puppies were destroyed, and the survivor was entrusted to this foster-mother of alien race. She adopted him at once, and lay on her side to suckle him.

To avoid exhausting his nurse, he was separated from her in a fortnight, and Jeanne undertook to bring him up herself on the bottle. She had called him Toto, but the Baron arbitrarily changed his name to Massacre.

The priest did not pay Jeanne another visit, but the following Sunday he hurled from the pulpit imprecations, denunciations and menaces against *Les Peuples*, declaring that wounds should be cauterised with red-hot iron, anathematising the Baron, who merely laughed, and making veiled, and at first timid, allusions to Julian's new love affair. Julian was very angry, but his wrath was restrained by his fear of a terrible scandal. In sermon after sermon the priest launched his threats of vengeance, saying that God's hour was at hand and that his enemies would be smitten.

In the end Julian wrote the Archbishop a letter, couched in respectful but forcible terms, and Abbé Tolbiac was threatened with disciplinary measures. He held his peace.

After this he was often seen taking long solitary walks, striding on his way in feverish excitement.

Gilberte and Julian were always coming across him on their rides. Sometimes they caught sight of him, looking like a black dot, far away on the moor or on the edge of the cliff; sometimes he would be reading his breviary in some narrow valley which they were approaching. Then, to avoid meeting him, they would turn their horses' heads in another direction.

Spring had come, kindling their passion anew and impelling them daily into each other's arms, in whatever convenient nook they chanced to find when they were out riding. The trees, clad in the light verdure of spring, afforded insufficient shelter; and Julian and Gilberte could not, as in the height of summer, hide themselves in the undergrowth of the woods. For this reason they generally concealed their love-making in a shepherd's hut on wheels, which had remained deserted since the autumn on the summit of Vaucotte Hill. It stood there solitary, high on its wheels, five hundred metres from the cliff, at the top of a steep incline leading abruptly into the valley. As they commanded a view of the whole plain, they felt safe from surprise. They tethered their horses to the shafts, to wait there until their riders had had their fill of kisses. One day, however, just as they were leaving their shelter, they caught sight of Abbé Tolbiac lurking in the rushes on the hillside.

"In future we had better leave our horses in the ravine," said Julian; "they would betray us miles away."

After this they used to tether their horses in a bushy nook in the valley.

One evening, as they were both returning to *La Vrillette* to dine with the Count, they met Abbé Tolbiac emerging from the house. He stood aside to let them pass, and raised his hat to them without meeting their eyes. They were seized with a sudden, though transitory, feeling of uneasiness.

One windy afternoon at the beginning of May, as Jeanne was reading by the fire, she caught side of Count de Fourville approaching on foot, in such haste that she thought something serious must have happened. She sped downstairs to meet him, and when she confronted him she thought he had gone mad. He had on a huge fur cap, which he never wore except at home, and his shooting-jacket, and he was so pale that his red moustache, which was not ordinarily conspicuous against his usual high colour, looked like a flame. His eyes were distraught and rolled vacantly.

"My wife is here, isn't she?" he stammered.

"No," replied Jeanne, losing her head, "I haven't seen her at all to-day."

He fell into a chair, as if his legs had given way under him, removed his cap and mechanically wiped his forehead with his handkerchief two or three times. Then, suddenly jumping to his feet, he approached Jeanne with outstretched hands and open mouth, as if to speak and confide to her some terrible affliction. But he stopped short, gazed at her fixedly as if in delirium, and exclaimed, "But he's your husband . . . You too . . ."

Then he fled in the direction of the sea. Jeanne ran after him to detain him; she called to him imploringly, in an agony of terror.

"He knows everything," she thought to herself. "What will he do? Oh, Heaven send that he may not find them."

But he was out of reach, and did not hear her. He went on his way deliberately, as if sure of his goal. He crossed the ditch, passed through the rushes with huge strides, and reached the cliff. Jeanne stood on the bank among the trees, and followed him a long time with her eyes, until he was out of sight; then she returned home in terrible distress.

The Count turned to the right and broke into a run. The waves were raging. Great black clouds, in swift succession, scudded wildly across the sky, and each, as it passed, deluged the countryside with torrential rain. The wind howled and moaned, sweeping over the grass, beating down the young crops, whirling before it great white birds, like flakes of foam. Squall after squall whipped the Count's face, drenching his cheeks and his moustache, which was dripping with water, filling his ears with clamour and his heart with tumult.

154

Before him lay the deep valley of Vaucotte, and there was nothing between him and the ravine except a shepherd's hut close to an empty sheep-pen. And to the shafts of this hut on wheels two horses were tethered. What had the lovers to fear in such a storm?

As soon as the Count saw the horses, he threw himself on the ground and crawled along on his hands and knees, looking like some monster with his great, mud-stained body and his fur cap. He crept up to the solitary hut and hid beneath it, so that he might not be seen through the cracks in the plank walls. The horses caught sight of him and moved uneasily. He cut their bridles deliberately with the open knife he carried in his hand. Another squall burst, and the horses galloped away, stung to madness by the hailstorm, which beat upon the sloping roof and shook the wooden hut on its wheels. He raised himself on his knees, applied his eyes to the crack beneath the door, and looked in.

He remained there motionless, as if he were waiting for something. Some little time elapsed. At last, covered in mud from head to foot, he suddenly stood erect. With a furious gesture, he shot home the bolt which fastened the opening on the outside, and, seizing the shafts, he began to shake the hut as if he meant to break it to pieces. Then all at once he put himself between the shafts, and, bending his great frame in a frantic effort, straining like an ox, and panting, he dragged the hut and its occupants towards the steep incline. Julian and Gilberte shouted and battered the walls with their fists, though without realising what was happening to them.

At the top of the slope he let go the shafts, and the lightly built hut began to roll down the side of the hill. Launched on its mad career, it travelled faster and ever faster, bounding and skipping like a living thing, while its shafts beat against the ground. An old beggar, who had taken refuge in a ditch, saw it shoot past above his head, and he heard shrieks of terror issuing from the wooden interior. Presently a wheel was wrenched off by a sudden jerk, the hut upset on its side, and began to roll over and over like a ball, or like a house torn from its foundations and hurled down a mountainside. Reaching the edge of the last ravine, it took a flying leap, and, striking the bottom, was shattered like an egg.

As soon as it lay in fragments on the stony ground, the old beggar, who had seen it pass him, made his way timidly down through the brambles. His rustic cautiousness restrained him from investigating the shattered hut, and he went to report the accident at the nearest farm. A rescue party hurried to the spot. When they had removed the wreckage, they saw two bodies, bruised, battered and bleeding. The man's forehead was cut open, and his face completely crushed. The woman's jaw hung down out of its socket, and all their limbs were broken and beaten to pulp. Nevertheless they were recognisable, and the cause of the accident was discussed at great length.

"What on earth were they doing in that hut?" exclaimed one of the women. The old beggar explained that they had doubtless sheltered there from a squall, and that the violent wind must have capsized the hut and hurled it down the hill. He added that he himself had intended to take refuge in the hut, but when he had caught sight of the horses tethered to the shafts he had realised that the place was already occupied.

"If it hadn't been for that, I should be in their place now," he added in self-satisfied tones.

"Wouldn't that have been better?" asked another voice.

At this the old fellow flew into a rage. "Why would it have been better? Because I'm poor and they are rich? Just look at them now . . ." Trembling, tattered, dripping with rain, a sordid figure with his tangled beard and his long hair beneath his battered hat, he pointed to the two corpses with the end of his crook-handled stick. "We're all equal when we're dead," he said.

Other peasants appeared on the scene, casting sidelong glances at the bodies, their faces expressing uneasiness, cunning, alarm, and selfish fears. They discussed what steps to take, and, in the hope of a reward, they decided that the bodies should be removed to their homes. Two carts were made ready. But a new difficulty arose. Some were for putting nothing but a layer of straw in the bottom of the carts; others considered that mattresses would be more seemly. The woman who had spoken before exclaimed, "But the mattresses will be all covered with blood. They will have to be bleached again."

A stout, jolly-faced farmer replied, "They'll pay for it. The more it's worth, the more it'll cost them."

This argument clinched the matter.

The two carts, on their high, springless wheels, set off at a trot, one to the right, the other to the left, shaking and jolting along in the deep ruts of the road with the remains of these two beings, who had loved and embraced, and now would never meet again.

As soon as the Count had seen the hut begin to roll down the steep incline, he had run away through the driving rain as fast as his legs could carry him. He ran on and on for hours, cutting across roads, leaping over banks, breaking through hedges. He had returned home at nightfall—how, he hardly knew.

The frightened servants were waiting for him, and told him that the two horses had returned without their riders, Julian's having followed the Countess's mare.

Monsieur de Fourville reeled, and in a broken voice he stammered, "Something must have happened to them in this dreadful weather. Send everyone out to search for them."

He set out again. But as soon as he was out of sight of the house he hid beneath some bramble bushes, watching the road along which the woman, whom he still loved with savage passion, must presently be borne—dead, or dying, or perhaps mutilated and forever disfigured. Presently a cart, with a strange load, passed by. It stopped on the road in front of the manor-house, then entered the gates. It was she. It was she. But a pang of agony held him rooted to the spot, a terrible dread of learning the truth. He did not stir, but crouched there like a hare, trembling at the slightest sound.

He remained there an hour, two hours, perhaps. The cart had not gone away. He told himself that his wife was dying, and the idea of seeing her, of meeting her glance, filled him with such horror that he was suddenly afraid of being discovered in his hiding-place and obliged to enter the house and witness her expiring agony. Once more he fled away into the depths of the woods. Then all at once it occurred to him that she might be in need of aid, and that there might be no one to attend to her. He ran madly homewards.

He met the gardener and exclaimed, "What news?"

At first the man did not venture to reply.

"Is she dead?" the Count almost shouted.

"Yes, sir," faltered the man.

The Count was conscious of a feeling of profound relief. The tumult of his blood and his quivering muscles suddenly subsided, and with a firm tread he went up the great flight of steps into the house.

Meanwhile the other car had reached *Les Peuples*. Jeanne caught sight of it in the distance, noticed the mattress, guessed that a corpse lay there, and realised the truth. The shock was so great that she swooned away. When she recovered consciousness, her father was supporting her head and bathing her temples with vinegar.

"You know . . . ?" he murmured.

"Yes, Father," she answered.

But, when she attempted to rise, she was in such pain that she could not move. That evening she gave birth to a dead child — a girl.

She saw and knew nothing of Julian's funeral. After a day or two, however, she was conscious that Aunt Lison had returned. In the feverish nightmares that haunted her, she tried persistently to remember at what period and in what circumstances her aunt had quitted *Les Peuples*. But this she could not remember, even in her lucid intervals. Only she was sure that she had seen her since her mother's death.

11

SHE remained three months in her room, and grew so weak and pale that her life was despaired of. Gradually, however, her strength returned. The Baron and Aunt Lison, who had taken up their abode at *Les Peuples*, never left her. The shock she had experienced had resulted in a nervous ailment. She fainted at the slightest sound, and the most trifling causes produced long attacks of syncope.

She had never asked for details of Julian's death. What did details matter? Did she not know enough? Everyone believed it was an accident, but she was not deceived. She bore in her heart a secret that tortured her—the knowledge of Julian's unfaithfulness, and the vivid recollection of the Count's sudden and terrible visit on the day of the catastrophe.

And now her soul was haunted by memories, tender and sad, of the brief joys of the early days of her wedded life. Again and again she was thrilled by some sudden pang of memory. She saw Julian such as he was during their engagement, and in those brief hours when her passion had ripened in the strong Corsican sun and she had loved him. His faults grew less, his unkindnesses were forgotten, and in the remoteness of the sealed tomb even his infidelities now seemed insignificant. Moved by a vague sense of posthumous gratitude towards this man who had held her in his arms, Jeanne forgave him her past sufferings, so that she might dwell exclusively upon her moments of happiness. As time went on, and month followed month, the dust of oblivion gathered thickly upon her memories and her sorrows, and she devoted herself entirely to her son.

The boy became the idol, the sole concern, of the three persons who surrounded him, and whom he ruled despotically. His three slaves were jealous of one another. Jeanne watched with an uneasy eye the hearty kisses he gave the Baron after a ride on his grandfather's knee. Aunt Lison, whom he regarded with the same indifference as others had, was ordered about like a servant by this tyrant, who could not talk yet; and she would go away to her room and cry, as she compared the casual kisses she coaxed from him with the loving embraces he reserved for his mother and grandfather.

161

In this manner passed two quiet, uneventful years, entirely devoted to the child. At the beginning of the third winter they decided to go to Rouen till the spring, and the whole family migrated.
But when they settled down in the damp old house, which had remained unoccupied, Paul caught such a severe attack of bronchitis
that pleurisy was feared. His distracted relations declared that he
could not thrive away from the air of *Les Peuples*, and, as soon as he
had recovered, they took him back. Then followed a period of happy,
uneventful years. The three adults were always with the child, either
in his room or in the big drawing-room or in the garden, rapturously
noting his lispings, his quaint expressions, his actions.

His mother's pet name for him was Paulet, but he pronounced it
Poulet, and this was an endless source of merriment. He was never
called anything else. He grew rapidly, and his three relations, whom
the Baron called his three mothers, took a passionate interest in
measuring him. Little notches, made month by month on the drawing-room door, marked his growth. Poulet's ladder, as it was called,
played an important part in their joint existence.

The family circle received an addition in Massacre, the dog, whom Jeanne, entirely monopolised by her son, had neglected. He was fed by Ludivine and housed in an old barrel outside the stable, where he was kept chained up. One morning Paul caught sight of him, and cried to be allowed to go and kiss him. With infinite apprehension, his mother led him up to Massacre, who fawned on the child. Paul howled at their parting, and Massacre was taken off the chain and allowed into the house. He and Paul became inseparable. They romped together, and slept side by side on the rug. Presently Massacre shared his playfellow's bed, to the concern of Jeanne, who was afraid of fleas. Aunt Lison had a grudge against the dog for monopolising so much of the child's affection. She felt that the animal had stolen love, which she herself would have given everything to possess.

Occasional calls were exchanged with the Brisevilles and the Couteliers. The visits of the mayor and the doctor were the only regular interruptions to the secluded existence in the old manorhouse. Jeanne no longer went to church. The priest's brutality to the dog, and his insinuations after the death of Julian and the Countess, had filled her with resentment towards a God who could endure such a minister.

From time to time Abbé Tolbiac made direct attacks on *Les Peuples*, anathematising it as haunted by the Spirit of Evil, the Spirit of Eternal Revolt, the Spirit of Error and Mendacity, the Spirit of Iniquity, the Spirit of Corruption and Impurity. By such terms did he designate the Baron.

His church, moreover, was deserted, and when he went through the fields where the farm-labourers were ploughing, the peasants did not pause in their work to chat with him, or turn to bid him good-day. They looked upon him, too, as a sorcerer, because he had driven out the evil spirit from a woman who was possessed. It was said that he knew mysterious words for breaking charms, which, according to him, were merely practical jokes of Satan. He laid his hands on cows who were giving blue milk, or who curled their tails, and by pronouncing certain unknown formulas he could find things that were lost.

His narrow, fanatical mind plunged passionately into the study of religious books which recorded instances of the Devil's appearance on earth, various manifestations of his power and of his occult and

163

manifold influence, all the resources at his command, and the wily methods he employed. He believed himself specially called to combat this mysterious and fatal Power, and he had learned all the formulas of exorcism contained in ecclesiastical manuals. He imagined that he could perceive the evil spirit forever prowling about in dark places, and the Latin phrase, *Sicut leo rugiens circuit quaerens quem devoret*, was continually on his lips.

People grew afraid of him and of his secret powers. Even his fellow-priests, ignorant country clergy, with whom a belief in Beelzebub was an article of faith, and who, confused by meticulous instructions dealing with rites that were to be observed in case this evil potency should manifest itself, came to confound religion and magic, looked upon Abbé Tolbiac as something of a sorcerer, and respected him as much for his supposed mysterious powers as for the irreproachable austerity of his life.

When he met Jeanne, he never raised his hat to her.

This state of affairs distressed and grieved Aunt Lison's timid and old-maidish soul. She could not understand people who would not go to church. Doubtless she herself piously went to Confession and Communion. But nobody knew or cared whether she did.

When she had Paul quite to herself, she would talk to him, in low tones, about God. He would pay some attention to her wonderful tales of the beginning of the world. But when she told him that he ought to love God very, very dearly, he sometimes said, "Where is He, auntie?"

Then she would point towards the sky and say, "Up there, Poulet, but you mustn't tell anyone." For she was afraid of the Baron.

One day Poulet announced, "God is everywhere, except in church." He had been telling his grandfather about his aunt's mysterious revelations.

The boy was now ten years old, and his mother looked forty. He was strong and boisterous and a bold tree-climber, but he knew hardly anything. Lessons bored him, and he was always escaping from them. Whenever the Baron kept him rather long at a book, Jeanne would come and say, "Let him go and play now. You mustn't tire him, he is so young."

She always thought of him as six months or a year old. She hardly realised that he could walk and run and talk like a little man. She was in a continual state of anxiety in case he should tumble down or catch cold or overheat himself, or eat more than was good for him or less than a growing boy required.

When he was twelve, the vexed question of the first Communion presented itself.

Lison came to Jeanne one morning, protesting that the child could not remain any longer without religious instruction and without fulfilling his earliest obligations. She argued the question from every point of view, alleging a thousand different reasons, and public opinion in particular. Perturbed and vacillating, his mother said hesitatingly that the matter could wait awhile. But a month later, when she was calling on Viscountess de Briseville, her hostess said to her casually, "I suppose your Paul is to make his first Communion this year?"

"Yes," replied Jeanne, taken by surprise.

This simple affirmation turned the scale. Without confiding in her father, she asked Lison to take the boy to be catechised. For a month all was well. But one evening Poulet came back hoarse, and the next day he had a cough. His distracted mother questioned him, and discovered that the priest had sent him to wait outside the church door in the draughty porch till the end of the lesson, because he had been naughty. After this, she kept him at home and herself taught him the rudiments of religion. But, in spite of Aunt Lison's entreaties, Abbé Tolbiac refused to admit him among the communicants, on the ground that he was insufficiently instructed. The next year the same thing happened, and the Baron declared in exasperation that it was quite unnecessary for the child to believe such a puerile absurdity as the doctrine of Transubstantiation in order to grow up a decent man. It was decided that he should be brought up a Christian, but not a practising Catholic, and that when he attained his majority he should be free to choose for himself.

Some time afterwards, Jeanne paid a call on the Brisevilles, which was not returned. Aware of her neighbours' punctilious politeness, Jeanne was surprised at the omission. But the Marchioness de Coutelier haughtily explained the matter to her. On the strength of her husband's position, his well-authenticated title and large fortune, she considered herself a sort of queen of the Norman aristocracy, and exercised despotic powers. She spoke her mind freely, condescended or snubbed according to circumstances, and was ever ready with admonishments, reproofs or praises. When Jeanne called on her, this lady, after a few icy remarks, observed drily, "Society is divided into two classes—people who believe in God, and people who do not. The former, even the humblest of them, are our friends and equals. The latter are nothing to us."

Aware of a hostile intention, Jeanne replied, "Is it impossible to believe in God without going to church?"

"Certainly it is," replied the Marchioness. "The faithful go to pray to God in His Church, just as people go to visit their friends in their houses."

Jeanne felt hurt.

"God is everywhere," she replied. "For my part, I believe with all my heart in His goodness, but I cannot feel His presence when certain of His priests interpose themselves between Him and me."

The Marchioness rose.

"The priest bears the banner of the Church. Whosoever does not follow that banner is against it and against us."

Jeanne, too, had risen. In a quivering voice she said:

"You, Madame de Coutelier, believe in the God of a single sect. I believe in the God of all good people."

She bowed and left the house.

The peasants, too, criticised her among themselves for not letting Poulet make his first Communion. They did not attend the services or take the Sacrament, except perhaps at Easter, according to the express injunctions of the Church. But children were another matter. None of them would have had the audacity to bring up a child outside the pale of this universal law, for after all religion is religion.

She soon became aware of the general disapproval she had incurred, and resented bitterly all these pacts and compromises on matters of conscience, the abject cowardice that lurks in all hearts and shows itself under one mask or another of respectability.

The Baron undertook to superintend Paul's studies and began to teach him Latin. "Do be careful not to tire him," was his mother's constant entreaty, and she roamed restlessly about outside the school-room. The Baron had forbidden her to come in, because she was always interrupting the lessons.

"Aren't your feet cold, Poulet?" "Doesn't your head ache, Poulet?" she would say, or "Don't make him talk so much; his throat will be tired."

As soon as lessons were over, the boy would go and garden with his mother and aunt. They had developed a passion for gardening, and in the spring all three of them planted trees and sowed seeds, watching them sprout and grow with intense interest. They trimmed the branches and cut posies of flowers.

The boy's special line was salads. He took charge of four large square beds in the kitchen garden, and devoted infinite care to his cos-lettuces, chicory, endive, and all known species of edible leaves. He dug, watered, hoed, and transplanted, with the help of his two mothers, whom he worked like day labourers. They spent hours on end kneeling on the beds, soiling their gowns and hands, planting seedlings in holes which they made by thrusting a finger into the earth.

Poulet grew up and reached the age of fifteen. His ladder on the drawing-room door recorded one metre fifty-eight, but he was still a child in mind, ignorant and simple, arrested in his development by the two women's sheltering petticoats and the benevolent old gentleman who belonged to a past century. At last one evening the Baron spoke of college, and immediately Jeanne began to cry. Aunt Lison shrank nervously away into a dark corner.

"What does he want with so much learning?" exclaimed his mother. "We are going to make him an out-of-doors man, a country gentleman. He will farm his own land, like many others of his class. He will live and grow old in perfect happiness in the home where we shall have spent our own lives. What more could one ask?"

The Baron shook his head.

"What answer will you give him if he comes to you at twenty-five and says, 'I am utterly useless and it's all your fault, all the fault of your maternal selfishness. I realise that I'm not fit for any kind of work and I shall never be anything, and yet I'm not suited for this obscure and humble existence of deadly monotony to which in your blind affection you have condemned me'?"

Still weeping, she appealed to her son:

"Tell me, Poulet, surely you will never reproach me for having loved you too well?"

"Of course not, Mamma," replied the big fellow in surprise.

"You promise?"

"Yes, Mamma."

"And you would like to stay here?"

167

"Yes, Mamma."

The Baron spoke out in loud, decisive tones.

"Jeanne, you have no right to dispose of his life for him. What you are doing is cowardly, almost criminal. You are sacrificing your child to your own personal happiness."

Sobbing violently, she hid her face in her hands, faltering through her tears:

"I have been so unhappy, so unhappy. And now that I am living with him in peace, you are going to take him from me. What will become of me now, all alone?"

Her father left his chair, seated himself beside her and put his arms around her.

"What about me, Jeanne?"

She flung her arms round his neck and kissed him passionately. Then, still half-stifled by her emotion, she faltered brokenly:

"Yes. Perhaps you are right, Papa. I felt frantic, but I have been through so much. I consent to his going to college."

Though he scarcely realised what was in store for him, Poulet too began to cry. His three mothers kissed him, petted him, and cheered him, but all of them went to bed with heavy hearts and wept on their pillows, not excepting the Baron, who had hitherto restrained his tears.

It was decided that at the beginning of term the boy should go to college at Havre. The rest of the summer he was more spoilt than ever. His mother groaned at the thought of this parting. She prepared his outfit, as if for an absence of ten years. At last, one October morning, after a sleepless night, the two women and the Baron and Poulet entered the carriage and the two horses set off at a trot.

One visit had already been paid for the purpose of selecting his place in the dormitory and in the class-room. With the help of Aunt Lison, Jeanne spent the whole day arranging Poulet's clothes in the little chest-of-drawers. As it would not hold a quarter of what had been brought, she asked the headmaster for another. The bursar was summoned. He suggested that such quantities of linen and other possessions were superfluous and would only be in the way. He quoted the rules and declined to provide a second chest-of-drawers. In despair, Jeanne resolved to rent a room in a hotel close by and to enjoin the landlord to go in person to Poulet with everything he required, as soon as the boy should send word.

The family then went for a walk on the quay and watched the ships arriving and departing. The melancholy gloom of evening sank down upon the town, and gradually the lamps were lighted. They went to a restaurant for dinner. But no one was hungry. With tearful eyes they gazed at one another, while dish after dish was sent away almost untouched. Then slowly they set out for the college. Boys of every size were arriving from all directions. They were accompanied by relations or servants, and many of them were in tears. A noise of weeping was heard in the large, dimly-lighted courtyard.

Jeanne and Poulet clung together in a long embrace. Aunt Lison, entirely overlooked, remained in the background with her face buried in her handkerchief. But the Baron, who felt himself weakening, cut short their farewells and drew his daughter away. The three of them entered the carriage, which was waiting at the door, and they drove through the night back to *Les Peuples*. At times a loud sob issued from the darkness.

Jeanne spent the next day in tears. The following morning she ordered the carriage and drove to Havre. Poulet seemed to have resigned himself to the separation. For the first time in his life, he had companions of his own age, and he fidgeted on the chair in the parlour in his eagerness to get back to his games.

Jeanne paid him a visit every other day, as well as on Sundays, when the boys were allowed out. As she did not know what to do with herself in class-time between the intervals for recreation, and lacked the strength of mind to tear herself away from the college precincts, she stayed in the parlour. The headmaster invited her into his study and asked her to pay fewer visits to the school, but she turned a deaf ear to this request. At last he warned her, that if she continued to interfere with her son's work and play, he would be obliged to send him home, and he gave a hint to the Baron. After this she was kept under close watch at *Les Peuples*, like a prisoner. She looked forward to the holidays more eagerly than the boy himself.

She gave herself no peace. Sometimes lost in idle dreams, she roamed the country all day long with Massacre, the dog. At other times she would sit the whole afternoon on the cliff, gazing at the sea. Now and then she walked through the woods to Yport, treading again the old ways with their haunting memories. How far away, how very far away, seemed the days when she had wandered over that same countryside, in the enchanting dreams of girlhood.

Whenever she saw her son again, she felt as if she had been parted from him for ten years. Between one month and another he grew into a man, while she became an old woman. Her father looked like her brother, and Aunt Lison, who had faded at twenty-five, and since then never appeared to grow any older, seemed like her elder sister.

Poulet did no work whatever. He remained two years in the fourth form. He did passably in the third form, but he had to do the second form course twice. At the age of twenty he was in the rhetoric class. He had grown into a tall young fellow, with budding whiskers and a suggestion of a moustache. It was now his turn to pay Sunday visits to *Les Peuples*. He had been having riding lessons for some time, and he would hire a horse and ride over in a couple of hours. In the course of the morning Jeanne would set out to meet him, and with her went her aunt and the Baron, who had grown somewhat bent and walked like a little old man, with his hands clasped behind his back, as if to prevent himself from falling on his nose. They strolled quietly along the highway, with an occasional rest by the roadside, straining their eyes to catch sight of the horseman. As soon as he came in view, a black blot on the line of white, his three relations waved their handkerchiefs. Then he would gallop up to them like a whirlwind, fluttering Jeanne and Lison, and evoking a rapturous bravo from his grandfather, who had all the enthusiasm of infirmity.

Although Paul was a head taller than his mother, she always treated him like a baby, and would still say to him:

"Aren't your feet cold, Poulet?"

When he strolled on the perron after luncheon, smoking a cigarette, she would open the window and cry:

"For goodness' sake, don't go out without a hat; you'll catch cold in your head."

When he rode back at night she trembled with anxiety.

"Be sure not to go too fast, my little Poulet. Do be careful. Think how heart-broken your poor mother would be, if anything happened to you."

One Saturday morning, however, she received a letter from Paul to say that he could not come home the following day, because some friends of his had invited him to go for an excursion with them. The whole of Sunday she was in agony, as if threatened by some catastrophe. By Thursday she could bear her anxiety no longer and set out for Havre.

In some indefinable way the boy seemed to her changed. He had an animated air and spoke in manlier tones. Presently he said to her, as if it were the most natural thing in the world:

"You know, Mamma, as you have come over to-day, I shan't go home next Sunday, because we have got up another excursion."

She was appalled; half stifled with emotion, as if he had announced his departure for the other hemisphere. At last when she had recovered her power of speech, she exclaimed:

"Oh, Poulet, what is it? Tell me what is the matter?"

He burst out laughing and kissed her.

"Nothing is the matter, Mamma. But at my age, one wants to enjoy oneself with one's friends."

She could think of no reply, and when she was alone in her carriage she was tormented by strange ideas. She had hardly recognised her Poulet, her own little Poulet of old days. For the first time she realised that he was grown up, and no longer hers, and that he meant to live his own life without troubling his head about the old people. It seemed to her that he had been transformed in a single day. Was this indeed her son, her own precious little boy, who used to make her transplant his lettuces, this strong young man with a moustache and a will of his own? For the next three months Paul paid his people only occasional visits, and even these he evidently desired to cut as short as possible. Each evening he tried to steal another hour from them. Jeanne was alarmed, but the Baron invariably comforted her.

"Let him alone," he would say. "After all, the boy is twenty."

One morning, however, a shabbily dressed old man, whose French had a strong German accent, asked to see the Viscountess. After much ceremonious bowing, he produced a disreputable pocket book, and remarking: "I have a little document for you," he unfolded and handed her a scrap of greasy paper. She read it twice, cast a glance at the Jew, and then re-read it.

"What does this mean?" she asked.

The man explained obsequiously.

"I will tell you. Your son happened to be in want of a little money. And, knowing that you are a kind mother, I lent him a little something to go on with."

"But why didn't he ask me?" she said, tremblingly.

The Jew explained at great length that it was a question of a gambling debt, which had to be paid the next day; that, as Paul was still a minor, no one would lend him any money and that, if he had not obliged him with this little service, the boy's honour would have been compromised. Jeanne wanted to call the Baron, but she was paralysed by her emotion and could not rise. At last she turned to the money-lender.

"Be so kind as to ring the bell."

Fearing some artifice, the Jew hesitated.

"If I am inconveniencing you, I will call another day," he said haltingly.

She shook her head. He rang the bell and they waited, looking at each other in silence. The Baron grasped the situation at once. The note was for fifteen hundred francs. He gave the man a thousand francs, and, looking straight at him, said:

"Don't show your face here again."

The Jew thanked him, bowed, and went away.

Paul's grandfather and mother left immediately for Havre. But when they arrived at the college, they were told that it was a month since Paul had been there. The headmaster had received four letters signed by Jeanne, reporting the boy's illness, and giving news of his progress. Every letter was accompanied by a medical certificate, and obviously the whole correspondence was forged. They were dumfounded and stood gazing at one another. The headmaster, in great concern, accompanied them to the police station. The Baron and Jeanne went to a hotel for the night.

The next day the young man was found living with a woman of the town. His grandfather and mother carried him off to *Les Peuples* and not a word was said during the whole drive. Jeanne wept into her handkerchief, while Paul looked out of the window with an air of unconcern. During the week it was discovered that the debts he had made in the last few months amounted to fifteen thousand francs. Aware that he would shortly come of age, the creditors had as yet made no sign. No explanations were asked or given. An attempt was to be made to win him back by gentle means. Delicacies were set before him; he was petted and spoilt. It was spring. In spite of Jeanne's nervousness, a boat was hired for him at Yport, so that he could go sailing as much as he pleased. He was not allowed a horse, in case he should ride over to Havre. But he remained idle, irritable, and sometimes surly. The Baron was troubled about his unfinished studies. Even Jeanne, miserable though she was at the idea of another parting, wondered what they were to do with him. One evening he did not return home, and they heard that he had gone out in a boat with two sailors. His distracted mother ran bare-headed through the night to Yport. There were some men on the quay waiting for the boat to return. Out at sea a small, swaying light appeared, and came close in. But Paul was not on board; he had had himself landed at Havre.

Search as they might, the police could find no trace of him. The woman who had hidden him on the occasion of his first disappearance had likewise vanished, leaving no clue. The furniture had been sold and the rent paid. In Paul's room at *Les Peuples* two of the creature's letters were found from which it was evident that she was madly in love with him. She spoke of a journey to England and said that she had raised the necessary funds.

The three occupants of *Les Peuples* dwelt in dismal silence in a gloomy inferno of mental torture. Jeanne's hair, prematurely grey, now turned white. She asked herself ingenuously why Fate should deal her so heavy a blow. She received a letter from Abbé Tolbiac.

"Madame,

"The hand of God is heavy upon you. You refused to give your child to Him, and for this He has taken him from you and thrown him into the arms of a prostitute. Will you still blind yourself to this admonishment of Heaven? The mercy of the Lord is infinite. Perchance He will forgive you, if you kneel at His feet. I, His humble servant, am ready to open to you the door of His house, as soon as you knock at it."

She sat a long time with this letter in her lap. Perhaps there was truth in what the priest said. And her conscience was torn with religious doubts. Could it be that God was vindictive and jealous like men? Perhaps if He did not show Himself a jealous God, no one would fear Him, no one would worship Him. Doubtless it was in order to make Himself better understood that He displayed Himself to mankind with qualities like their own. Actuated by the cowardly misgivings which impel those in doubt and perplexity churchwards, at dusk one evening she hurried secretly to the parsonage, and, throwing herself on her knees before the gaunt priest, she prayed for absolution. He accorded her a semi-pardon. God, he said, could not pour all His blessings upon a roof which sheltered a man like the Baron. Nevertheless, he assured her, she would soon experience the workings of divine forbearance.

It so happened that, two days later, she received a letter from her son. In her affliction she regarded this as the first of the alleviations promised by the Abbé.

"My dear Mamma,

"Don't worry about me. I am in London and in the best of health, but hard pressed for money. We haven't a penny left and there are days when we have nothing to eat. My companion, whom I love with all my heart, has spent five thousand francs, all she had, for the sake of staying with me. You will understand that I am bound in honour to repay this sum before anything else. It would be very good of you if you would advance me fifteen thousand francs out of Papa's property, as I am almost of age. You would get me out of a very tight corner.

"Good-bye, dear Mamma. I send my best love to you and Grandpapa and Aunt Lison, and I hope to see you again soon.

"Your loving son,

"PAUL DE LAMARE."

He had written. He had not forgotten her. She was not distressed at his demand for money. Money should be despatched, as he had none. What did money matter, when he had sent her a letter? She ran in tears to the Baron with the letter. Aunt Lison was summoned and this scrap of paper, which brought news of him, was read over and over again, word by word. Every phrase of it was discussed. Jeanne, soaring from the depths of despair into a delirium of joy, defended Paul.

"He will come back. He has written, so he is sure to come back."

The Baron, who was less enthusiastic, remarked:

"The fact remains that he left us for that creature. So he cares for her more than he does for us. He did not hesitate between us."

A sharp and terrible pang pierced Jeanne's heart, and suddenly she conceived, against the woman who had stolen her son from her, a fierce, flaming, implacable hatred, the jealous hatred of a mother.

174

Hitherto, wholly obsessed by Paul, she had scarcely given a thought to the hussy, who was at the bottom of all his wild behaviour. But the Baron's remark suddenly conjured up the idea of her rival and brought home to her her fatal power. She felt that a fierce struggle had begun between this woman and herself, and that she would rather lose her son than share him with the other. All her joy lay in ruins.

They sent the fifteen thousand francs, and for five months heard no further news. Then they received a visit from an agent to arrange the details of Julian's inheritance. Jeanne and the Baron made over the accounts to him without any discussion, and even conceded the life interest, which was legally Jeanne's. Paul returned to Paris and received the sum of one hundred and twenty thousand francs. In the next six months he wrote four letters, curt in style and ending with cold protestations of affection.

"I am working on the Stock Exchange," he stated, "and I hope to come and see you, dear Mamma, at *Les Peuples* some day."

He never mentioned his mistress, and this reserve had more significance than if he had written a whole sheet about her. Lurking implacable behind these frigid letters, Jeanne divined the woman, the mistress, who is ever a mother's sworn enemy.

The three lonely people considered what they could do to save Paul, but could think of nothing. A journey to Paris? What was the use of it?

"We must let his passion exhaust itself," advised the Baron, "then he will come back to us of his own accord."

In the meantime their life was deplorably dreary.

Jeanne and Lison went to church together behind the Baron's back. Some little time passed without news. Then, one morning, came a frantic letter which terrified them all.

"My poor dear Mother,

"I am lost. There is nothing for it but to blow my brains out, unless you come to the rescue. A speculation, which had every prospect of success, has failed, and I owe eighty-five thousand francs. If I do not pay this debt I shall be ruined and dishonoured, and my future will be blasted. I am lost. As I said before, I will blow my brains out rather than endure such disgrace. Probably I should have done so already had it not been for the encouragement of a woman who, though I never mention her, has been my guardian angel.

"I send you my fondest love, my dear Mamma, perhaps for the last time. Farewell.

"PAUL."

With this letter were enclosed bundles of business papers, which gave detailed explanations of the disaster. The Baron replied by return of post that suitable measures would be considered. Then he went to Havre to make enquiries, and he mortgaged some land to raise the money to send Paul. Paul replied with three letters of rapturous gratitude and passionate affection, and announced his intention of paying an immediate visit to his dear people. But he never came, and a whole year passed away.

Jeanne and the Baron were on the point of setting out for Paris to find him and to make one last attempt to win him back when they received a brief note to say that he was in London again, promoting an enterprise in steam packet boats, under the business name of Paul Delamare & Company.

"It means a competency and perhaps wealth, and I am risking nothing. This will give you some idea of the advantages of the scheme. When we meet again I shall have made a good position for myself in the world. There is nothing like business, nowadays, for extricating oneself from difficulties."

Three months later the steamboat company failed, and the director was prosecuted for irregularities in his accounts. Jeanne had an attack of nerves, which lasted several hours; then she took to her bed.

The Baron paid another visit to Havre, interviewed barristers, business men, solicitors and bailiffs, and verified that the deficit of the Delamare Company amounted to two hundred and thirty-five thousand francs. Again he mortgaged some more of his property, namely, *Les Peuples* and the two farms, for a large sum.

But one evening, as he was completing the final formalities in the lawyer's office, he fell on the floor in a fit of apoplexy. A man on horseback was despatched to Jeanne with the news. When she arrived at Havre he was dead. She brought the body back to *Les Peuples*. She was so utterly prostrated by this blow that she felt stunned rather than desperate.

In spite of the passionate entreaties of the two women, Abbé Tolbiac refused to admit the body into the church. The Baron was buried at nightfall without any rites whatever.

Paul heard of the Baron's death through one of the liquidators while he was still in England in hiding. He wrote to apologise for his absence; he had not heard of the calamity till it was too late.

"However, my dear Mamma, as you have rescued me from my predicament, I am returning to France and shall soon come to see you."

Jeanne was in such a state of depression that she seemed to have lost interest in everything.

Towards the end of the winter Aunt Lison, who was now sixty-eight, had an attack of bronchitis which developed into pneumonia. She expired peacefully, sighing:

"My poor little Jeanne, I shall ask God to take pity on you."

Jeanne followed her bier to the cemetery, watched the earth fall upon the coffin, and just as she was swooning away, in her yearning for death, for an end to sorrow and thought, a buxom peasant woman caught her in her arms and carried her home as if she had been a child.

When they reached the house Jeanne, who had spent the last five nights by her aunt's couch, passively allowed this unknown peasant woman, who treated her with gentle authority, to put her to bed. Worn out with weariness and grief she fell into a sleep of exhaustion. Towards midnight she awoke. A night-light was burning on the mantelpiece and she saw a woman asleep in an armchair. Who was she? Jeanne did not recognise her, and leaning out of bed she endeavoured to make out her features in the flickering light of the wick, which was floating in oil in a kitchen tumbler. She thought she had seen her face before. But when and where? The woman was sleeping peacefully, with her head on her shoulder, and her cap on the floor. She might be forty or forty-five. She was stout, of ruddy complexion, squarely built and powerful. Her large hands hung down on either side of the chair. Her hair was turning grey. Jeanne looked at her fixedly in that uneasiness of mind in which one wakes from the feverish sleep that succeeds a deep sorrow.

She was sure she had seen that face before. But was it long ago or recently? She did not know, and this obsession troubled and unnerved her. Softly she crept out of bed and tiptoed up to look at the sleeper. It was the same woman who, she vaguely remembered, had raised her in her arms at the cemetery and had put her to bed.

But had she really met her elsewhere at some earlier stage of her existence? Or was she merely haunted by some vague recollection of the preceding day? And how did she come to be in her room? And why?

The woman opened her eyes, caught sight of Jeanne and sat up suddenly. They were face to face, so close that their bosoms touched.

"What are you doing out of bed?" scolded the stranger. "You'll catch your death at this time of night. Go back to bed, will you?"

"Who are you?" asked Jeanne.

But the other clasped Jeanne in her arms, picked her up, and carried her back to bed, with all the strength of a man. Then, as she laid her down on the sheets, leaning, almost lying, upon her, she burst into weeping, frantically kissing Jeanne's cheeks and hair and eyes, and bathing her face with tears.

"My poor mistress, Miss Jeanne, my poor mistress! Don't you recognise me?"

"Rosalie, my child," exclaimed Jeanne, and throwing both arms round her neck she hugged and kissed her. And they clung together sobbing, mingling their tears, each loath to let the other go. Rosalie was the first to regain her composure.

"Come," she said, "we must be sensible and not catch cold."

And she picked up the blankets, smoothed the bed, and replaced the pillow beneath Jeanne's head. But Jeanne continued to choke with emotion, quivering with old memories that surged anew within her soul. At last she asked:

"How did you come here, my poor child?"

"Good Heavens," replied Rosalie, "do you think I'd leave you all alone as you are now?"

"Light the candle," replied Jeanne, "and let me look at you."

When the light had been placed on the table by the bedside they gazed long and silently at each other. Then Jeanne held out her hand to her old servant and murmured:

"I should never have recognised you, child, you have changed a great deal, you know, but not as much as I have."

Rosalie looked at the thin-faced, white-haired woman, whom she had left young and pretty and fresh.

"It's true that you have changed, Madame Jeanne, and more

than you ought to have. But you must remember that it is twenty-four years since we met."

They were silent, each busy with her own thoughts. At last Jeanne murmured,

"But you, at least, have been happy?"

Rosalie, fearing to arouse memories unduly painful, said halt-ingly, "Why, yes, Ma'am. I have not had much to complain of. I have had a happier life than you, to be sure. Only, one thing has always weighed on me. It is that I didn't stay here."

Then she suddenly broke off, in concern at having involuntarily touched on the very subject she wished to avoid. Jeanne, however, replied gently:

"What would you have, my child? One can't always do as one pleases. You are a widow, too, are you not?"

Then, in a voice trembling with painful emotion, she asked:

"Did you . . . did you have any other children?"

"No, Ma'am."

"And your son . . . what has become of him? Are you pleased with him?"

"Yes, Ma'am. He is a good lad, who puts his back into his work. He got married six months ago, and he will take over my farm now that I have come back to you."

"Then you'll never leave me again?" whispered Jeanne, quiver-ing with emotion.

"Certainly not, Ma'am," said Rosalie in a resolute voice, "I have made my arrangements accordingly."

There was a prolonged silence.

In spite of herself, Jeanne found herself comparing their two lives. But she felt no bitterness; she was resigned now to the cruel injus-tice of fate.

"How did your husband treat you?" she asked.

"Oh, he was a good fellow, with no humbug about him, Ma'am, and he knew how to put by a little. He died of consumption."

Jeanne sat up in bed. She longed to hear the whole story.

"Come, tell me everything, Rosalie, all about your life. It will do me good."

Rosalie drew up a chair and sat down and began to talk about herself, her house, her little world, entering into all the minute details in which country people delight, describing her farmyard, and laughing sometimes at old memories of past moments of happiness, and gradually raising her voice to the loud tones of a bustling farmer's wife. "I have my little bit of property now. I'm not afraid." Then she added softly, and with compunction, "It's to you I owe all this. And you must know I won't take wages from you. I won't. Indeed, I won't. If you won't agree to that I'm off."

"But you really can't give your services for nothing," Jeanne protested.

"Why not, Ma'am? Money! Take money from you? Why, I have about as much as you have. Do you know how much you have left, after all the tomfoolery about mortgaging and borrowing, with the interest unpaid and mounting up year by year? You haven't the least idea, have you? Well, I assure you that your income doesn't amount to as much as ten thousand francs. Not ten thousand francs even, believe me. But I shall see to all that, and as soon as possible."

She had raised her voice again. She spoke heatedly, indignant at the thought of her mistress's neglected interests and the ruin that menaced her. As a faint smile flitted over Jeanne's face Rosalie exclaimed resentfully:

"It's nothing to laugh at, Ma'am; without money one's nothing but a vagabond."

Jeanne seized her hands again and held them. Then, still obsessed by one fixed idea, she said deliberately:

"Oh, I have never had any luck. Everything has gone badly with me. Fate has been against me all along."

But Rosalie shook her head.

"You mustn't say that, Ma'am. You mustn't say that. You made a bad marriage, that's the whole secret. One has no business to marry without knowing anything about one's husband."

Then she went on discussing their concerns, like two old friends. At sunrise they were still talking.

12

IN a week's time Rosalie had taken complete charge of the entire household. Jeanne resigned herself and did as she was told. Feeble in body, dragging her feet just as her mother used to do, she went for walks leaning on the arm of her maid, who led her slowly along, lecturing her, cheering her with curt but kindly words and treating her like a sick child.

They were always talking of the past, Jeanne with a lump in her throat, Rosalie with a peasant's solid composure. The old servant returned on several occasions to the question of the interest that was due. Then she insisted on taking over the documents, which Jeanne, who knew nothing of business, had been hiding from her, out of shame on her son's behalf.

Rosalie spent a week in daily visits to Fécamp, having matters explained to her by a notary of her acquaintance.

One evening, after she had put her mistress to bed, she sat down beside her and said abruptly:

"Now that you are in bed, Ma'am, we will have a talk."

And she made the situation clear to her.

After all obligations had been settled Jeanne would have an income of seven or eight thousand francs. That was all.

"What does it matter?" replied Jeanne. "I know I shall never make old bones. There is enough for me."

But Rosalie was indignant.

"Possibly for you, Ma'am. But what about Monsieur Paul? Do you intend to leave him nothing?"

Jeanne shuddered.

"For Heaven's sake don't talk about him. It's such agony to think about him."

"On the contrary, that's exactly what I'm going to do, Ma'am, because you have no courage. He is sowing his wild oats, but he won't do so always. Some day he will get married and have children. He will need money for their education. Now, listen to me. You must sell *Les Peuples.*"

Jeanne started up in bed.

"Sell *Les Peuples?* What are you thinking of? Never. Not for anything in the world."

Rosalie remained unperturbed.

"I tell you, Ma'am, you have no choice. It is absolutely necessary."

She expounded her calculations and plans, giving reasons for everything. After the sale of *Les Peuples* and the two adjoining farms, for which she had found a purchaser, there would remain four farms at Saint Leonard, which, freed from their mortgages, would bring in an income of eight thousand three hundred francs. Thirteen hundred francs would be put aside for keeping up the property, leaving seven thousand francs, of which five thousand would be devoted to current expenses, while the remaining two thousand would form an emergency fund.

"Everything else has been run through. I warn you that I shall keep the purse strings, and as for Monsieur Paul, he shan't have another penny, not a penny. He wouldn't leave you a farthing."

Jeanne, who was silently weeping, murmured,

"But suppose he is starving?"

"If he is hungry, he can come to us. There will always be a bed, and a knife and fork for him. Do you suppose he would have played the fool like this if you had refused to give him a penny right from the beginning?"

"But he had made debts. He would have been disgraced."

"When you've nothing left, will that stop him from getting into debt? You have paid up for him. Very good. But you shan't do it again, I shall see to that. And, now, good-night, Ma'am."

She went away.

Jeanne could not sleep. She was in despair at the idea of selling *Les Peuples*, at having to leave the house with which every moment of her life had been linked.

The next morning, when Rosalie entered her room, she said:

"Rosalie, my dear, I shall never be able to tear myself away from here."

"You'll have to, all the same, Ma'am," said the servant sourly. "The notary is coming here presently with the person who wants to buy the property. If you don't sell, in four years' time you won't own a blade of grass."

Jeanne remained prostrate, murmuring again and again:

"I can't, I can't."

An hour later the postman brought her a letter from Paul with a request for another ten thousand francs. What was to be done? In despair she consulted Rosalie, who threw up her hands.

"What did I tell you, Ma'am? There would have been a nice pair of you if I hadn't come to the rescue."

Yielding to her servant's domination, Jeanne sent Paul the following reply.

"My dear Son,
    "I can do no more for you. You have ruined me; I find myself actually forced to sell *Les Peuples*. But do not forget that you will always find a refuge with your old mother, to whom you have brought so much sorrow.
                                        "JEANNE."

When the notary arrived with Monsieur Jeoffrin, a retired sugar refiner, she received them in person, and invited them to inspect the whole property in detail. A month later she signed the deed of sale, and at the same time bought a small, middle-class house near Goderville, on the highroad to Montivilliers, in the village of Batteville.

After this transaction she wandered all alone till evening in the Baroness's avenue. Heart-broken, in agony of mind, she took a despairing and tearful farewell of all those intimate things which seemed to possess her eyes and soul, the distant prospect, the trees, the worm-eaten bench beneath the plane trees, the little wood, and that bank overlooking the moor where she had sat so often, and whence she had seen Count de Fourville running towards the sea on that terrible day of Julian's death, the old pollarded elm against which she used to lean, the garden she knew so well.

Rosalie came and took her by the arm and forced her away.

A tall peasant, about twenty-five years of age, was waiting at the door. He greeted her in friendly tones, as if he had known her a long time.

"Good-evening, Ma'am. I hope you are well. My mother told me to come about the removal. I want to know what you are going to take with you, so that I can cart it at odd times, without interfering with the farm work."

He was Rosalie's son, Julian's son, Paul's brother. Her heart stood still for a moment, and yet she had an impulse to kiss him. She gazed at him, seeking a resemblance to her husband and her own son. He was ruddy and strong, with his mother's fair hair and blue eyes. And yet he bore a likeness to Julian. In what did this likeness consist? She hardly knew, but there was something of Julian in the general cast of his features.

"If you could show me now," the young fellow continued, "I should be much obliged."

Her new house was very small and she had not decided yet what she would take with her. She asked him to come back at the end of the week. During the following days she was fully occupied with the business of the removal, which lent a melancholy interest to her life of hopeless dreariness. She went from room to room choosing such pieces of furniture as recalled incidents of the past. In process of time chairs and tables become friends to us, part of our lives, almost of our persons, familiar to us from childhood; they record memories of joys or sorrows, dates in our private chronicles; they have been the silent companions of bright and gloomy hours, and before our eyes they have grown old and worn, their covers rent, their linings torn, their joints infirm, their hues faded.

She made her selection slowly and hesitatingly, perplexed, as if confronted by some momentous question. She was continually reversing her decisions, weighing the merits of two armchairs, or balancing the claims of an old writing desk against those of some ancient work table. She would open drawers in an effort to conjure up some bygone memory. When she had at last made up her mind the article selected was removed to the dining-room. She proposed to keep all the furniture in her own room, bed, tapestries, clock, and everything. She chose some of the drawing-room chairs, with the designs that had been her favourites from early infancy; the fox and the stork, the fox and the crow, the cricket and the ant and the melancholy heron. One day, in the course of her roamings through all the corners of the home she was so soon to leave, she went up to the attic. She was struck with amazement. It contained a medley of things of every description, some broken, some merely soiled, some that had been relegated there for no particular reason, simply because they had fallen out of favour, or had been replaced. She recognised a thousand knickknacks, whose sudden disappearance she had never noticed, trifles that she had handled, little odds and ends, which had been lying about for fifteen years, and which she had seen, unconsciously, every day. Unexpectedly discovered there in the attic, together with other objects even older, whose place in the house she remembered perfectly in the early days of her first home-coming, they suddenly assumed an importance as of witnesses that had been forgotten, as of friends lost and found. They impressed her like old associates who have never revealed their true selves until one evening, for no special reason, they confide, in an unending flow of words, all the unsuspected secrets of their souls. Her heart thrilling with emotion she went from one to the other.

"Oh, here is that Chinese cup I broke one evening a few days before my marriage. This is Mamma's little lantern, and this is the stick Papa broke trying to open the gate when the wood was swollen with rain."

The attic contained, too, much that she had never seen before, and which stirred no memories, objects that had come down from grandparents or great-grandparents. Thick with dust, they had an air of exiles, saddened by neglect, in an age not their own, exiles whose history and associations were forgotten, since no one was left now who had ever seen those who had chosen, bought, owned and loved these discarded treasures, no one who had known the familiar hands and the eyes which they had gladdened.

Jeanne touched them and turned them over, leaving finger-prints on the coating of dust. She lingered among these old relics, in the dim light which fell through a few small squares of glass let into the roof. In the hope that they might stir some memory she examined minutely chairs with only three legs, an old copper warming pan, a dented foot-warmer, which she thought she recognised, and a quantity of worn-out household utensils. At last she made a collection of everything she wished to take away and sent Rosalie up to fetch it. Rosalie refused indignantly to bring down "such rubbish." But Jeanne, who had seemed to have no will of her own, remained firm for once, and Rosalie had to obey.

One morning Denis Lecoq, the young farmer, Julian's son, came with his cart for the first load. Rosalie accompanied him to superintend the unloading and to see that the furniture was properly arranged.

When she was alone, Jeanne wandered again through the house in a terrible paroxysm of despair, kissing in an access of passionate affection everything she could not take away with her, the great white birds in the drawing-room tapestry, old candlesticks, whatever she happened to come across. With tears pouring down her cheeks she roamed distractedly from room to room. Then she went out to bid farewell to the sea. It was towards the end of September. A grey lowering sky seemed to weigh upon the earth. The drear expanse of livid waves stretched away out of sight. She stood a long time on the cliff, revolving thoughts that tortured her. At nightfall she returned to the house, after a day of suffering as severe as she had experienced in her greatest afflictions.

Rosalie had returned and was waiting for her. She was delighted with the new house, and remarked that it was far more cheerful than this great box of a place, which was not even close to a road. Jeanne spent the whole evening in tears.

As soon as they knew the house was sold the farmers showed Jeanne no more respect than they thought due to her. Among themselves they referred to her as the Mad Lady, hardly knowing why. Doubtless their ruder instincts led them to divine her morbid and increasing sentimentality, her overheated imagination, and all the confusion of her stricken soul.

On the eve of her departure she happened to enter the stable and was startled by a sudden growl. She saw Massacre of whom she had not thought for months. Blind and paralysed, of an age to which dogs rarely attain, he lingered on. He lay on a litter of straw and was cared for by Ludivine, who never forgot him. Jeanne clasped him in her arms and kissed him and carried him into the house. Round as a barrel, he could hardly drag himself along on his stiff straddling legs, and he barked like a child's toy dog.

The day of their departure arrived. Jeanne, whose own room was dismantled, had slept in Julian's old room. When she rose from her bed she was exhausted and panted as if she had been running. A waggon loaded with the trunks and the rest of the furniture was standing in the courtyard. Behind it a two-wheeled trap was made ready for mistress and maid.

Old Simon and Ludivine were to stay on at *Les Peuples* by themselves until the arrival of the new owner. Then they intended to retire and live with their relations. Jeanne had provided them with a small annuity, and they had their savings. They were very old

and garrulous now and past work. Marius had married and left long ago.

Towards eight o'clock rain set in, an icy drizzle, drifting in from the sea, and the cart had to be covered over. The trees were already shedding their leaves.

Steaming cups of coffee and milk stood on the kitchen table. Jeanne sat down and drank her cup slowly. Then she rose.

"Let us go now," she said.

She put on her hat and shawl, and while Rosalie fastened on her galoshes for her, she said in a choking voice:

"Do you remember, Rosalie, how it rained that day when we left Rouen to come here?"

She was seized with a spasm, clasped her hands to her bosom and fell back unconscious. For more than an hour she remained as if she were dead. Then she opened her eyes, and went into convulsions and floods of tears. When she grew calmer, she was so completely exhausted that she could not even rise to her feet. Rosalie, however, in dread of fresh attacks, if the departure were postponed, went to fetch her son. They pleaded with her, lifted her up, and carried her to the trap and deposited her on the wooden, waxcloth-covered seat. Rosalie climbed up beside Jeanne, spread a wrap over her mistress's knees, threw a big cloak round her shoulders and held an umbrella over her head.

"Quick, Denis, let's be off," she cried.

The young farmer jumped up beside his mother, making the most of the small space left, and urged his horse into a fast trot, which jolted the two women.

Turning out of the village they saw a figure walking up and down the road. It was Abbé Tolbiac, who seemed to be lying in wait for their departure. He halted to allow the carriage to pass. With one hand he held his cassock out of the way of the wet road, revealing lean, black-stockinged legs which ended in enormous muddy shoes.

Jeanne lowered her eyes to avoid his glance, but Rosalie, who was aware of everything that had happened, flew into a rage.

"Brute," she ejaculated, "brute." Clutching her son's arm she exclaimed, "Fetch him one with your whip."

But just as they were passing the priest the young farmer drove the wheel of his old rattle-trap as fast and as violently as he could through the mire, and a jet of mud spirted up and covered the priest from head to foot. Rosalie, highly delighted, turned round and shook her fist at him, while the Abbé wiped himself down with his large handkerchief.

They had been five minutes on the way when Jeanne suddenly remembered Massacre. They stopped and Denis got down and ran back for the dog, while Rosalie held the reins. Presently he returned with the fat, shapeless, almost hairless animal in his arms, and placed him between the women's skirts.

13

TWO hours later the trap drew up in front of a small brick house standing in a garden planted with clipped pear trees, close to the highroad. A trellised arbour, overgrown with honeysuckle and clematis, stood at each of the four corners of the garden, which was arranged in little squares of vegetables, separated by narrow paths bordered with fruit trees.

The property, which was divided by a field from the neighbouring farm, was entirely surrounded by a high hedge. A hundred feet further along the road was a smithy. There were no other dwellings within half a mile. The house commanded an extensive view of the flat country of Caux, with its sprinkling of farms, each in its apple orchard, enclosed by double rows of tall trees.

As soon as Jeanne arrived she wanted to rest, but Rosalie, fearing that she would relapse into her reveries, would not hear of it. A carpenter from Goderville had come to settle them in, and they at once set to work to arrange the furniture, which had already been brought while they waited for the arrival of the last cart. This task involved much labour, thought and discussion. In an hour's time the cart appeared at the gate and had to be unloaded in the rain. By the evening the house was in a state of complete chaos, full of articles in haphazard heaps, and Jeanne was so weary that she fell asleep as soon as she was in bed.

The next few days she found herself overwhelmed with work and had no time for regrets. She even took a certain pleasure in making her new home attractive, for she was always haunted by the idea that her son would return to her there. The tapestries that used to be in her bedroom were hung in the dining-room, which also did duty for a drawing-room. She took special pains with the arrangement of one of the two rooms on the first floor, which she secretly thought of as Poulet's. She occupied the other herself, while Rosalie slept in the one above, next to the attic.

The tiny, carefully furnished house was not without charm, and for some time Jeanne was pleased with it, although something she could not define was missing.

One morning the clerk of the notary at Fécamp brought her three thousand six hundred francs, the proceeds of the furniture left at *Les Peuples*, which had been valued by an upholsterer. She felt a thrill of pleasure at receiving this money, and as soon as the man left her she hastily put on her hat, intending to walk to Goderville as quickly as possible in order to send this windfall to Paul. But as she was hurrying along the highroad she met Rosalie coming back from market. The maid had her suspicions, although she did not hit upon the truth immediately. But Jeanne could conceal nothing from her, and when she had discovered her mistress's intention, she put down her basket, to give free rein to her indignation. She placed her hands on her hips and shouted. Then, seizing her mistress with her right hand and the basket with her left, and still in a passion, she continued her way towards the house. As soon as they were indoors Rosalie demanded the money. Jeanne handed over all but six hundred francs, but the suspicious Rosalie saw through this deceit, and she was obliged to surrender the entire sum. In the end, however, Rosalie agreed that the odd hundreds should be sent to Paul.

In a few days' time she received a letter of thanks.

"My dear Mamma, you have done me a real service. We were in great distress."

Jeanne, however, could not reconcile herself to Batteville. She felt that she could not breathe there, that she was lonelier, more forlorn, more desolate than ever. She would take a walk as far as the village of Verneuil and come back by Trois-Mares. As soon as she returned home she would leave her chair, feeling impelled to go out again, as if she had forgotten to visit the one spot to which her duty and her desire urged her. Every day she had the same, inexplicable sensation. But one evening a chance remark revealed to her the secret of her restlessness.

As she sat down to dinner she exclaimed:

"Oh, how I long for a sight of the sea!"

It was the sea that she missed so intensely, the sea, for twenty-five years her mighty neighbour, the sea with its salt breath, its passions, its angry voice, its strong winds, the sea which she had viewed every morning from her window at *Les Peuples*. Night and day she had breathed its saltness and felt its nearness till all unconsciously she had grown to love it, as one loves a human being.

Massacre, too, showed a similar uneasiness. On the evening of their arrival he had established himself in the bottom of the kitchen cupboard and refused to budge. He remained there all day long, scarcely moving, merely turning over now and then with a low growl. But as soon as it grew dark he got up and dragged himself to the garden gate, creeping close to the walls. After he had been out a few minutes he would return to the house, sit down on his haunches before the kitchen range, which still threw out some heat, and as soon as his two mistresses had gone to bed he would begin to howl. All night long he howled in a mournful, lugubrious way, occasionally pausing for an hour, only to begin again in still more piercing tones. Jeanne had him chained up in a barrel outside the house, but he merely howled under her windows, and as he was feeble and near his end, he was restored to the kitchen. He banished sleep from Jeanne, who heard the old dog ceaselessly groaning and scratching, and trying to adapt himself to this new abode, where he did not feel at home. Nothing soothed him. He spent the day in a torpor, as if his failing sight and his sense of his infirmities prevented him from stirring abroad at a time when all other creatures were alert and active. But at nightfall he would roam restlessly, as if he only ventured to live and move in darkness when all living things were blind. One morning, to Jeanne's great relief, he was found dead.

Winter drew on and Jeanne fell into a mood of deep despondency. It was not an agony of the soul that tortured her but a profound and dismal melancholy. There was nothing to rouse her. No one took an interest in her. Before her door lay the highroad, stretching away to left and right, and almost always deserted. Now and then a gig went by at a trot, driven by a red-faced man whose smock was blown back and puffed out behind like a blue balloon. Sometimes a cart moved slowly along, sometimes a pair of peasants, man and wife, could be discerned, tiny figures in the distance, slowly increasing in size until they passed the house, and gradually dwindling again to the proportions of insects till they reached the far end of the white line, which ran on and on out of sight, rising and falling with the gently undulating ground. When the grass began to grow again a little girl in short petticoats passed the gate every morning, driving two lean cows which grazed in the ditches by the wayside. Every evening she returned home, with the same dreary gait, taking one step every ten minutes behind her cattle.

Each night Jeanne dreamed that she was living at *Les Peuples* as in the old days, with her father and mother, and sometimes even Aunt Lison. Old and forgotten incidents returned to her mind, and she dreamed that the Baroness was with her in the avenue leaning on her arm. And always when she awoke she wept.

Paul was continually in her thoughts.

"What is he doing?" she wondered. "How is he? Does he ever think of me?"

As she wandered slowly about the sunk roads between the farms she revolved in her mind all these agonising thoughts. Above all, she suffered torments of implacable jealousy against the unknown woman who had robbed her of her son. It was this hatred alone which held her back and prevented her from taking action, from going to him and seeking him out in his dwelling. She seemed to see his mistress standing on the threshold and demanding:

"What is your business here, Madame?"

Her maternal pride revolted against the possibility of such an encounter. She had all the haughty disdain of a pure woman, free from stain or weakness, a steadily increasing disgust for the baseness of a man enslaved by all the ignoble devices of sensual love, which degrades the very heart. All humanity seemed to her unclean, as she thought of all the indecorous secrets of the senses, degrading caresses, all the surmised mysteries of sexual union.

Spring and summer went past. But when autumn returned with its continuous rain, grey skies, and heavy clouds, she grew utterly weary of this existence, and resolved to make a great effort to win Paul back. By this time the boy's passion must have worn itself out.

She wrote him a despairing letter.

"My dear boy,

"I beseech you to come back to me. You must have realised that I am old and ill, and am living all alone with a maid the whole year round. I am now occupying a small house by the roadside. It is very dreary. But if only you were here everything would be changed for me. I have no one in the world but you, and I have not seen you for seven years. You will never know what I have suffered and what a solace you used to be to me. You were my life, my dream, my only hope, my only love; you have deserted me and I miss you.

"Oh, come back to me, my little Poulet, come back and embrace me. Come back to the arms of your broken-hearted old mother,

"JEANNE."

A few days later she received his reply.

"My dear Mamma,

"I should be only too glad to pay you a visit but I haven't a penny. Send me some money and I'll come. I had intended to come and see you, to tell you of a plan which would enable me to do what you ask. There are no bounds to the disinterested affection of the woman who has been my companion in these bad times. I can no longer refrain from acknowledging publicly such faithful love and devotion. I may add that she has excellent manners, which would appeal to you. She is very well informed and reads a great deal. You cannot imagine all that she has been to me. I should be a brute if I did not give her proof of my gratitude. I therefore ask your permission to marry her. If you would forgive me my past escapades we might all live together in your new house.

"If you knew her you would give your consent at once. I assure you she is perfection and has real distinction. I am sure you would love her. As for me I could not live without her.

"I shall look forward to your reply impatiently, my dear Mamma.

"With fondest love from us both.

"Your affectionate son,

"PAUL DE LAMARE."

Jeanne was thunderstruck. She remained motionless with the letter on her knees. She divined the subtle intentions of this woman who had kept her son from her, who had not allowed him to pay her even a single visit, but had bided her time, awaiting the moment when the broken-hearted mother could no longer resist her yearning for her son's embrace, and would weaken and yield on all points. Her heart was rent by the bitter pain which Paul's obstinate preference for that creature caused her.

"He does not love me," she repeated again and again, "he does not love me."

Rosalie came in.

"He wants to marry her now," faltered Jeanne.

The maid gave a jump.

"Oh, Ma'am, but you'll never allow that. Monsieur Paul can't tie himself up with that baggage."

Overwhelmed though she was Jeanne protested in horror. "No, I will never consent to such a thing. And as he won't come home, I shall go to him, and we shall see which of us will triumph, she or I."

She wrote at once to Paul, announcing her visit, and asking for an interview in some place, other than that hussy's domicile. While she was waiting for his reply she began her preparations for the journey. Rosalie set to work to pack her mistress's clothes and underlinen in an old trunk. But as she was folding a gown, an old countrified garment, she suddenly exclaimed:

"You haven't a thing to put on your back. I can't allow you to go away like that. Everyone would be ashamed of you. The ladies in Paris would look down on you, as if you were a servant."

Jeanne gave way to her. The two women went together to Goderville and chose a green check which was entrusted to a dressmaker in the market town. Then they paid a visit to the notary, Maître Roussel, to ask his advice. He spent a fortnight every year in the capital, whereas Jeanne had not been in Paris for twenty-eight years. He gave her many instructions as to how to get out of the way of traffic and to avoid being robbed, and advised her to sew her money into the lining of her clothes, and to keep only a minimum in her pocket. He spoke at great length on the subject of moderate-priced restaurants, and gave her the names of one or two which women could frequent. Finally, he recommended to her the Hotel de Normandie, where he himself stayed, close to the railway station. She could mention his name there.

For the last six years the much discussed railway had been open between Paris and Havre. But Jeanne, obsessed by her sorrows, had not so much as seen one of these steam coaches, which were revolutionising the whole country.

No answer, however, came from Paul. She waited a week, a fortnight. Every morning she went along the road to meet old Malandain, the postman.

"Have you nothing for me?" she would ask him, in trembling tones.

"Nothing yet, lady," he invariably replied, in a voice roughened by exposure in all weathers.

Doubtless it was that woman who was preventing Paul from answering.

At last Jeanne made up her mind to go to Paris at once. She wanted to take Rosalie with her, but the maid refused to accompany her for fear of adding to the expenses of the journey. Moreover, she would not allow her mistress to take with her more than three hundred francs.

"If you want more," she said, "you can always write to me, and I will get the notary to send it to you. If I give you any more Monsieur Paul will pocket it."

One December morning they climbed into Denis Lecoq's trap which was to take them to the station, Rosalie accompanying her mistress on this first stage of her travels. First they asked the price of tickets. When everything was in order, and the trunk registered, they stood looking at the iron rails trying to understand how the thing worked, and so much engrossed in its mysteries that they forgot the painful reasons for the journey.

A distant whistle made them turn their heads, and they caught sight of a black engine, which grew larger and larger, till it thundered into the station and clanked past them, dragging a long chain of small houses on wheels. A guard opened a door and Jeanne kissed Rosalie tearfully and climbed into one of the little huts.

Much affected, Rosalie cried:

"Good-bye, Ma'am, a pleasant journey, and come back soon."

There was another whistle, and the whole string of carriages began to glide out of the station, slowly at first, then faster and faster, until it attained a terrifying speed.

There were two gentlemen in Jeanne's carriage, each fast asleep in his corner. She watched fields, trees, farms and villages go past. She was frightened at the rapidity at which she was travelling, and felt herself in the grip of a new existence. It seemed to her as if she were being borne away to a new world, not her own, a world alien from that of her tranquil youth, and of her present monotonous days.

It was evening when the train reached Paris. A porter took Jeanne's trunk. Frightened and jostled, she awkwardly made her way after him through the moving throng, almost running in fear of losing sight of him.

In the office of the hotel she lost no time in announcing:

"I have come here on Monsieur Roussel's recommendation."

"Monsieur Roussel? Who is that?" asked the landlady, an enormous woman of solemn aspect, who was seated at her writing table.

"Why, the notary from Goderville," replied Jeanne in confusion, "who stays here every year."

"Possibly," conceded the stout lady, "but I don't remember him. Do you want a room?"

"Yes, please."

A waiter took the luggage and preceded her upstairs.

With a heavy heart she seated herself at a small table and ordered soup and a wing of chicken. She had had no food since the early morning. She took her melancholy meal by the light of a single candle, her mind busy with many thoughts. She recalled her flying visit to Paris on her return from her honeymoon, and how the first glimpses of the real Julian had been revealed to her during their stay in that city. But in those days she was young and full of hope and courage. Now she felt that she was old, harassed, timid, weak and perturbed by the merest trifles. After her meal she went to the window and looked out upon the crowded street. She wanted to go out, but did not venture. She felt sure that she would get lost. So she went to bed and blew out her light.

But the noise, the feeling of strangeness in an unknown town, and the excitement of the journey kept her wakeful. Hour after hour went by. Gradually the sounds in the streets died down, but still she could not sleep. Her nerves were affected by the incompleteness of the nightly repose of the great cities. Accustomed to the calm deep slumber of the country, which casts its spell upon men, animals, and plants, she was conscious of a mysterious restlessness all around her. Voices almost inaudible reached her ear as if they had filtered through the walls of the hotel. Sometimes she heard a board creak, a door open, or a bell ring.

About two in the morning, just as she was falling asleep, a woman suddenly began to shriek in an adjoining room. Jeanne started up in bed, and she thought she heard a man's laughter.

198

Towards morning she became more and more obsessed with the idea of Paul. As soon as it was dawn she rose and dressed.

He lived in the Rue du Sauvage, in the City. In obedience to Rosalie's injunctions of economy, she intended to make her way there on foot. It was a fine day. Her skin tingled with the cold air. Busy people were hurrying along the pavements. She walked as fast as she could down a street which had been pointed out to her. At the end of the street she was to turn first to the right and then to the left. Then she would come to a square and here she was to ask again. But she could not find the square, and consulted a baker, who gave her various directions. She wandered on, missed her bearings and went astray, took further advice, and in the end lost herself completely.

Utterly bewildered, she walked on almost at random. At last, just as she had decided to hail a cab, she caught sight of the Seine, and she proceeded along the quay. After about an hour she entered the Rue du Sauvage, a narrow, gloomy side street. Outside the door of Paul's dwelling she stood still in such a state of agitation that she could not take another step.

Poulet was there, in that very house.

Her knees and hands were trembling. At last she entered the house and at the end of a passage she found the porter's lodge. She held out a coin.

"Could you go up and tell Monsieur Paul de Lamare that an old lady, a friend of his mother's, is waiting for him downstairs?"

"He doesn't live her now, Ma'am," replied the porter.

She shuddered violently.

"But where . . . where does he live now?" she stammered.

"I don't know."

She felt ready to swoon, and for some little time she could not speak. At last, with a violent effort, she controlled her faculties.

"When did he go away?" she faltered.

The man gave her full details.

"A fortnight ago. They went off all of a sudden one evening, and never came back. They owed money all over the place, so as you can imagine they left no address."

Lights danced before Jeanne's sight, vivid flashes of flame, as if someone were firing a gun close to her eyes. But she was fortified by her fixed idea, and stood there outwardly calm and collected. She wanted information which would enable her to find Poulet.

"Then he did not say anything when he went away?"

"No, nothing at all. You see, they ran away so that they shouldn't have to pay up."

"But he must have sent someone for his letters?"

"About as likely as my letting him have them. Besides they didn't get ten letters a year. But I did take one up to them two days before they left."

Doubtless he referred to her own letter.

"Listen," she said impulsively. "I am his mother, and I have come to find him. Here are ten francs for you. If you have any news or information about him send me word at the Hotel de Normandie, Rue du Havre, and I will pay you well."

"You can depend on me, Ma'am," he replied.

Then she made her escape. Without thinking where she was going, she hurried along as if on urgent business. She pressed close to the wall and was jostled by people carrying parcels. She crossed roads without regard for the traffic, and was abused by the drivers; she stumbled blindly over the curbstones and, utterly distracted, hastened on and on. Suddenly she found that she had entered a garden and she felt so weary that she collapsed on a bench. There she remained for what seemed a long time, unconscious of the tears that were rolling down her cheeks, and of the passers-by who stopped to look at her. Presently she felt very cold, and rose from her seat to walk on. She was so utterly crushed and exhausted that her legs could hardly carry her.

She wanted to have some soup, but she shrank from entering a restaurant. She felt that the signs of her grief were too evident, and she was restrained by a nervous feeling of shame and embarrassment. She stopped for a moment outside the door, and looked in at all the people seated at table. But her courage failed her and she passed on, saying to herself:

"I will go into the next one." But at the next restaurant the same thing happened.

At last she bought at a baker's a small crescent shaped roll, which she ate as she went along. She was very thirsty but did not know where to go for something to drink, so she went without. She passed under an archway and entered some gardens, surrounded by ar-

cades. She recognised the Palais Royal. Somewhat warmed by the
sun and the exercise, she sat down for another couple of hours.
Presently the gardens were invaded by a fashionable throng, talking, laughing, bowing, the happy throng whose women are always
handsome, whose men are always rich, the throng that lives entirely
for dress and pleasure.

In consternation at this brilliant gathering Jeanne rose to make
her escape. Suddenly it occurred to her that she might perhaps find
Paul here, and she roamed backwards and forwards, with quick
timid steps, from end to end of the gardens, scrutinising all the
faces she saw.

Some of the people turned to look at her; others pointed her out
and laughed. She noticed this and fled from the gardens, supposing
that they were making fun of her green check, which had been
chosen by Rosalie, and made up, according to Rosalie's directions,
by the Goderville dressmaker. She did not even venture to ask the
way of persons in the street. Fortune, however, favoured her, and
eventually she found her hotel. She spent the rest of the day motionless in a chair at the foot of her bed. Then she dined, as on the
previous evening, on soup and a little meat. Afterwards she went to
bed, force of habit prompting her in her usual routine.

The next day she went to the police station to ask the police to
find her son for her. No promise was made, but she was told that
steps would be taken. Then she roamed the streets, still in the hope
of meeting him. But, surrounded as she was by busy crowds, she
felt even more forlorn and desolate than in the deserted fields.

When she returned to the hotel that evening she was told that
a man had asked for her, on behalf of Monsieur Paul, and that
he would come back again the next day. She had a rush of blood
to the heart and did not close her eyes all night.

Supposing it were Paul himself? Surely it must be, although she
would never have recognised him from the description she was given.

Towards nine o'clock the next morning there was a knock at her
door.

"Come in," she cried, ready to dart forward with open arms. A
stranger entered. He apologised for disturbing her, and explained
his business: a debt of Paul's, which he was anxious to recover. She
felt her tears rise, and endeavoured to conceal them, brushing them
away as they welled into her eyes. The man had heard of her visit

203

from the porter at the Rue du Sauvage, and, as he could not discover the son's whereabouts, he addressed himself to the mother. He presented a paper, which she accepted mechanically. She read the figure—ninety francs—took out her purse and paid the bill.

All that day she remained indoors.

The next day, other creditors appeared. She gave them all the money she had left, except twenty francs, and she wrote to Rosalie, explaining her position.

She spent her days wandering about, awaiting Rosalie's reply. She did not know what to do with herself, nor how to kill the dismal, interminable hours, without a soul to say a kind word to her or to sympathise with her distress. Throughout her aimless rambles she had a frantic longing to leave Paris and to return home to her little house by the side of the deserted highroad.

A few days ago she had felt that she could no longer endure its oppressive monotony. Now, on the contrary, she realised that she could not bear to live anywhere else but there, where her joyless habits had taken root.

At last, one evening she received a letter and two hundred francs.

"Madame Jeanne," wrote Rosalie, "come home at once, because I shall not send you any more money. As for Monsieur Paul, I'll go and find him myself, when we hear from him. With respects,

"From Rosalie."

One cold, snowy morning Jeanne left for Batteville.

14

AFTER her visit to Paris, Jeanne never went out or exerted herself in any way. She rose every day at the same hour, looked out of the window at the weather, and then took a chair by the sitting-room fire. She remained there motionless, day after day, gazing into the fire, her thoughts roaming dreamily and at random, while she brooded over the depressing series of her misfortunes. Dusk gradually invaded the little room, and still she made no movement, except to put fresh wood on the fire. Rosalie brought in the lamp, exclaiming, "Come, Madame Jeanne, you must rouse yourself, or you won't eat any dinner again to-night."

She was often a prey to fixed ideas and tortured by infinitesimal worries, which, in her disordered mind, assumed an exaggerated importance. She lived chiefly in the past—the remote past—obsessed by her early years and her honeymoon in far-away Corsica. In the embers of the fire she saw Corsican landscapes, long ago forgotten, and she recalled all the details, all the little incidents, all the faces she had seen on the island. She was haunted by the figure of Jean Ravoli, the guide, and sometimes thought that she heard his voice. Then she would dwell upon the happy years of Paul's childhood, when he had made her plant out his salads, and she had kneeled on the rich earth beside Aunt Lison, the two of them vying with each other in their efforts to please the boy, each endeavouring to show her superior skill in making the young plants strike root and in raising more of them than her rival.

Softly she murmured, "Poulet, my little Poulet," as if she were speaking to him. At this name her reverie broke off, and sometimes for hours at a time she tried to write on the air with her fingers the letters that composed it. Seated in front of the fire, she traced them slowly, imagining that she could see them; then, thinking that she had made a mistake, she would trace the "P" over again, her arm trembling with fatigue as she endeavoured to write the whole name from beginning to end. When she had finished, she began her task again, until she found herself mixing up the letters and forming other words, and, worn almost to imbecility, was obliged to stop. She had

205

all the insane fancies of those who live alone. The least thing out of its usual place vexed her.

Rosalie often took her for a walk on the road, but after twenty minutes Jeanne exclaimed, "I can go no farther, Rosalie," and sat down by the roadside.

Soon every exertion became intolerable, and she stayed in bed as late as she could.

Hitherto she had always clung to one habit, which she had acquired in her childhood. As soon as she had drunk her coffee and milk, she was accustomed to get up and dress. She had a craving for this early morning cup, and would have missed it more than anything else in the world. Every morning she awaited Rosalie's entrance with an almost sensual impatience. As soon as the brimming bowl was placed on the table by her bedside, she sat up and drank it off somewhat greedily. Then she would throw off the bedclothes and begin to dress.

But gradually she acquired a habit of dreaming for a few moments after she had put the cup back on the saucer, then she lay down again in bed; and every day she indulged more and more in these idle ways, until Rosalie entered in a fury and dressed her almost by force.

Moreover, she seemed to have no will of her own, and whenever her maid asked her advice or opinion, or put a question, she answered, "Do as you please, my dear."

Firmly convinced that she was directly pursued by implacable misfortune, she became as fatalistic as an Oriental. Accustomed to see her dreams dissipated and her hopes blighted, she no longer ventured upon any enterprise. She hesitated for days before she attempted the simplest thing, convinced that she would always take the wrong turning and that her efforts would end in failure.

She was continually complaining, "I have never had any luck in life."

Rosalie would reply, "What would you say, I should like to know, if you were obliged to earn your bread, to get up at six every morning and to go out to work all day? There are plenty of women who have to do that, and when they're too old to work they die of want."

"Remember that I'm alone in the world, and that my son has deserted me."

At this Rosalie worked herself into a rage. "What a fuss about nothing! What about sons who have to do their military service, and sons who go and settle in America?"

America she regarded vaguely as a country where one made one's fortune, but from which one never returned.

"There always comes a time," she added, "when one has to part with one's children. The old and the young are not intended to live together." Then she said fiercely, "What would you say if he were dead?"

To this Jeanne had no reply.

When the air grew milder, in the early days of spring, she recovered some degree of strength. But she used it merely to plunge deeper and deeper into her gloomy thoughts. One morning, when she had gone up to the attic to fetch something, she chanced to open a box full of old calendars, which had been preserved, according to the custom of country people. It seemed to her that she had recovered the actual years of her past life, and a strange vague emotion seized her as she contemplated the pile of cardboard squares.

She took them down to the drawing-room. They were of all sizes, big and little. She arranged them on the table according to their dates, and presently she came upon the earliest one, which she had brought with her to *Les Peuples*. For a long time she gazed at it, with the dates she had crossed out on the morning of her departure from Rouen, the day after she had left the convent. She wept. She shed slow, bitter tears—the tears of old age—confronted with her own wretched life, of which the record lay there before her on the table. She was seized with an idea, which speedily became a terrible obsession, persistent and fierce. She endeavoured to remember everything she had done, day by day. She pinned in rows upon the tapestry on the walls these squares of cardboard, yellow with age, and spent hours gazing at one or the other, wondering what had happened to her in some particular month.

She had put marks against all the important dates in her history, and sometimes succeeded in reconstructing a whole month—recovering one by one, grouping and linking together, all the little incidents which had preceded or followed some important event. By dint of fixed attention, efforts of memory and concentration, she succeeded in piecing together almost the whole of her two first years at *Les Peuples*. The distant memories of her early married life came back to her with a curious facility, and brought her a certain solace.

But the subsequent years seemed to lose themselves in a mist, to mingle and overlap. Occasionally she remained an endless time poring over a calendar, her mind straining into the past, unable even to remember if it was on this particular square of cardboard that such-and-such a memory could be recaptured.

One after the other, she contemplated these pictures of vanished days, which hung all round the room, like engravings of the Stages of the Cross. She would suddenly place her chair in front of one of them, and remain there gazing at it until nightfall, deep in her investigations.

When the sap began to rise in the heat of the sun, the corn to sprout in the fields, and the trees to clothe themselves with verdure, when the pink buds of the apple trees in the orchard were diffusing their perfume abroad, she was seized with sudden and intense restlessness. She could not keep still. She wandered about, went in and out twenty times a day, and roamed far away among the farms, as if in a fever of regrets.

The sight of a daisy nestling in a tuft of grass, a ray of sunshine stealing through the leaves, the blue of the sky reflected in a puddle, moved her, touched her, affected her profoundly, stirring in her forgotten sensations, an echo of her girlish emotions in the days when she had roamed, dreaming, over the countryside.

She had felt the same tremors, tasted the same sweet and distracting intoxication of early spring, in those days when she had looked forward to the future. And now that the future was closed to her, these sensations came back to her. They still filled her heart with delight, but it was mingled with pain, as if the immortal joy of the newly awakened world, though it penetrated her withered frame, her chilled veins and prostrate soul, held for her now a weaker and sadder charm. It seemed to her, moreover, that everything around her had suffered some slight change. The sun had somewhat less warmth than in her youth; the sky was a shade less blue, the grass a shade less green; the flowers were paler of hue and less fragrant, and had no longer all their former intoxicating power. There were days, however, when she had such a deep sense of wellbeing that she began once more to dream, to hope, to look forward. For, in spite of the relentless persecutions of fate, may one not always hope, when the sun is shining? She wandered on and on for hours on end, spurred by the feverish excitement of her mind. Sometimes she would suddenly halt and sit down by the wayside, and yield herself up to melancholy thoughts. Why had she never been loved like other people? Why had she not been granted even the simple joys of a quiet life? At times she would forget for a moment that she was old, that there was nothing to look forward to except a few sad and solitary years, and that her race was run. Just as she had done at sixteen, she would fondly build her castles in the air, and piece together delightful schemes for the future. Then the harsh reality overwhelmed her once more. She would rise to her feet, bowed down as if under a back-breaking load, and turn slowly homewards, muttering, "Old fool! Old fool!"

Rosalie was always saying to her, "Why don't you keep quiet, Ma'am? What makes you so restless?"

Jeanne replied sadly, "I can't help it. I'm like Massacre before he died."

One morning Rosalie entered her mistress's room earlier than usual with the customary cup of coffee, which she placed on the table.

"Come, drink it quickly. Denis is waiting for us at the door. We are going to *Les Peuples;* I have some business to attend to there."

Jeanne was so much agitated that she thought she was going to swoon. She dressed, trembling with emotion, bewildered and faint at the prospect of seeing her beloved home once more.

Overhead the sky was radiantly blue, and the pony, in a skittish mood, occasionally broke into a gallop. Entering the parish of Etouvent, Jeanne could hardly breathe for the rapid palpitations of her bosom. When she caught sight of the gate with its brick pillars she exclaimed involuntarily, "Oh, oh, oh!" as at some overwhelming event.

The trap was put up at the Couillards' farm. While Rosalie and her son were attending to their business, the farmer suggested that Jeanne should visit the house, as the owner was away. The keys were handed over to her.

She went all by herself. In front of the old manor-house, on the side facing the sea, she stood and gazed. Externally nothing was changed. The sun was smiling down on the weather-beaten walls of the massive grey building. All the shutters were closed.

A small twig from a dead branch fell upon her gown. She raised her eyes: it came from the plane tree. She went up to the great tree, with its smooth pale bark, and caressed it as if it were a living creature. She stumbled over a piece of mouldering wood, hidden in the grass. It was the last fragment of the bench, on which she and her family had sat so often, the bench that had been placed under the tree on the very day of Julian's first visit. She made her way to the double door of the hall, but could hardly open it, for the heavy, rusty key refused to turn. At last, however, the springs of the lock yielded with a harsh, grinding noise, and the door, which was likewise a little stiff, burst open when she pushed it.

First of all, Jeanne made with all speed for her own room. She hardly recognised it, with its new, light-coloured paper. Throwing open a window, she stood there, moved to the very depths at the sight of the prospect she loved so dearly — the copse, the elm trees, the moor, and the sea with its sprinkling of brown sails, which seemed motionless in the far distance. Then she roamed all through the great, empty house. She recognised old marks on the walls, and stopped to contemplate a little hole in the plaster, made by the Baron, who often amused himself, in memory of his young days, by lunging with his stick against the partition whenever he passed that particular spot. Behind the door of her mother's room, in a dark corner near the bed, she found a slender gold-headed pin, which she now remembered to have stuck there one day, and which she had sought for years. No one had ever found it. She seized it like a priceless relic, and kissed it. She visited every corner of the house, recognising in the old wallpapers patterns now almost invisible, discovering again fantastic faces, which the imagination traces in the designs of materials and marbles and in the shadows on time-blackened ceilings.

With noiseless step, she wandered all alone through the great, silent mansion, as if through a cemetery where all her past lay buried. She went downstairs to the drawing-room. It lay in darkness behind its closed shutters, and for some time she could distinguish nothing. When her eyes grew accustomed to the gloom, she gradually recognised, high up on the walls, the tapestries with their flights of birds. Two armchairs stood before the fireplace, as if their occupants had just left them. The very odour of the place — an odour vague yet characteristic, individual, as that of a living being — the sweet, elusive perfume that clings about old rooms — stole into Jeanne's soul, enfolding her and intoxicating her with memories.

She stood there panting, drawing in this breath from the past, with her eyes fixed upon the two chairs. In a sudden hallucination, begotten of her obsession, she thought she saw—yes, undoubtedly she saw, as so often before—her father and mother warming their feet at the fire.

She started back in terror; her back struck against the edge of the door; she clung to it to keep herself from falling, while her eyes never left the armchairs.

But the vision had vanished.

For some minutes she felt light-headed. Then, slowly recovering her self-possession and fearing for her reason, she turned to make her escape. Her glance fell on the panel against which she had been leaning, and she caught sight of Poulet's ladder. There was a series of faint marks, one above the other, scratched on the paint with a pen-knife, figures recording the month and Poulet's age and height. Sometimes they were in the Baron's large hand, sometimes in her own smaller script, sometimes in the rather tremulous writing of Aunt Lison. It seemed to her as if the fair-haired child of long ago were there before her, pressing his forehead against the door, to allow his height to be measured.

"Jeanne," the Baron exclaimed, "he has grown a centimetre in six weeks."

She kissed the ladder in a passion of love. A voice outside was calling her. It was Rosalie.

"Madame Jeanne, Madame Jeanne. Luncheon is ready for you."

She went out with her head in a whirl. She did not understand anything that was said to her. She ate whatever was set before her, listened without comprehension to the conversation around her, chatted away, no doubt, to the farmer and his wife, who asked after her health, gave and received kisses, and at length climbed again into the trap.

When the lofty roof of the mansion disappeared from sight among the trees, an agonising pang pierced her soul. She felt in her heart that she had taken an eternal farewell of her old home.

She and Rosalie returned to Batteville.

Just as she was entering her new home, she caught sight of something white under the door; it was a letter, which the postman had slipped there while they were away. She saw at once that it was from Paul, and, trembling with apprehension, she opened it.

211

"My dear Mamma," it ran, "I did not write to you sooner, because I did not want you to make an unnecessary journey to Paris, as I always intended to come and see you myself. A great misfortune has befallen me, and I am in a terrible predicament. My wife is dying, after having given birth to a little girl three days ago, and I am penniless. I do not know what to do with the child. My porter's wife is bringing her up on the bottle as well as she can, but I am afraid of losing her. Could you not take charge of her? I am simply at my wits' end, and have no money to put her out to nurse. Please answer by return of post.

"Your loving son,
"PAUL."

Jeanne sank into a chair, and could hardly summon sufficient strength to call Rosalie. Together they re-read the letter, then gazed at each other long and silently.

"I'll go and fetch the child myself, Ma'am," said Rosalie at last. "She can't be left like that."

"Yes, you must go," replied Jeanne.

Again they fell silent. Then Rosalie resumed: "Put on your hat, Ma'am, and let's go and see the notary at Goderville. If the woman is going to die, Monsieur Paul must marry her, for the sake of the child later on."

Without a word, Jeanne put on her hat. Into her heart surged a deep joy—a joy that she could never confess, a traitorous joy which at all costs she must conceal, one of those shameful emotions for which one blushes, but in which one takes a passionate pleasure in the secret recesses of the soul. Her son's mistress was going to die.

The notary gave Rosalie detailed instructions, which she made him repeat several times. Then, confident of making no mistake, she said, "Don't worry. I'll do what is necessary."

She left for Paris the same night.

Jeanne spent the next two days in an agitation of mind which rendered her utterly incapable of thought. On the morning of the third day she received a line from Rosalie, announcing her return by the evening train: nothing more. About three o'clock she ordered a neighbour's trap, and was driven to the Beuzeville railway station to meet Rosalie.

She stood on the platform straining her eyes along the straight

lines of rails, which ran on and on, converging far away in the distance. From time to time she looked at the clock. Another ten minutes. Another five. Another two. And now the train was due. But there was nothing in sight. Suddenly she saw a white wisp of steam, and then beneath it a black dot, which grew steadily larger as it approached at high speed. At last the heavy engine slowed down and panted past Jeanne, who scanned the windows with eager eyes. Doors were opened and passengers alighted—peasants in smocks, farmers' wives with baskets, and small shopkeepers wearing soft caps. At last she saw Rosalie with something that looked like a bundle of linen in her arms.

She wanted to hurry towards her, but her legs suddenly threatened to give way under her. Rosalie caught sight of her, and went up to her with her usual imperturbability.

"Good afternoon, Ma'am," she said, "I'm back again, but I've had rather a time of it."

"Tell me about it," faltered Jeanne.

"Well," replied Rosalie, "she died last night. They were married first. Here is the baby."

She held out the child, who was almost lost in her wrappings. Jeanne took her mechanically. They left the station and climbed into the trap.

"Monsieur Paul is coming home after the funeral," resumed Rosalie. "To-morrow at the same time, I expect."

"Paul," murmured Jeanne, and could say no more.

The sun was setting, flooding with light the flat green country, flecked here and there with the gold of flowering rape and the crimson of poppies. Over the quiet earth, full of vitalising sap, brooded an infinite calm. The peasant encouraged his horse with clicks of his tongue, and the trap drove along at a rapid pace.

Jeanne gazed straight in front of her into the air, into the sky, which was intersected by the curving, rocket-like flight of swallows. All at once, through her clothes, she grew conscious of a gentle warmth penetrating her limbs and her body, the warmth of the little creature asleep on her knee.

She was overwhelmed by a boundless emotion. Swiftly she drew away the covering, and looked for the first time on the face of this child, her son's daughter. And when the frail little atom, roused by the bright light, opened her eyes and moved her lips, Jeanne embraced her passionately, clasping her to her bosom and showering kisses upon her.

Rosalie, who was delighted, checked her with assumed peevishness: "Come, come, Ma'am; give over. You'll make her cry."

Then, doubtless in answer to her own unspoken thought, she added: "Life, you see, is never so good or so bad as people think."